COVERUP

An Adam Drake novel

SCOTT MATTHEWS

Chapter One

THE MANAGER OF TEAM OMNI, the hottest team in the world of competitive video game playing, known as esports, finished watching a qualifying round of a tournament in Hong Kong. It was two thirty in the morning.

He'd been scouting the Chinese HK Lightning team they were scheduled to play in an upcoming Defense of the Ancients (Dota 2) tournament. In a sport that was watched by more people than NFL football, with major tournaments that featured million-dollar prize winnings, knowing your opponent's favorite plays was a key to winning. He had a file on his laptop for every team, except for the team that called itself HK Lightning.

Kevin McRoberts, the young head of the IT division of Puget Sound Security, was used to playing video games until the sun came up. Watching the action tonight was tempting him to do it again, but he couldn't tonight. His report on the hacking assaults of a client's IT system wasn't ready to be presented and he was scheduled to meet with that client the day after tomorrow.

He yawned, got up out of his gaming chair and walked from the back of his apartment toward his bedroom. Halfway there, he remembered that he'd left his iPhone on the end table next to his gaming chair and he hadn't used it to turn on his security system before going to bed. The neighborhood he lived in didn't have many break-ins but working at an international security firm had taught him to be vigilant and careful.

He started back down the hall and caught a flash of movement in his peripheral vision a microsecond before his head exploded in pain.

When he regained consciousness and opened his eyes, a man was standing in front of him wearing a black balaclava over his head. His wrists and ankles were duct-taped to his gaming chair and his mouth had a strip of the tape over it.

It wasn't the balaclava or the look in the man's eyes that worried him as much as the wicked-looking knife in his right hand.

The intruder watched him for a minute and then leaned down until his head was directly in front of Kevin's.

"You have something that doesn't belong to you and I've been sent to retrieve it. I'm not here to kill you, just to inflict enough pain to get you to tell me where it is. I saw you looking at my knife. It's a Spyderco Matriarch 2 and it's very good at slicing and dicing, if that becomes necessary.

"You need to be able to speak, so I will take the duct tape away from your mouth. If you call for help or scream, I will cut off an ear and maybe the tip of your nose. I would rather not have to do that. Will you promise me that you won't make me do that? Nod your head if you agree."

Kevin nodded his head and the man ripped off the duct tape.

"What do I have that doesn't belong to me?"

"A laptop."

"Who are you and why do you think I have someone's laptop?"

"Because when a terrorist by the name of Nazir was taken into custody, his laptop wasn't with him. The company you work for flew him to the mainland and you're the company's IT guy."

"That still doesn't explain why you think I have this laptop."

"We know you had the laptop because we know you tried to open it without the password. That triggered the information on a file in the laptop being sent to the FBI Tipline."

Kevin blinked and started to say something when the man held up his hand.

"Mr. McRoberts, you are wasting my time. Tell me where it is, and I will leave."

Kevin stared at the man and shook his head. "I have three problems with your proposal. First, if I tell you, you will kill me. You would have no reason not to. Second, if I tell you that I don't know where the laptop is, and I don't, you'll probably kill me anyway. And third, if you're from the government, and I think you are, you can't let anyone find out that you broke in and took me hostage. It looks like a zero-sum situation to me; if you win, anyway you slice it or dice it, I have to die."

The man smiled and stepped back. "You're a smart kid, but you have this all wrong. You don't know who I am, and you will never find out. So, you'll never be able to prove that I'm from the government. Even if you could, the reason for my being here trumps any grievance you might have against your government. Make it easy on yourself and when I will leave, you will have all of your body parts attached."

Kevin was a gamer, but he didn't see a way to win this one. He knew his company had sent the laptop on to Washington when he'd been unable open it without the password. And he really didn't have any idea where the laptop was.

"All right, I'll tell you what I know, but you won't like it. I did try to open the laptop and you're right, I wasn't successful. But the last time I saw the laptop was in my office when a legal courier service came to pick it up."

"Where was it going and which courier service was it?"

"It was sent to Washington. The courier service was Capitol Courier Services, LTD."

"Good choice, kid. But if you're not telling me the truth, I will be back. You're going to have to spend the night in your gaming chair, but I bet you have done that before. Just pray that I don't find out you lied to me."

With that, the man tore off another strip of duct tape, slapped it across Kevin's mouth and left the apartment.

Chapter Two

THOMAS R. Danforth, III was reading the *Washington Post* on his iPad and drinking a second cup of coffee in the breakfast nook of his McLean, Virginia French country house when the call came.

His wife, Charlene, was driving their two girls to school and he had the quiet house all to himself to enjoy the early fall sun streaming in through the bay windows. As the head of the FBI's Counterintelligence Division, it was a rare pleasure he seldom got to enjoy.

Danforth accepted the call.

"He doesn't have the laptop."

"Does he know where it is?"

"He said he doesn't."

"Do you believe him?"

The man Danforth was talking with was a former FBI agent. He'd been fired because he'd enjoyed his work for the FBI's High-Value Detainee Interrogation Group a little too much.

"I did. He told me that he'd been unable to open the laptop and that it had been sent to Washington via a courier."

"To whom?"

"He didn't know, but he did know the name of the courier

service, Capitol Courier Services, LTD. He said it was sent to Washington as evidence."

"Capital Courier Services is a legal courier service."

"What do you want me to do?"

"Find out who received the laptop and find a way to get it back. Do whatever it takes."

"Understood."

Danforth ended the call and stared into the light reflecting off the surface of the Jamaican Blue Mountain café noir in his cup for a long moment.

He needed the laptop in his hands. The information on it that had been sent to the FBI Tipline had been successfully discredited and was no longer under investigation. He had taken care of that by arranging for the owner of the laptop, a terrorist by the name of Zal Nazir, to be turned over to the CIA instead of being in the custody of his own agency.

When the FBI had been unable to interrogate the author of the Tipline information, because he was already in the custody of the CIA who said it believed he was an Iranian agent, the FBI had agreed to look the other way and drop its investigation of the man's activities last summer in America.

Danforth knew that Nazir was the founder of a group of American Muslim hackers. He had participated in a social media campaign to assist the efforts of a Russian oligarch and a radical university professor. The Russian and the professor had wanted to spark a Marxist-style revolution by riding on the coattails of the recent anarchist and Antifa protests against the election of the new president. Nazir and his hackers had used fake news and ransomware attacks on white supremacist and loosely affiliated conservative groups and to fuel the flames of partisan anger in the country.

Danforth had played a minor role in the efforts of the Russian oligarch, one Mikhail Volkov, and the radical professor, Mason Bradley, that he'd rather no one ever found out about. He had tipped off the Russian and let him know that his shipment of AK-

47s was going to be intercepted when it arrived at the port of Seattle.

He'd provided the information to Volkov for a couple of reasons. The primary reason was that he didn't want the new president to be able to stop the anarchist violence so that he'd be seen as someone who secretly sided with the white supremacist fascists.

The secondary reason was his sincere belief that America needed to be profoundly changed. His parents were professors at the University of Illinois Chicago and were openly Marxists, with a small "m". He agreed with many of their beliefs and hadn't felt that he was really betraying his country by aiding the struggle against fascism and arming Antifa. The hate speech on the right had to be silenced and he'd seen Antifa was the perfect tool to do that.

The only thing he worried about was the possibility that he would be exposed for helping the shipment of the AK-47s get through the port of Seattle safely by the men who had tracked down the Russian oligarch and the radical professor.

Danforth had learned of the attorney from Oregon, and the security firm where he served as special counsel, from FBI files investigating the death of the radical professor on the Hawaiian estate of the Russian oligarch. The attorney and his friend, the CEO of the security firm, had served together as Special Forces operatives in the Army Compartmented Elements, or ACE, the special missions unit most people knew as Delta Force. They had been the ones who had learned that the Russian and the professor had been funding and assisting the anarchist violence.

The two needed to be sidetracked so that they no longer had time to stick their noses into things they didn't fully understand. He knew just how to accomplish that.

He took out an iPad Pro from his old brown leather briefcase, with its concealed firearm compartment for his Glock 17M, and scrolled through his private list of FBI agents he trusted. The agent he was looking for, William Ferrar, was in the FBI's satellite office in Kona Hawaii.

Danforth called him at home.

"Bill, Thomas Danforth here. I apologize for calling you so early in the morning, but I need you to do something for me."

"It's actually 2:00 a.m. here, Tom, but go ahead. What can I do for you?"

"You remember the incident on the Big Island at the villa of the Russian oligarch?"

"Yes."

"Did your guys recover a laptop when they searched the villa?"

"Not that I remember, why?"

"Something has developed and it may have information on it that could be useful in another case. I want you to send everything you have on that matter to Allen Chappell, the SAC in Seattle. He needs the information to get a search warrant and see if that laptop turned up in the headquarters of that Puget Sound Security outfit that was involved at the villa in Hilo."

"Wouldn't it be quicker for Seattle to get the warrant, based on what you're already working on?"

"Yes, but I want it tied to the incident at the villa, not what I'm working on."

"All right, I'll head to the office and send it within the hour."

"Thanks Bill."

"Anytime."

Chapter Three

IT WAS mid-morning on the first Monday of October. Adam Drake was having a hard time keeping his mind focused on the file open on the desk in front of him.

A client was still having a problem with someone trying to hack into its IT system. The hacker he had believed was responsible had been captured last month in Hawaii and was now in federal custody.

The terrorist's name was Zal Nazir, a software engineer and American Muslim working for Intel Corporation in Hillsboro, Oregon. In the last year, he'd been found to have been involved in a social media campaign aimed at starting a second civil war in the United States.

The person or persons who were continuing to harass his client now had not been identified and the company was anxious to put an end to the matter. The white hat hacker he'd asked to identify the hacker or hackers hadn't yet been able to do so.

But it wasn't the lack of progress on the matter or the inevitable meeting with his client that was distracting Drake. It was something more personal. Where was he going to keep living, on his farm in the heart of the Oregon wine country or in Seattle, where the woman he loved had moved across the country to live and work?

He'd spent the previous week with his vineyard manager and crew planting the grape vines that had been growing in one-gallon pots since the spring on his forty-acre farm. The farm and the restoration of the old vineyard, abandoned by a dentist from New Jersey, was the dream of his former wife, Kay. They'd bought the farm for their first home and when she died three years later, he had promised her that he would fulfill her dream for the place and replant the vineyard.

It was a promise he'd kept. But he wasn't a farmer, which was what you had to be if you owned and operated a vineyard. With the vineyard now planted and in the capable hands of his neighbor, who had agreed to be his vineyard manager, he had the opportunity to end the long-distance relationship with the woman who had made him love again.

Liz Strobel was a former FBI agent, former executive assistant to the secretary of the Department of Homeland Security, now the vice president of governmental affairs for Puget Sound Security where he served as the company's special counsel.

Moving to Seattle, Washington, to be with her meant that he would have to give up his law practice in Portland, Oregon. It meant abandoning his long-time secretary and her husband, Margo and Paul Benning, who were leasing the condo above his office. Margo had been his senior secretary when he was a prosecutor in the District Attorney's Office. Her husband, Paul, was a detective in the Multnomah County Sheriff's Office who had recently retired to work as a private detective out of Drake's law office.

Moving to Seattle or somewhere nearby also meant that his dog Lancer would no longer have his farm to patrol and scare off the deer who loved to nibble on grape his grape vines.

Moving to Seattle to be with Liz was complicated, to say the least.

To make things even worse was the guilt he felt over the boredom he was experiencing when he was confined in his office doing the routine and monotonous legal work that you were never told about when you were in law school. Trial work, as a prosecutor, had been invigorating and meaningful. But serving the legal needs of corporations and business clients in Portland wasn't. It just paid well.

Not that he needed the money. Kay had left her trust fund to him and it had grown nicely since she died, but working the long hours just to have more money in the bank wasn't what he wanted to live for.

The vibration of his phone scuttling across his desk brought him out of his reverie.

"Hi Liz, how are things in the Emerald City?"

"Lonely, but that's not why I called. Kevin was attacked in his apartment last night. He's okay, but I think you should get up here."

"What happened?"

"Some guy wearing a balaclava got into his apartment, knocked him out and duct-taped him to his gaming chair. When he came to, he asked him where Nazir's laptop was. He threatened him with losing a finger or an ear if he didn't talk. Kevin figured it wouldn't hurt to tell him that it had already been couriered to Washington."

"Was Kevin hurt?"

"He spent the night duct-taped to his chair until we sent someone to his apartment to check on him when he didn't come to work. He may have a concussion and will need stitches in the back of his head where he was hit, but other than that he's okay."

"Does Kevin have any idea who the guy was?"

"He thought he was from the government, but get this. The guy said he'd never be able to prove it and even if he could, his reason for being there trumped any grievance Kevin might have against the government."

"That's a pretty damning admission that he's government, using the old 'this involves national security' B.S. The only agency we know that knows anything about the laptop is the FBI."

"That's what Mike and I think."

"Is Kevin there with you?"

"He's still in the emergency room."

"I'll drive up and be there as soon as I can. Call Senator

Hazelton and let him know about Kevin. He arranged for the legal courier to take the laptop to Washington. He'll want to make sure it's somewhere safe."

"All right. Apologize to Margo for me for pulling you out of the office. I know she has a number of files she wanted you to finish this week."

"I'm regretting the day I introduced you to her."

"You shouldn't. We're both just trying to take care of you."

"I'm going to hang up now."

"Drive carefully."

He knew Liz and Margo were friends, but this mothering conspiracy between them was starting to annoy him.

Chapter Four

WHEN DRAKE STOPPED his company car, a Porsche Cayman GTS, at the security gate at Puget Sound Security's headquarters in Seattle, a uniformed officer from the Kirkland Police Department blocked his way and told him that no one was allowed to enter or exit the premises.

Drake took out his wallet and handed the officer his Puget Sound Security business card.

"What's going on, officer?"

"The FBI asked for our assistance while they search the premises."

"Then I suggest you call the agent in charge and tell him that Puget Sound Security's attorney is here and wants to see the search warrant right now before he searches anything."

The officer stepped away from the car and studied the business card before taking a handheld radio off his belt. "Tell the agent in charge the company's attorney is here demanding to see the warrant before any search."

While he waited, Drake used his own smartphone to call Liz. "What's going on? I'm at the gate and not being allowed to enter."

"The FBI arrived about five minutes ago with a warrant to search the building."

"What does the warrant say they're looking for?"

"They're looking for a laptop taken from the villa in Hawaii."

"The one Mike brought back from the Big Island. How did they find out that we had it?"

Drake saw that the officer was waving him forward. "They're letting me in. I'll be there in a minute. Tell the agent in charge to meet me in my office."

He pulled forward and entered the day's code on the keypad. When the security gate rolled back, he drove across the gated compound and down the ramp to his reserved spot in the building's underground parking.

Taking three steps at a time, he sprinted up the stairs to the executive offices three floors above. When he opened the fire door from the stairwell, he saw half a dozen FBI agents down the hallway and two more standing at the door to his office. Mike Casey, PSS's CEO, was there with Liz standing next to him.

Drake marched down the hall, brushing aside FBI agents in his way, and stopped in front of the two FBI agents at the door of his office.

"May I see the warrant?" he asked, holding out his hand.

"Certainly," the taller of the two agents said and handed it over along with his business card.

Drake took the warrant and stepped into his office to read it. The warrant named Zal Nazir specifically and a laptop belonging to him that was believed to be in the possession of Puget Sound Security, Inc.

He turned back to the FBI agent and said, "Agent Chappell, may I see you in my office?"

Agent Chappell was six feet three or four tall and had a narrow face and a thin beak of a nose that made him look even taller. Drake motioned for him to be seated and sat down behind his desk.

"The warrant you obtained claims the laptop has evidence of criminal conduct. Whose criminal conduct? Can you be more specific?"

"You know I'm not going to do that."

"Zal Nazir, of course. Are you also investigating the others he was involved with?"

"Same answer, Drake. I'm not discussing our investigation."

"Why do you think his laptop is here?"'

"Are you saying you didn't have it when you flew back with him from Hawaii?"

Drake leaned back in his chair and smiled. "By now you know that he's a terrorist and was involved in the plot to kill innocent people attending mass in Portland. He was also engaged in social media warfare recently to stir up things and start a civil war in America. Why do you believe anything he's telling you?"

"Let's stop dancing around, Drake. We know all about Nazir and we know all about your raid on Volkov's villa. Personally, I think you and everyone who participated in that little adventure in Hawaii should be in jail. You know what we're looking for. Why not just hand it over before we have to tear your offices apart looking for it?"

"The laptop's not here. We sent it to Washington. If you don't believe me, call my father-in-law, Senator Hazelton. He's the chairman of the Senate Intelligence Committee. For all I know, he found someone in your agency or the NSA or CIA to work on it."

Agent Chappell sat back in his chair and glared at Drake. "Why would you do that? Why not give it to us in the first place?"

"It involves something I'm handling for a client. There are other reasons, but client confidentiality is the main one."

The FBI agent considered the information and made his decision. "All right, I'll pull my guys off, for now. If Senator Hazelton doesn't confirm what you've told me, I'll be back, and you won't recognize this place when we're finished."

Agent Chappell stood up and walked out of Drake's office.

Liz and Mike Casey walked in and stood in front of Drake's desk.

"He just told his second in command to call off the search," Casey said. "What did you say to him?"

"I told him the truth. The laptop's not here."

"Did you tell him where it is?" Liz asked.

"I told him he should ask my father-in-law where it is. I didn't want to put us in the crosshairs of the FBI, the CIA and who knows what other agencies by refusing to cooperate. Let them deal with the chairman of the Senate Intelligence Committee instead and explain what they're after."

"They have the information Nazir sent to the FBI Tipline, why do they need the laptop?" Casey asked.

"They have Nazir in custody. They know by now he was working with Volkov and Russia. They don't need more evidence to prove that. My guess is that someone in the intelligence community, the FBI, the CIA or the NSA wants to make sure there's no evidence on that laptop that will prove that someone knew what Volkov or Bradley were up to."

"If this warrant is part of some coverup, Volkov's friend is pretty far up the food chain to orchestrate this. Do you want me to reach out to people I trust in Washington and see if we can find out who it is?" Liz asked.

Drake looked to Casey before he answered. "That's a step that could put us on someone's enemy list. Are you willing to take that risk?"

Casey didn't hesitate to answer. "Absolutely. It's no coincidence that Kevin was attacked and asked about the laptop and the next day we get served with a search warrant looking for the same thing. Injuring Kevin crossed the line. Find out who's responsible and we'll decide where we go from there."

Chapter Five

CASEY LEFT to see if Kevin McRoberts was back from the ER and Liz went to her office to call a friend she worked with when she was an FBI agent herself.

Drake thought for a moment about what he was going to say to Senator Hazelton. Zal Nazir was in custody somewhere but there'd been no news about his arrest. What was the FBI doing with him? Why send someone to Kevin's apartment before serving the search warrant? If Nazir told the FBI that they had his laptop, why not serve the warrant first? And why serve the warrant at all if Kevin had told his abductor that the laptop had been sent to Washington? It didn't make any sense.

It had been his idea to send the laptop by legal courier to the law firm PSS used in D.C., to keep his father-in-law out of the chain of custody. That way, the senator and the committee, small "c", the senator had organized to work around the Deep State, if necessary on matters of national security, wouldn't be directly involved. But the law firm that had the laptop would be and there was no way it could refuse to hand over the laptop if the FBI served it with a search warrant.

He had deflected a little when he told Agent Chappell that the laptop involved something he was working on for a client, but it was the truth. Just not all the truth. Zal Nazir had been involved in a hacking assault on a client, Caelus Research, Inc., and had communicated with others in his group from his laptop. Their client wanted the hacking assault resolved and he needed to know the identity of the others who had been involved with Nazir. If the FBI took possession of the laptop, there would be little or no chance for him to ever extract that information from the laptop.

He scrolled through the contacts on his iPhone and called Senator Hazelton's office.

The receptionist told him the senator was having lunch in his office, before a committee hearing in half an hour, but she would see if he had time to take his call.

"Hello Adam, you caught me with a mouthful of a roast beef sandwich. I'll keep eating while you tell me what you needed to talk to me about."

"The FBI served a search warrant on us this morning, looking for Nazir's laptop. Last night, Kevin McRoberts was attacked in his apartment and asked where the laptop was. He told his attacker, in lieu of having a finger sliced off, that the laptop had been sent by legal courier to Washington. It won't take the FBI long to find out which law firm received the laptop. Have you had any luck finding someone to get past the encrypted password and open the laptop?"

"I have the top private security consultant in the world picking up the laptop sometime today. He says he might need a week to get it open."

"Do you have someone who can get the laptop to him as quickly as possible? I don't know how long we have before the FBI finds out which law firm we used."

"I'll get someone to deliver it to him as soon as I get off the phone. Did you find out where Nazir is being held?"

"No, but if he's been arrested, someone has to know."

"Secretary Rallings might be able to find out," Senator Hazelton said. "Homeland Security had agents waiting in Montana to take custody of Nazir when you flew him to the mainland from Hawaii. As the former Secretary of DHS, he might be able to find out who the FBI agents were and if they said where they were taking him. It might be a long shot, but I'll give it a try."

"It can't hurt. Let me know if you get the laptop somewhere safe before the FBI show up."

"I will. Say hello to Liz for me."

Drake stood up and stretched, rolling his head around to loosen his neck muscles. He'd been tense at times on the drive from Portland to Seattle, gripping the steering wheel so hard his knuckles had turned white. Casey was right, someone had crossed the line and that had to be dealt with.

He walked out of his office and stopped at the open door of the PSS vice president for governmental affairs.

When Liz turned around in her chair to face the door, he saw that she was on her smart phone. He also saw she was blushing.

She held up her hand for him to wait a minute and turned her chair back around. "Thank you, Sam. I really appreciate this. Dinner's on me the next time you're in Seattle."

Drake leaned against the door frame with his arms folded across his chest when she turned back around. "Who's Sam?"

Liz didn't look up as she wrote something on the legal pad on her desk. "Sam Gregory. I worked with him in the San Diego Field Office before I transferred to headquarters."

"Is he going to help us find out who ordered the search warrant?"

"He is, and before you ask, we also dated when I was in law school. Dinner was his quid pro quo for helping me. What are you grinning about?"

"Because you were blushing when you turned around. You're still blushing. Should I be worried?"

It was Liz who was grinning now. "Not if you take me to dinner tonight. Then we'll see."

"And my quid pro quo for doing that?"

"Like I said, we'll see. Now, let's go down and see how Kevin's doing. He's back in his office."

Chapter Six

THOMAS R. Danforth, III, the head of the FBI's Counterterrorism Division, left FBI headquarters on a 'personal errand' to return a call from Allen Chappell, the FBI SAC in Seattle. Chappell had submitted the application and affidavit for the search warrant and conducted the search of the headquarters of Puget Sound Security.

He walked south on 9th Street NW toward the National Mall and the Smithsonian Museum and used his personal iPhone to make the call.

"Did you get it?" Danforth asked.

"No, but then I guess you knew that."

Danforth was silent as he looked around to make sure there wasn't anyone within range to record his conversation. The FBI had developed an app for smartphones that boosted the power and range to record conversations at a distance. If they had the app, someone else probably had the same thing.

"What are you talking about?"

"One of my agents overheard a couple of PSS guys talking about their head IT guy being duct-taped to his gaming chair and asked if he knew where some laptop was. I got the search warrant you wanted, but I'm not risking my career by getting involved in some off-the-books operation you're running."

"I don't know what you're talking about, Allen."

"Listen, I don't expect you to tell me what's going on, but I can't help you unless I'm fully briefed and know that it's an official investigation. You don't need my help, anyway. Adam Drake, special counsel for PSS, said the laptop had been sent by legal carrier to some law firm in D.C. He told me to call Senator Hazelton to verify that PSS didn't have the laptop. I haven't called the senator, you'll have to. You've got the juice to find out where the laptop is, I don't."

Danforth crossed Constitution Avenue and turned around on the sidewalk to look back at the J. Edgar Hoover Building a block away.

"Keep my name out of your report on the search warrant. With the information you had from Agent Ferrar on the raid on Volkov's villa in Hawaii, you had a legitimate reason for asking for the warrant. I'll handle the rest from here. But don't cross me, Chappell. I'm at headquarters and you're not. Do what I tell you and you might just have a long career with us."

He waited for the light to change and headed back to headquarters. He had to find a way to get a hold of Nazir's laptop, for two reasons. The most important one, of course, was making sure it didn't have anything on it that would link him to the Russian oligarch.

But there was another reason. The senior level CIA man, who gave him the information about the AK-47 arms shipment the Russian was involved with, wanted to use Nazir's band of Muslim hackers to conduct cyber warfare against America and make it look like Iran was behind it.

The president had promised that any cyberattacks by a nation state against America would amount to an act of war. If he was provoked to attack Iran, and Russia acted to defend its ally, a simmering new cold war would become a raging fire and the devious CIA would be important again.

On his way back to headquarters, Danforth called his CIA

friend at the George Bush Center for Intelligence, the CIA head-quarters, in Langley, Virginia.

"Meet me at CCR tonight, nine o'clock. I'll buy you dinner."

"Can't tonight. I have plans."

"Change them. We have a problem."

"How about breakfast tomorrow?"

"Because we might have a bigger problem by then. There's something that needs attention tonight."

"Does this involve our Persian?"

"It does. See you tonight."

Danforth smiled as he thought of the perverse pleasure he enjoyed whenever he had a chance to make James T. Oliver squirm. Oliver was currently the associate deputy director of the CIA's Directorate of Digital Innovation (DDI).

CCR was what the locals called the Crystal City Restaurant Gentleman's Club in Arlington, Virginia. A restaurant with a decent New York strip and a smoking lounge, it was also a strip club. Oliver would have preferred to meet in some dark gay bar, but he wasn't calling the shots. His sexual orientation wasn't the only secret he was keeping, as Danforth reminded him from time to time. He had been a frequent client of a drug-dealing MS-13 gang.

Danforth had discovered that little secret when he was investigating Transnational Organized Crime groups out of the FBI's Chicago Field Office. MS-13 had expanded its turf from Chicago to the D.C. area and surveillance there had captured Oliver making a buy from one of its dealers.

The video wasn't clear enough for a positive identification of Oliver, but Danforth had become interested in finding out who he was because of the location of the buy in the parking lot of J. Gilbert's Wood-fried Steak and Seafood restaurant in McLean, Virginia. J. Gilbert's had the well-known reputation as being a favorite watering hole of the CIA in the past and was located just two miles south of its headquarters.

Danforth needed to know more about Drake and his company and Oliver was just the man to accomplish that. Oliver was also the man who was going to find out which law firm had Nazir's laptop and then hire someone to break in and get it for him.

Chapter Seven

KEVIN MCROBERTS WAS SITTING at his desk in the corner office when Liz and Drake walked through the IT Division of PSS on the second floor. There was a red rash stretching across his cheeks on both sides of his mouth where the duct tape had been.

"How's your head?" Drake asked from the door of Kevin's office.

"Heck of a headache, but the worst part is the bare patch of my hair where they did the stitches. Might have to start wearing a watch cap."

Liz moved to the side of his chair and leaned down to have a look. "Ouch. You got whacked pretty hard, by the looks of this, but I think the bald patch is kind of endearing."

Kevin smiled bravely. "That's what one of the nurses said too. I think I'll still go with a watch cap."

Liz sat down in the one chair in front of his desk, while Drake remained standing at the door. "Did the guy who broke into your apartment say why he thought you might have Nazir's laptop?"

"He did, in a way. He said he knew that when Nazir was taken into custody in Montana, the laptop wasn't with him. He also said they knew I had it because when I tried to open it without the pass-

23

word, it triggered Nazir's file being sent to the FBI Tipline. The only way they would know that is if they were monitoring his laptop."

"Is the 'they' our government?"

"That's my guess. We know from the WikiLeaks Vault 7 release of documents the CIA has software called "Brutal Kangaroo" that can remotely monitor a computer, even if it isn't on the internet. I'm sure they've developed something even better than that by now."

"I can understand the involvement of the FBI," Liz said, "but not the CIA. It isn't authorized to conduct electronic surveillance of U.S. citizens. Only the FBI is and, even then, a FISA warrant is required."

"Could there be anything on Nazir's laptop that will tell us if the CIA was monitoring his laptop?" Drake asked Kevin.

"If his laptop was infected with malware from the CIA, you can find it if you're looking for it. But you need to get into it first. That's something I couldn't do. Senator Hazelton might be able to find someone who can get around encrypted passwords."

"I'll pass that along to him about looking for the malware. Kevin, no one expects you to be here working today. Why don't you go home and rest until your headache gets better?"

"Thanks, Mr. Drake, but I can rest here where I feel a little safer."

Liz and Drake left Kevin and took the stairs to their offices.

"We should make sure Kevin feels safe in his apartment. Maybe install a security system and give him a little close quarter combat training. This could happen again with some of the things we ask him to do," Liz said.

"Good idea. I'll call the senator. See if your 'Sam' found out who was behind the search warrant and I'll think about making a reservation for dinner."

"Sam will probably want to go for Italian food, so why don't we do French tonight? It might get me in the mood for some 'quid pro quo'," Liz said with a flirtatious smile as she brushed past him and entered her office.

Drake closed the door to his office and made a mental note to

Google Sam Gregory when he had a moment. He knew she was teasing him, but it never hurt to know as much as possible about someone she was willing to take to dinner. He wasn't really worried, although he had to admit that one of the reasons he was willing to move to Seattle was to make sure he didn't need to be worried.

Senator Hazelton was back from the afternoon hearing he chaired for the Senate Select Committee on Intelligence when Drake called his office again.

"I had one of my staffers pick up the laptop," the senator told him. "He and I are the only ones who know where it was taken. It's safe for now. Have you made any progress?"

"Liz asked a former FBI colleague, Sam Gregory, to find out who wanted our headquarters searched. I don't think she's heard back from him yet."

"Is that the agent she dated for a while? He dropped by to see her at my office when she worked here. He introduced himself as her old boyfriend."

"Apparently."

"I take it you haven't met him."

"Haven't had the pleasure."

"Oh, I don't think it will be much of a pleasure. Agent Gregory fancies himself as quite a ladies' man."

"Thanks for warning me. Senator, have you ever had a briefing by the CIA about a cyber espionage tool they call Brutal Kangaroo?"

"I'm aware of it, but I don't know much about it. Why?"

"Kevin thinks someone in the government was monitoring Nazir's laptop, even when it was off the internet. They knew Kevin was the one who tried to get into it and triggered the file being sent to the FBI Tipline."

"Nazir's a U.S. citizen. The CIA shouldn't be involved. Even the FBI would need a FISA warrant for that kind of surveillance."

"That assumes the surveillance was authorized. Could you find out if a FISA Court warrant was approved?"

"FISA Court records aren't available to the public, but I can probably find out. Is that what you want me to do?"

"Yes, if you would."

"What are you planning?"

"I'm going to find out who ordered the search of our offices and then find out why Nazir's laptop is so important to the FBI."

"If I can help, let me know."

"I will. Thanks, senator."

FISA warrant applications are handled out of the FBI's headquarters in Washington, D.C. If a warrant from the FISA Court was approved, they would know who wanted the laptop so badly. If a warrant wasn't approved and the CIA was involved, then more than just someone in the FBI was colluding with the Russian oligarch.

Drake knew he had made a few enemies in the FBI when he had responded to threats to the homeland before the government had. If the CIA was involved, it looked like he'd probably be making a few enemies in that agency as well.

If that was the case and he continued his search, he needed to start thinking about the risks involved, not only to himself but to those around him.

Chapter Eight

THOMAS R. Danforth, III selected a table at the Crystal City Restaurant Gentlemen's Club close to the raised dance floor. He wanted to give his guest the best possible view of the topless dancers who would be performing a few feet away.

He ordered a glass of his favorite Laphroaig Scotch and waited for James Oliver to arrive. It was early in the evening and there were plenty of empty tables. The late crowd would arrive later and there would be standing room only to watch the lovely ladies sway and turn on their poles.

Sex had never been that big a deal for him. He had carefully chosen his wife, the daughter of a wealthy and powerful Chicago attorney, and she had given him two sons that fulfilled his procreational needs. After their births, sex had been required with her from time to time to prove his fidelity, leaving him free to use an occasional escort when he needed one.

Oliver walked across the floor to his table, after surveying the room for a full minute, and sat down exactly at nine o'clock.

"I hope you're hungry," Danforth said. "I ordered prime rib for us with a nice crab dip for starters."

A blonde cocktail waitress came over and placed a coaster on the table in front of Oliver, leaning down to give him the best view of her well-endowed assets. "What can I get you, handsome?"

"Double Grey Goose over one ice cube with a lemon twist," Oliver said without taking his eyes off Danforth's smirking face.

When the waitress left, he asked, "What problem required meeting here, of all places?"

"Relax, enjoy the ambience and break bread with me, James. We have things to discuss that must be considered carefully."

The cocktail waitress returned and sat his drink down on his coaster. "You need anything else, you just call me. I'm here to make your evening memorable."

Danforth laughed as she walked away. "I don't think we'll need her to achieve that, will we?"

"I know you're enjoying yourself, Danforth. If there's something that we need to take care of tonight, I suggest we get to it."

Danforth raised his empty glass and motioned to the cocktail waitress that he wanted another Scotch.

"Let's get to it then. Our Persian friend's laptop is here in Washington and we need to recover it. I need you to find out which law firm the attorney in Seattle sent it to and if it's still there. If it isn't, I need to know who has it and how we get our hands on it. I need it to make sure the information you provided me about the arms shipment isn't discovered so we both don't go to jail. You need the laptop to identify Nazir's other hackers, if you want to use them. Nazir isn't cooperating. Is that clear enough for you?"

"Why tonight? Why did we have to meet tonight?"

"Because I suspect the laptop was sent to Washington so that Senator Hazelton, the attorney's father-in-law, could keep it safe. He'll try to find someone to get around Nazir's encrypted password. If that happens, it's over for both of us."

"I never should have told you I knew what Volkov was doing."

"We crossed that bridge a long time ago. We know things elected officials don't need to know. Sometimes we need to act on the things we know and sometimes we need to keep the information to ourselves. Volkov was doing the right thing and just needed a little help."

"By tipping him off that the harbor patrol was waiting for the ship with the AK-47s, you didn't just act on the information I gave you, "Oliver said. "You aided and abetted someone working on behalf of Russia. There's no way he developed his billions as quickly as he did without help from Putin."

"So, what do you want to do, James? There's no turning back."

Their crab dip appetizer was brought to their table and Oliver ordered another double Grey Goose. But before his second drink arrived, the music started. The first trio of dancers waved to their patrons as they took the stage and strutted to their assigned poles.

"Do you know which courier service brought the laptop here?" Oliver asked.

"Capitol Courier Services. The laptop was to be delivered to a law firm."

"Do we have any idea which law firm?"

"Start with any law firm Puget Sound Security has used here in Washington in the past. If it isn't one of those, see if there's a law firm Senator Hazelton has used for personal matters or outside legal services for the committee he chairs, the Senate Committee on Intelligence."

"I know which committee he chairs. I've testified before it. Is there anything else you need from me?"

Two platters of prime rib were brought out from the kitchen to their table and when the waitress was far enough away, Danforth leaned forward and said, "If the laptop has already been delivered to some IT security expert, find a contractor who is willing to do whatever is necessary to get it back."

Danforth cut a bite of prime rib off and leaned back. "Now, enjoy your dinner. The prime rib here is excellent."

Chapter Nine

JAMES OLIVER LEFT the strip club in a silent and furious rage as he drove to his condo in the Watergate West.

Thomas R. Danforth was a member of the Washington elite that he hated, the politically-connected public servant working in government to enrich himself at the expense of the country.

Every agency in the intelligence community had men like Danforth. Mediocre talents who graduated from the right universities, with the right connections and the innate gift for sucking up to anyone with the ability to boost their careers.

Danforth was one of the worst talentless insiders in the FBI. His transfer from the Chicago field office to FBI headquarters had coincided with the election of the last president. It was rumored to have been due to the large campaign donations by his parents to the president and not the stellar work he did while on the gang taskforce in Chicago.

Oliver knew for a fact that Danforth hadn't played a major role in the arrest and conviction of the Chicago leader of MS-13, the ruthless and blood-thirsty gang of El Salvadoran immigrants who settled in Los Angeles in the 1980s. Danforth had taken credit for the arrest, of course, but Oliver knew it was information he'd given him, gleaned from electronic surveillance of the leader's communication with members of the gang back in El Salvador.

As much as he loathed and despised Danforth, there wasn't much he could do about his subservience to the man at this point. He was being blackmailed and couldn't do anything about it, as long as the man was still breathing.

Danforth had asked him to keep an eye on the Russian oligarch named Mikhail Volkov, who was a citizen of both the United States and the Ukraine, the Russian's place of birth, and he had no choice but to agree.

The surveillance amounted to domestic spying, so he'd used an off-the-books contractor for the electronic surveillance. That had led him to the radical professor who was working with Antifa activists as well as the Muslim hacker the FBI had in custody.

He had provided Danforth with the information and it was that sharing of intelligence with Danforth that would put them both in prison for the rest of their lives, if it was discovered.

Oliver instructed his Bluetooth-paired smartphone in his E 400 Mercedes coupe to call his favorite hacker-for-hire.

"Busy tonight?"

"Not if the pay's right."

"Isn't it always?"

"Good point. What do you need?"

"Meet me tonight where we met last time. I'll tell you then."

"I'll be there in half an hour."

Oliver was seated in a green leather booth in his favorite cocktail lounge in Georgetown when a Japanese man with the build of a gymnast nodded to him and walked over. Tony Yamada had worked for the NSA for six years before leaving to work as a private contractor.

"I'm not sure it's safe to sit down, from the look on your face."

"Sorry, I was thinking about another problem I'm going to have to solve someday."

Yamada sat across from Oliver and asked with raised eyebrows, "What's the job?"

"Would you like something to drink?"

"Sure, Akashi White Oak if they have it."

Oliver waved to the cocktail waitress and ordered the whisky for Yamada.

"I need you to find something."

After he explained what little he knew about the location of Nazir's laptop, he told Yamada he needed to find out who had it as soon as possible.

"What's on the laptop that's so important?"

"I have a good idea, but that's not something you need to worry about. Just tell me where it is."

"Do you care if anyone knows you're looking for this laptop?"

"I think the people who have it know that we're looking for it. Just don't allow anything to be traced back to you. I need to be able to use you in the future."

"Same rate as before?"

"Same rate as before. I'll even throw in a bottle of that expensive whisky you just ordered."

Yamada grinned. "I didn't think you knew anything about Japanese whisky. You're a vodka guy."

"There are quite a few in the agency with expensive tastes. It pays to be informed."

Oliver ordered another Grey Goose so that Yamada wasn't drinking alone. When their glasses were empty, Yamada left to get started on his new assignment.

Alone in his booth, Oliver made a call to another contractor he used for a different kind of assignment.

"I may need your services on short notice. Are you available for the next couple of days?"

"Who's the target?"

"I'm waiting for that information."

"Is he or she here in the district?"

"Here or nearby, I expect."

"I'll reserve the next three days for you. Will that be long enough?"

"It should be."

"Full menu?"

"Special order one, as well as special order two, may be required."

"You got it. Send the information the usual way."

Oliver took his time finishing his drink while imagining the day when he would make a similar call to take care of his FBI problem, one Thomas R. Danforth, III.

Chapter Ten

DRAKE AND LIZ left PSS headquarters in his gray Porsche Cayman at six o'clock. Liz wanted French cuisine and that's what she was going to get. He'd made dinner reservations at the Le Grand Bistro Amercain at Carillon Point in Kirkland, a short drive away.

When they were seated at the window with a view of Lake Washington, Drake gave Liz the lead.

"I don't know much about French food, so you order everything. The only thing you can't order for me is escargot. Been there, done that and didn't like it."

"Fair enough. I'll find something you'll like."

After a quick glance at the wine offerings, she told the sommelier they would begin with the white Bordeaux and some steamed clams.

"You do eat steamed clams, don't you?"

"Can't get enough of them."

Liz chuckled and reached her hand across to lay it on top of his. "This is wonderful, but we didn't have to go to a French restaurant just because I mentioned it."

"Once you told me that Sam would probably take you to an Italian restaurant, it limited my options somewhat."

She sat back in her chair with a look of amused puzzlement.

"You're not seriously worried about me having dinner with Sam, are you?"

"Well, I hear he's quite the ladies' man."

"Yes, I would agree with that. It's why I stopped seeing him."

Their wine and steamed clams arrived and gave Drake the opportunity to change the subject.

"Did you decide to buy that condo you liked?"

Liz sipped her wine and shook her head. "I'm having a hard time making up my mind. The furnished apartment is okay for now, until I get to know Seattle a little better. I don't know what else is out there."

Drake dipped a clam into the melted garlic butter and casually said, "Would you help me find a place, if I decide to move up here?"

Her head snapped up and she dropped her fork on her plate. "Are you teasing me?"

He shook his head. "No, I started thinking about it as soon as you agreed to come work for us."

"But what will you do with your law practice and your vineyard? What about Margo and Paul?"

"I have some ideas. They may or may not work out. My neighbor up the road, Chuck Crawford, has agreed to manage the vineyard. He has a master's degree in viticulture from U.C. Davis and manages several other small vineyards. He'll keep an eye on the house for me, so I wouldn't have to move everything here.

"I'm already spending more time here than in my office in Portland. Mike's asked me to help him expand PSS and come work fulltime. I think I'd like that. Paul could lease my office for his P.I. business and I'll keep leasing them the condo upstairs. If they want, I'd sell them both units. We need an investigator and Paul doesn't have to be in Seattle.

"I don't think I could live here in the city. I've looked online at some places out on Vashon or Bainbridge Islands that I think I'd like. It would mean commuting on a ferry, but even that sounds intriguing."

"Wow! You sure know how to take a girl's breath away. I've been trying to think of reasons for PSS opening a satellite office in Portland, so I would be closer to you. Are you sure about this?"

"Yes, I am. Are you sure you want me to?"

Liz picked up the napkin in her lap, laid it on the table and said with an alluring smile, "Why don't you pay the bill and let's go to my place? I think we should explore these ideas in greater detail."

Drake furrowed his brow and nodded with a serious look on his face. "I agree, we have to explore these ideas much more thoroughly."

The exploration of Drake's "proposal" lasted all night and was only interrupted early the next morning when Senator Hazelton called.

"I know it's early, did I wake you?"

Drake sat up quickly on the edge of the bed. "No sir, I was just getting up."

"I was able to get someone to look at the FISA Court's records for last year and this year. No warrant was approved for the electronic surveillance of a U.S. citizen named Nazir."

"Someone would have to been doing it illegally then, but why? Surely the FBI could make up something to justify a warrant. They seem to be pretty good at getting whatever they want, whenever they want it."

"I agree, it doesn't make any sense, if it was the FBI, to go off the reservation like this. Why risk it?"

"Unless it wasn't the FBI."

"You mean one of the other agencies?"

"There are others who must have the capability."

"I'm sure there are."

"Maybe your security expert can unlock Nazir's laptop and tell us who was monitoring it. Tell him to look for malware on it that might tell us."

"I'll give him a call today."

"Thanks senator. Let me know."

Drake turned to look at Liz. "Want to go for a run?"

She sat up and rubbed her sleepy eyes, letting the sheet fall to her lap. "I'd have to get up and put something on. May I make another suggestion?"

Chapter Eleven

JAMES OLIVER WAS FINISHING a second cup of coffee, standing at the window of his condo looking down at the Potomac River, when his phone dinged with the arrival of a text message.

I have the information you want.

He looked at the time on his vintage Hamilton wristwatch and saw that he had enough time to squeeze in a meeting with Tony Yamada on his way to Langley.

Starbucks on the harbor in twenty.

Oliver wasn't surprised that Yamada had located the laptop so quickly. The former NSA cyber spy was the best digital detective he knew and, as the associate deputy director of the CIA's Directorate of Digital Innovation, he knew them all. Finding talent for his directorate was one of his responsibilities.

He emptied the remainder of the coffee in his cup in the kitchen sink, grabbed his black leather laptop case and left for the short walk to his meeting.

It was cloudy but the air was crisp. The temperature was in the mid-sixties and would probably climb another ten degrees in the afternoon; a nice enough day for October. As he lengthened his stride and quickened his pace, he reminded himself that he needed to get out and walk more often. He was only fifty-one, but he saw every morning when he got out of the shower how far from fit he was. Five years ago, he'd played tennis three times a week religiously, before having a skiing accident and needing knee surgery. Since then, the most exercise he got was an occasional rush to catch an elevator.

Thinking about the fit younger man he was about to meet, Oliver squared his shoulders and tightened his stomach muscles. Maybe he would start using the fitness center in his complex and see what a regular workout would do for his flabbiness.

Yamada was seated at a small table smiling with a copy of the *Washington Post* and a venti-size cup of something sitting on it. "Do you want to get something?" he asked.

Oliver sat down and shook his head. "Already had my two cups. Where's the laptop?"

"You asked me to find out who has the laptop and I did. But you're not going to like what I found out."

"Explain."

"I found the legal courier service that brought the laptop from Puget Sound Security to a law firm they use here in Washington. I hacked into the law firm's CCTV system and reviewed the footage from the day it arrived until yesterday."

"This law firm has the laptop?"

"Not anymore. Someone came and left with a laptop under his arm that he didn't walk in with. I used the D.C. cops' facial recognition database to identify the person. That's what I think you're not going to like. The person who left with the laptop is a staffer who works for Senator Hazelton, the chairman of the Senate Intelligence Committee."

Oliver's eyes widened just enough to tell Yamada that he was alarmed.

"What did you get me into, Oliver?" Yamada asked.

"Nothing that you need to know about. You think Senator Hazelton has the laptop because his staffer left with what you think might be the laptop I'm after, is that correct?"

"That's right."

"But the laptop he left with might not be the one I'm looking for. The laptop might still be at the law firm, correct?"

"Right again."

Oliver leaned over the table and said softly, "Then you really haven't earned your pay, have you?"

Yamada squinted his eyes and leaned forward until his face was a foot away from Oliver's. "Why don't you talk with the staffer and find out? We both know that I've done everything you asked me to do. But I don't do break-ins and I don't haul people away to black sites to interrogate them. That's what you do, and you probably need to do it again if you want to know where your precious laptop is. I expect the money to be in my account by the end of the day."

Yamada stood up and walked out.

Oliver watched him leave and calmly considered adding Yamada to the list of loose ends to be eliminated one day soon.

Yamada left his folded newspaper on the table and when Oliver picked it up, a folded page of white paper fell out. When he picked it up, he saw that it was a copy of the senate staffer's congressional security clearance.

On the walk back to the underground parking where his car was, he cursed the day when he'd made the cocaine purchase that Thomas Danforth had found out about. One moment of weakness had made him a pawn in another man's game.

All he could do now was keep doing everything he could to get a hold of Nazir's laptop. Once he had that, he would have evidence of Danforth's involvement with the Russian Volkov and leverage of his own to break the chains that bound him to the FBI agent.

Sitting in his Mercedes before he drove to CIA headquarters, Oliver used his iPhone with its encrypted communication app to message the contractor he wanted to go interrogate the senate staffer.

I have someone I want you to have a talk with.
Let's meet at the mall at noon. I'll buy you
a burrito.

The man he was meeting had been hired and trained by Black-water USA, the private security contractor, after 9/11 to be an assassin in the CIA's anti-terrorism program. When the program was cancelled in 2009 by Director Panetta, he'd offered his services as a private contractor.

The food truck that served the man's favorite burrito was on the Capital Mall. It was where they met the last time Oliver needed his help.

Chapter Twelve

VINCENTE MARTINEZ FOLLOWED the young senate staffer as he walked from the Hart Senate Office Building. He hadn't had time to establish the target's routine, let alone where he lived, due to the time constraints he'd been given.

He wasn't concerned though. He'd worked with less information before, improvising along the way as he'd been trained. Riley Garrett, the twenty-three-year-old college graduate from the University of Oregon, wasn't going to be a challenge unless he ran. The kid looked like he couldn't weigh more than a hundred and sixty pounds dripping wet and had the build of a long-distance runner.

Martinez was ten years older than his target, but he had continued his workout routine since leaving the army. Working as a wet-work contractor for the CIA and now on his own, for people like James Oliver, required a high level of fitness if you wanted to survive.

The problem Martinez was having was deciding where to have a conversation with the young staffer. He wasn't going to hurt him, just ask him one question and leave, making sure he knew that it was in his best interest to forget they'd ever met.

When the young man suddenly turned to his right and walked to the front door of a row house, the decision was made for him. Their conversation was going to have to take place inside the house, unless he wanted to wait for him to come out again. That could be next morning, if this was where he lived.

Judging by the look of the old brick row house, he assumed that Riley Garrett didn't live there alone. He knew from his time in D.C. that a lot of the young people who migrated to the capital after college lived in group houses, sharing the rent. If that was the case, he would just have to find a way for the two of them to talk inside privately.

Martinez walked on past the row house to the next corner and then turned back. Nothing he'd been able to see gave him any information about Garrett's living arrangement. He would have to go in blind.

He walked to the front door and knocked.

Riley Garrett opened the door still wearing his gray overcoat.

"Are you Riley Garrett?"

"Yes."

"And you are a senate staffer working for Senator Hazelton?"

"Yes. What's this about?"

Martinez grabbed the lapels of Garrett's overcoat and pulled him outside, leaving the door open behind him.

"I need to know where the laptop is that you picked up the other day. If you tell me right here, right now, I'll leave. You'll never see me again. If you don't tell me where it is, I will hurt you."

"Who are you? Why should I tell you anything? It's not your laptop!" Garrett said loudly, trying to step back inside.

"Riley, what's going on out there?" a male voice shouted from inside.

Martinez looked over his shoulder and saw a couple on the sidewalk stop to watch. He shoved Garrett inside, kicking the door closed behind him, and pushed the young staffer up against the wall with his left hand. In his right hand was a Walther P22 pistol with its barrel pointed under Garrett's chin.

"I don't have a lot of time here, kid. Tell me where it is, and you'll walk away from this. If you don't, you won't."

Before Garrett could answer, his six-foot-five, two-hundred-and-eighty-pound roommate came down the hallway. "What's going on out here?"

Martinez' right hand was a blur as he fired a single shot, hitting the roommate between the eyes, before sticking the barrel of the pistol back under Garrett's chin.

Garrett's eyes opened wide and his knees buckled.

Martinez held him up and kept him from falling. "I didn't want to do that, but it became necessary when you didn't cooperate. Your roommate's death is on you. Don't make this any worse than it already is. Where's the laptop?"

Garrett moaned and shook his head from side to side. "I don't know. I met a man at Union Station and gave it to him. I don't know where it is now."

"What was his name?"

"I don't remember, honest."

"You can do better than that. How did you know who to give it to if you didn't know his name?"

"I'd seen him before. He's the security expert who checks our computers every other week, but I don't know his name."

Martinez looked into the frightened eyes of the young staffer and knew he was telling the truth. "Thank you."

He brought the Walther P22 up to Garrett's temple and shot him. After taking a handkerchief from his pocket and wiping his fingerprints from the pistol, he put it in Garrett's hand and helped him fire another shot in the direction of the dead roommate. Then he positioned the staffer's body to look like there had been a deadly confrontation that ended badly for the two roommates; one murder, one suicide.

Martinez walked through the row house and left by the back door. An alley led to the next street over and he walked away into the fading light of a cool October night.

A phone call the next morning to Senator Hazelton's office, posing as a staffer from another senator's office, asking for a referral to the IT security firm they used would get him the information he needed.

He regretted the necessity of killing the two roommates, but in his line of work it wasn't something he was going to lose a night's sleep over. Oliver wanted the laptop and killing again to get it for him was a likely possibility.

Chapter Thirteen

SENATOR HAZELTON WAS in his study enjoying his favorite nightcap, a dark rum and amaro concoction over a cube of ice, when his wife knocked lightly on the open door.

"Honey, there's an officer from the Metro police at the door. He says he needs to talk with you."

"Did he say why?"

"No, he didn't. He just apologized for it being so late."

Senator Hazelton got up and followed his wife down the stairs to the front door of their three-story row house in the historic section of Georgetown. A plain-clothed detective was standing just inside the door.

"Senator Hazelton, I apologize for the late hour, but I thought you would want to know as soon as possible. One of your young staffers, Riley Garrett, was killed tonight."

"Oh, no," Meredith said. "His parents are friends of ours. Have they been notified?"

"Not yet, ma'am. We're still investigating the scene."

"Where did it happen?" Senator Hazelton asked.

"In the group home where he lived with some other staffers. His roommate was also killed. It looks like a murder and suicide, but we're still investigating. Do you know anything about his living arrangements? Did he get along with his roommates?"

"As far as I know. They were all from Oregon. Two of them work in my office and the third works in the office of one of our state's congressmen. Who was the roommate that was killed?"

The detective checked his notes. "His name is Troy Walters."

"Troy worked in Congressman Waller's office," Senator Hazelton said. "Is the other roommate okay, Paul Simmons?"

"He found the bodies when he came home. He's pretty shaken up, but otherwise he's okay. According to him, Garrett and Walters were good friends. He's having a hard time accepting what appears to be true, that Garrett killed his friend."

"He's not the only one. Riley was one of the best staffers I've ever had. I've never heard him raise his voice to anyone or even get angry about anything. We have constituents who visit us on occasion who would try the patience of a saint. Riley is the staffer we usually ask to deal with them."

"Do you know if Garrett owned a gun?"

"I wouldn't think so," Meredith Hazelton said. "His parents won't allow a gun in their house."

"What kind of gun was it?" Senator Hazelton asked.

"A Glock 26. It's a compact 9 mm pistol that's a favorite for concealed carry."

"Does Garrett have a concealed carry license?"

"I don't have that information, senator."

Senator Hazelton put his left arm around his wife and reached out with his right hand to the detective. "Thank you for letting me know about Riley, detective. If there's anything you need from me for your investigation, don't hesitate to ask."

As soon as the door closed behind the detective, Senator Hazelton said, "I have a bad feeling about this. I may be the reason Riley's dead."

"Whatever are you talking about?"

"I asked Riley to do something for me that didn't have anything to do with his duties as a senate staffer. I had him take a laptop to a security expert for examination. I learned, after I had him pick it up from a law firm Drake and Casey use here in D.C., that the FBI is looking for that laptop. Some dangerous people might also be looking for it. That might be the reason he was killed—he knew where the laptop is."

Senator Hazelton turned to walk away when Meredith took a hold of his arm. "You know where this laptop is as well. Are you in danger?"

He turned back and put his arms around her. "I don't think so. I have bodyguards, like so many others in Congress these days. Whoever killed Riley may already know where it is, if he told them. If he didn't, they won't compound their problem of his death by coming after me. They know I'll be protected."

Meredith kissed him on the cheek. "Go finish your nightcap and come to bed."

Senator Hazelton followed her upstairs and returned to his study, closing the door behind him.

The first call he made was to the office of the security firm he'd hired to see what information could be retrieved from the encrypted laptop. He left a message on the firm's answering machine for them to call him first thing in the morning.

The next call went to his son-in-law in Seattle, who answered on the third ring.

"Adam, I think we have a problem here. My young staffer I sent to pick up the laptop from the law firm where you sent it was killed tonight. The police say it looks like he killed his roommate and then killed himself. I don't believe it."

"Why not?"

"I know him. I know his parents. His mother was the one who found his grandfather when he shot himself. They've never allowed a gun in the house and would never allow Riley to have one."

"Is there anything that points to anyone else?"

"It's not a coincidence that the FBI show up with a search warrant at your offices looking for the laptop and the next day my staffer is killed."

"Have you told anyone what you think might be behind this?"

"Who would I tell? Certainly not the FBI."

"Do you still have your bodyguards?"

"Yes."

"Tell them what you suspect and be on the alert. You're a potential target as well."

"You're the second person who's told me that tonight."

"Is Mom worried?"

"I told her not to worry but I'm sure she is."

"You might want to alert the people who have the laptop to double their security."

"I left a message with them minutes ago to call me first thing in the morning."

"Is there anything you want me to do from here?"

"Not that I can think of. Did you find out who ordered the FBI search warrant?"

"Liz is having dinner with her old boyfriend tomorrow night. If he comes through, we might know something then."

"All right. Let me know. If it came from someone here in Washington, I can find out."

"Thank you, senator. You and Mom be careful. If someone with enough pull to get our offices searched is behind this, he's risking everything by killing your staffer. There's no reason to think he won't do it again if he thinks it's necessary."

Chapter Fourteen

VINCENTE MARTINEZ WAITED for the cyber security consultant to drive home from his office in his black BMW Z4 roadster. William Nielsen, aged thirty-seven and a former naval intelligence officer, worked for RTX Security Services in Hanover, Maryland.

Martinez had identified Nielsen as the person who visited Senator Hazelton's office twice a month to test the cyber security of its computers and then take his wife in the office to lunch. He was the one the young staffer said he delivered the laptop to for the senator.

He'd planned initially to find a way into the RTX offices and retrieve the laptop Nielsen was working on. The RTX office building was in a suburban corner of the D.C. area where several cyber security start-up firms were located. Those firms were hiring government cyber security talent, former spies, intelligence analysts and hackers to provide cyber security services to corporations and smaller government agencies in and around the capitol.

But the RTX building's architects had taken the need for physical and personnel security seriously. The ten-story building had a controlled perimeter, with anti-ram barriers, remote controlled gates into its underground parking, and personnel access control that used biometrics and identification cards he assumed were used to access the different secured areas of the building. It also had video and CCTV surveillance technology evident on its exterior.

To get the laptop, he was going to have to do it the old-fashioned way, by getting Nielsen to bring the laptop to him.

As soon as he recognized the RTX building's level of security features that morning, he turned his focus to Nielsen and had been lucky. It was one of the days when Nielsen went to Senator Hazelton's office. He'd taken his wife to lunch at a restaurant in the Eastern Market with outside patio seating. He'd followed him there and taken pictures of Nielsen and his wife from his car parked across the street.

Now it was just a matter of finding a place to speak to Nielsen.

From the RTX building parking lot, Martinez followed Nielsen's black convertible to a small strip mall where he parked in front of a wine and spirits shop called Cork and Bottle and went inside.

Martinez parked on the left side of Nielsen's Z4 and waited for him to come out. Five minutes later, Nielsen did with a tall bottle of wine in a purple paper sack in his left hand and his key fob in his right hand.

Martinez got out with his camera and walked around the back of his Audi A4 to meet him.

"How do you like your Z4?" Martinez asked.

"Great car. This is the four-cylinder. I'll get the six-cylinder next time though."

"Is it Bill or do you prefer that I call you William?"

"What is this? How do you know my name?"

"That's not important, I assure you. What is important is that you listen to me carefully. You have a laptop that doesn't belong to you that I want. I'm willing to trade you for something that I know you want."

Nielsen took a step back and shifted the bottle of wine to his right hand. "What would that be?"

Martinez brushed his coat back with his right hand and took the Glock 19 from its paddle holster on his belt. "You don't want to do that. Toss the bottle in your car."

Nielsen hesitated and said, "I'm tossing the bottle in my car. Now, what is it that I want?"

"You want your wife to stay alive."

"You son of a—"

"Unfortunately, that is a correct description of my parentage. I'm very good at what I do, Bill. You need to know that. If you cooperate with me, you can continue taking your wife to lunch at trendy restaurants with patio seating outside and enjoying her company every night at home. If you don't, there's no way you can keep me from killing her.

"I want you to bring me the laptop Senator Hazelton gave you. Take the cell phone I'm going to give you and call me tomorrow morning at ten o'clock. A number is taped on the back of it. I'll give you directions on where to take the laptop. If you do as I say, you'll never hear from me again. If you don't, you will never hear from your wife again either. Do not involve the police or the FBI. I will know if you do. Do you understand what I'm telling you, Bill?"

"I can't just walk out of the office with the laptop, be serious!"

"Find a way, if you want your wife to live."

Martinez took a burner phone out of his left coat pocket and tossed it to Nielsen.

"Now get in your car. Go home and enjoy a glass of that wine with your wife. Think about your future together and call me tomorrow morning at ten o'clock."

Martinez waved his pistol toward Nielsen's roadster. "Go."

He watched Nielsen back his car out and drive away before getting in his Audi and turning on his own burner phone. The one he'd given Nielsen had an app installed that Oliver had borrowed from the CIA's Directorate of Digital Innovation. The app let him send a command to the phone and turn it on remotely. Using its microphone, he could hear all audio communications and any sound in the room where the smartphone was located.

He didn't expect Nielsen to use the phone to call anyone before calling him tomorrow, but he did expect him to talk to someone about the threat on his wife's life. In fact, he was banking on the consultant reaching out to someone for help. If it was the police, he would know it. If it was someone at RTX Security Services, he would know it and have some idea of whether Nielsen was going to cooperate or not.

In the event he didn't cooperate, he would have to turn up the heat and show the man he didn't make idle threats.

Chapter Fifteen

FOR THE SECOND time in as many nights, Meredith Hazelton came downstairs to answer the door to find they had an unexpected visitor. Emma Nielsen, one of the senator's senior staff members, looked like she had been crying.

"Emma, come in. Is something wrong?"

"Is Senator Hazelton here? I need to talk with him."

"He's upstairs in his study getting ready for tomorrow's hearing. Come with me."

Meredith took Emma's trembling hand and led her up the stairs.

"Robert, Emma's here to see you," she said as she opened the door to his study.

Senator Hazelton dropped the file he was reading on the floor next to his old leather armchair and stood to greet her. When he saw the look on her face, he walked over and put his hands on her shoulders. "Emma, what is it?"

"A man approached Bill on his way home tonight. He said to bring him the laptop tomorrow morning you have him working on. The man said if Bill didn't, he would never hear from me again."

Meredith Hazelton gasped as her husband beckoned Emma to sit in his armchair and tell them everything.

"Take your time. Would you like a glass of water?"

She took a deep breath and said, "No thank you. The man told Bill he would know if he involved the police or the FBI, so Bill sent me a text message explaining what had happened and told me to come here."

"What did this man look like?" the senator asked.

"Bill said he was Hispanic, dark complexion in his late thirties or early forties. Five seven or five eight and wearing a black leather overcoat and black slacks. Bill didn't see what car the man was driving, but he has the license number of a white Audi that was parked next to him. He thinks it's probably the man's car."

"Does Bill have any idea who the man is?"

"He has no idea, senator. He wants to know what you think he should do."

Senator Hazelton turned to his wife. "Why don't you take Emma downstairs and get her a glass of wine or something? I need to make a couple of calls."

He helped Emma up and waited until the two women were out of the study before sitting down in his armchair to call his son-in-law.

"Adam, are you still in Seattle?"

"I stayed around to hear if Liz finds who in the FBI wanted our offices searched."

"Are you driving back to Portland tonight?"

"I thought I would. Liz doesn't need me hanging around when she has dinner with her old boyfriend."

"Good, because I may need you here tomorrow morning. The man I asked to work on Nazir's laptop was approached tonight. He was instructed to bring a man the laptop or his wife would be killed. She's one of my senior staffers and came here to ask me what he should do. What do you think we should do?"

"They're pretty desperate if they killed your younger staffer and are brazenly threatening another one. Have you been able get anything from Nazir's laptop?"

"Bill Nielsen, the cyber security expert at RXT Security Services, tells me that Nazir used a disk encryption software that's immune to brute-force attacks to crack the encrypted password. Without having Nazir's password, it could take years to get information from the files on his laptop."

Drake thought for a moment. "If someone in the FBI has Nazir in custody somewhere, they'll get the password from him sooner or later. But without the laptop, it won't do them any good. We have the laptop, but without the password it won't do us any good. What if we let this guy have the laptop and find a way to track it? It could lead us to where they're holding Nazir."

"What's our downside?"

"If your guy at RXT can get a GPS tracking transmitter on the laptop case it was in, or something on the laptop itself, there isn't a downside. The downside is they find the GPS transmitter, we lose the laptop and it's the end of the trail."

"We'll need to follow the laptop ourselves because I'm not willing to bring the FBI into this," Senator Hazelton said. "How soon can you get here if we decide to let him have the laptop?"

"If Mike's willing to let me use the Gulfstream, we can be there tonight."

"Are you bringing Liz?"

"No, she has a dinner engagement I'd like her to keep. I'd like to bring a couple of Mike's best people."

"The people you took to Hawaii?"

"Yes, if they're available on short notice. If not, Mike has others I can bring. In fact, we hired a new guy today who used to command an FBI HRT unit. He knows the FBI and still has friends in D.C."

"I like your plan," Senator Hazelton said. "I'll send Emma back to her husband to tell him what we want him to do. Let me know when you're getting here. I'll have someone there to meet you."

"We'll be there before the sun comes up. We'll make sure your guy is safe when he hands over the laptop. We're dealing with some dangerous people and I intend to find out who they are."

Chapter Sixteen

IT WAS a hasty departure for Drake and the PSS team he'd been able to quickly assemble for the flight in the company's Gulfstream G-650.

Mike Casey, the PSS CEO and Drake's best friend, had jumped at the chance to provide protection for Bill Nielsen. Not only had he offered the best members of his close protection VIP division, as well as his newest hire, the former FBI HRT commander, he had insisted on joining the team and coming along.

As always, the G-650 was flown by Steve Carson, a former F-16 close air support jockey in Iraq. Marco Morales, a former long-range reconnaissance patrol Army Ranger who was used to operating behind enemy lines without being detected, argued that operating in D.C. was something he was uniquely qualified for. Two of the company's SEALs, Don Borden and Nick Manning who were tapped for duty, were experienced urban warriors and trained to operate among civilians on covert assignments.

The last member added to the team was Dan Norris, the former FBI HRT commander. Norris had left the FBI after being made the scapegoat for a hostage rescue attempt that was doomed from the git-go because of the bad operational intelligence he received.

In addition to his HRT experience, Norris knew most of the senior staff at FBI headquarters and was familiar with Washington, D.C. He'd spent fourteen years operating out of the FBI's training facility at Quantico, Virginia, where the HRT was based.

While the departure from Seattle had been hurried, it had also involved a minor skirmish between Drake and Liz. He wanted her to stay and have dinner with her old boyfriend.

Liz was adamant that she didn't need to stay behind to have dinner, that Sam Gregory would tell her what he knew without a face-to-face exchange. She felt Drake was insisting that she stay behind because he couldn't get over the fact that she had agreed to Sam Gregory's quid pro quo in the first place.

A compromise resolved the issue; Liz would catch the red-eye flight to Washington after the dinner and be there to help monitor the laptop exchange.

An hour into the flight, Drake and Casey were sitting in the main cabin, facing each other across a dark Indian Rosewood fold-out table. Casey had poured each of them a glass of his new favorite small batch bourbon.

"How are we going to protect Nielsen when he hands over the laptop?" Casey asked.

"It's not going to be easy. We won't know where he's supposed to go until he calls this guy and we can't be seen following him. We'll have to be with him when he calls and work from there."

"Have you wondered why he was told only to use the burner phone he was given?"

"Because it makes it harder to track a burner phone, I suppose."

"There could be another reason," Casey said. "The CIA's supposed to be able to remotely activate a phone's microphone, so they can listen to any sound in the room where the phone is located. What if that's what this guy is doing to make sure Nielsen doesn't get the police or FBI involved?"

"Then he'd be CIA and we'd have a bigger problem than I want to think about right now."

"I'm not sure he'd have to be CIA. Some of their toys have

found their way into the public domain and are being used by all types of bad actors; drug cartels, terrorist groups and criminal hackers."

Drake shook his head. "How would any of these bad actors know about Nazir's laptop? We know about it because we have it. The FBI knows about it because they want it. It has to be someone in the government."

"Or someone working for the government."

Drake agreed. "Or someone working for the government. We've considered that possibility all along. With that in mind, how do we protect Nielsen and then track the laptop?"

"Well, we need to get a mike on Nielsen to know if he's in danger at the handover. And then we need to be able to protect him if he is, even from a distance," Casey added with a sly smile.

Drake smiled as well. "Do we have any idea how we would do that?"

"Find someone who's good with a long gun, like a sniper, I guess."

"Maybe even a former Delta Force sniper, like you?"

"I will humbly offer my services. I even have my favorite M24 sniper rifle onboard, along with all the other things you thought we might need."

Drake raised his glass in toast and said, "I'm glad we settled that minor detail. Now we just need to find out who's waiting for the laptop on the other end. That's the person I want to get my hands on, literally."

"You will. Be patient, like we had to be stalking targets in Iraq and Afghanistan."

"I'm not sure we have the luxury of waiting for the right time to take a shot, like we did then," Drake said. "Someone's in a hurry and is willing to take big risks to get this laptop. Whoever it is must know we're on to them. If they have Nazir and force him to give up his encrypted password and then erase whatever it is they don't want us to discover, we'll never be able to prove who they are."

"Then we have two problems. Protecting Nielsen and tracking

the laptop is one. Finding Nazir in time to keep him from erasing what's on his laptop is another. How do we find Nazir in time?"

Drake thought for a moment. "We find the FBI agents who took custody of him, when you flew him from Hawaii to Montana, and ask them."

Chapter Seventeen

DRAKE AND LIZ waited at eight o'clock with a group of morning walkers at the main entrance to the Arundel Mills Mall in Hanover, Maryland. They were there to meet Emma Nielsen. She had been told by Senator Hazelton to look for a couple wearing Seattle Seahawk ball caps who would walk with her, once they were sure she wasn't being followed.

Liz squeezed Drake's hand as a petite brunette wearing black running tights and a pink tank top joined the group. She looked their way and nodded then looked forward as the doors opened for the mall walkers.

Drake started forward with Liz and then stopped and bent down as if he needed to re-tie a shoe. "Go ahead, I'll catch up."

When he finished, he stood up and saw that Liz was walking beside Emma Nielsen at the back of the pack of walkers. He looked around the parking lot to see if anyone was rushing to join the walkers he should be worried about and then jogged ahead to catch up with Liz and her walking companion.

When he fell in step beside Liz, he said, "Emma, my name is Adam Drake. I think you know Liz from the time she worked in Senator Hazelton's office with you. How are you?"

"Worried about Bill, but thankful you and Liz are here to keep him safe."

"How is Bill?" Liz asked.

"Calmer than I am, but he worked as an intelligence officer. He's as interested in finding out what this is all about as he is in making sure I'm safe, although he won't admit it."

"Was he able to load a GPS transmitter on the laptop case or on the laptop itself?" Drake asked.

"Here," she said and took a smartphone out of her running waist pack. "He slipped the transmitter into the laptop case. He couldn't find a way to get it on the laptop itself. The password for monitoring the GPS transmitter is taped on the back of the phone. It's active now."

"Emma, we have four men in two SUVs waiting to follow Bill to the location where he's told to take the laptop. We will coordinate with them and make sure he's safe before we use the tracker to follow the laptop. Did he decide how he's going to let us know where he's going?"

"Just before he calls the man who gave him the burner phone, he'll call you on his phone to the phone I just gave you. He'll keep it open, so you can hear him. He'll repeat the instructions he's given out loud."

They reached an alcove that was lined with benches and Liz guided Emma to one and sat down beside her. Drake stood watch at the entrance to the alcove.

"I know you're planning on going to Senator Hazelton's home to wait with Meredith. We want to take you there, just to be safe in case they want to snatch you to make sure Bill cooperates. Is there anything else we can do for you?"

"The only thing you can do; keep my husband safe. I know he's trained for this kind of thing and he's carrying his Glock, but please protect him for me. I'll be with Meredith waiting for him to call me when it's over."

After driving Emma Nielsen to the Hazeltons' home in Georgetown, Drake and Liz stopped by the Savoy Suites Hotel in Georgetown to pick up Mike Casey.

Before getting into their rented black GMC Yukon, Casey slid a M24 Pelican tactical rifle case across the back seat. "How's Mrs. Nielsen doing?"

"Nervous but handling it like a former intelligence officer's wife," Liz said.

Drake pulled out of the hotel's parking lot and asked Casey if their guys at Nielsen's office had reported anything yet.

"Nothing so far. They have eyes on Nielsen's Z4 roadster. They're each parked near one of the two exits, so they won't have any trouble following him. They haven't seen anyone waiting for him."

Drake checked his watch. "We have thirty minutes before Nielsen makes his call. There are five major routes out of Hanover with Maryland Route 30, the Hanover Pike, being the highway that runs east and west. If Nielsen's meeting our guy closer to the capitol, he'll probably take the Hanover Pike. If it's closer to Hanover, there's a cemetery just north of town that would be a good place to meet. We have no way of knowing where the drop site is. Let's find a place close to the center of Hanover. That way we'll have a chance to get ahead of Nielsen wherever he's told to go."

Liz turned in her seat to look back at Casey and then to Drake beside her. "I have a bad feeling about this. There's a good chance we're not going to be there in time to protect Nielsen. We'll be able to track the laptop but we're really asking Nielsen to take a big risk."

"I know," Drake said. "I'd feel better if we could bring in the police or the FBI to handle this. But with what we know, that it's possible someone in the government is involved, he could be in more danger that way."

"He'll be okay, Liz," Casey said. "We have talented people protecting him. If everything goes as planned, he should be back in time to take his wife to lunch."

"That's what's bothering me," Liz said. "Things never go as planned."

Chapter Eighteen

AT TEN O'CLOCK DRAKE, Liz and Casey were sitting in their Yukon in the parking lot of the Candlewood Suite near the intersection of the Paul T. Pitcher Memorial Highway and the Baltimore-Washington Parkway.

Liz put the smartphone Emma Nielsen gave them on the center console so they all could hear Bill Nielsen when he made the call. When it buzzed, Casey leaned forward from the back seat so that his nose was six inches from the phone.

They heard the call ring twice and a male voice answered. "Don't say a word. I will know if you do. I'm sending your instructions as text messages."

Casey slapped his leg and sprang back. "No way to get ahead of Nielsen now. All we can do is follow him."

"Liz, tell the others that Nielsen is getting directions by text messages. I'm going to get us closer to his office. Then send Nielsen a message on that phone he gave us to text the directions he's given to us, if he can while he's driving. If this guy plays games and sends him racing from point to point, he might not be able to."

Drake drove quickly through the parking lot and accelerated out onto Dorsey Road heading west. The RXT Security Services building was a quarter of a mile away.

He slowed down when they were half a block away and parked on the street in front of the RXT building.

Liz finished talking with Morales a second before they received a text from Nielsen on the smartphone he'd loaded the GPS tracker app on.

Told to drive south on 295, the Baltimore-Washington Pkwy.

Liz responded: **Copy that.**

Drake waited until Nielsen left the parking lot and pulled in behind the two Yukons following him.

Casey checked the MapQuest app he had open on his smartphone. "He'll probably take Hanover Road to Coca Cola Drive and then onto the Paul T. Pitcher Memorial Highway. That will get him to the Baltimore-Washington Parkway. Do you want to get ahead of him?"

"Where does the highway go?" Drake asked.

"Southeast for a couple of miles and then it reaches the cloverleaf that will put him on the Baltimore-Washington Parkway."

"Then where?"

"The Annapolis Junction is the next major intersection that would put him on the Patuxent Freeway that runs northwest to southeast past Fort Meade toward D.C."

"Let's get in front of him. Liz, text him just before we pull alongside that it's us and tell him to let us know if he's leaving the parkway. Mike, call Morales and tell him we're trying to get to the drop site before Nielsen does. If we can't get there and set up before he arrives, he needs to be right on his tail."

Drake pulled into the fast lane and drove past the first Yukon, then a white Camry that got between their two SUVs, and slowed to match the speed of Nielsen's Z4 for a minute. They saw Nielsen turn to see why Drake had slowed and then nod when he saw Liz hold up her right hand to signal okay and then the smartphone he'd given them.

"He looks like he's handling this pretty well for a swabbie," Casey said as Drake pulled ahead and in front of the black roadster.

Liz turned around and corrected him. "A swabbie refers to a Naval man of low rank. Nielsen was a lieutenant colonel. He won't like you calling him that."

Casey laughed. "They never do. That's why we do it."

They passed a traffic sign advising that the exit for the Patuxent Freeway was two miles ahead when Nielsen sent another text message.

Exiting parkway onto 32, the Patuxent Freeway, driving east.

Copy that, Liz responded.

"Where's he heading, Mike?" Drake asked.

Casey studied MapQuest on his phone and said, "There's a huge wildlife research refuge south of the freeway. That would be a good place to make sure no one was coming with Nielsen. Fort Meade is not far, north of the freeway, but I can't see Nielsen being told to go there. He's probably going somewhere closer to the capitol."

Liz's smartphone pinged.

Turning south on 198, Laurel Fort Meade Rd.

Copy that, she responded.

"Looks like you're right, Mike," Drake said. "It's the wildlife refuge. Any place there that stands out?"

Casey held his smartphone closer. "We might have a problem. There's a local general aviation airport just off Fort Meade Road. They could fly Nielsen from there so we can't follow him."

"No, no, no." Drake exhaled loudly. "I should have thought of that, had you up in a bird just in case."

"It still might be the wildlife refuge," Liz said. "We haven't lost him yet."

Her phone pinged again.

Told to take Exit 198 to Airport Road.

Drake slammed on the brakes and slid the Yukon to a stop then burned rubber as he spun the SUV around. Airport Road was just a hundred yards back and they'd driven past it.

Tipton Airport is a former U.S. Army airfield that was privatized for general aviation operation in 1988. Its 366 acres and single runway are bordered by Fort Meade and the Patuxent National Wildlife Research Refuge.

Drake pulled to the side of the road and let Nielsen's BMW Z4 drive by. Straight ahead down an entrance road he saw a two-story tower and beyond that six single-engine planes on a tarmac tie-down area. A black Sikorsky S76 helicopter was parked on a run-off area next to the runway with its rotors spinning.

"That's where Nielsen's going. Mike, can you cover him from here with your M24?" Drake asked.

Casey already had the sniper rifle out of its case and jumped out to stand behind the SUV's open rear door with the window down. He put the rifle barrel through the open window and sighted on the Z4 that was stopped fifty yards in front of the helicopter.

"Nielsen's just sitting there," Casey reported. "It looks like the pilot is the only one in the helicopter. What do you want to do if Nielsen gets in the helicopter?"

"We'll have to let this play out. It could be just a chartered helicopter to fly Nielsen or the laptop somewhere else."

Casey slowly scoped the immediate area from right to left. "Wait, movement at nine o'clock. Someone on a motor scooter is headed toward Nielsen."

"If he's armed and threatens Nielsen, take him down," Drake ordered.

Casey watched as the motor scooter stopped next to the driver's side door of the Z4. "Some young guy in coveralls. He's gesturing for Nielsen to hand him something. Nielsen's giving him the laptop. He's taking it to the helicopter. The pilot has his door open and is handed the laptop case. Looks like Nielsen is going to be okay."

They watched the black helicopter gain elevation and turn to the south and then speed off over the Patuxent National Wildlife Research Refuge.

Chapter Nineteen

VINCENTE MARTINEZ WAITED in the Signature Flight Support Lounge for the Sikorsky S76 he'd chartered from Talon Air to land at Ronald Reagan Washington National Airport. The pilot had called during the short flight from Tipton Airport to tell him he had the laptop. He was pushing it so there would be plenty of time for Martinez to get to his meetings that morning.

There were no meetings, of course, and the last-minute charter could never be traced back to him or the company he'd said he worked for. Doing contract work for men like James Oliver required total anonymity if you wanted to stay alive and out of jail. The collection of identities the CIA had prepared for him when he worked for them was as good as any you could buy anywhere in the world.

Martinez tipped the lounge attendant generously for running out to the Sikorsky and bringing him his laptop. He'd faked a conference call he said he had to be on and sent the attendant out to the helicopter so the pilot would never be able to describe him.

By eleven o'clock he was negotiating traffic in his Audi A4 on his way to the old warehouse he leased in Ivy City, an old industrial area in Northeast Washington, D.C. The city had been laid out as a suburban development for African Americans in 1873. Despite some gentrification, people living in the residential core of the city remained poor and unemployment rates were always high.

It was perfect for his needs. You didn't wander into Ivy City unless you had a reason to or you were looking for someone, which was why he'd installed the best security systems money could buy; fiber-optic intrusion detection, integrated video surveillance and electronic access control doors and all of it could be monitored remotely.

The building was also sound-proofed so well that you could stand outside at a door when he was using his indoor gun range and not hear a thing. That included times when he practiced with unsuppressed weapons like his FN Five-seveN pistol or his FN P90 submachine gun.

To excel as he had in his chosen profession, you had to be the best and stay the best in all the killing arts.

Martinez stopped in front of the sliding security gate to enter the day's code on the key pad and drove forward across a large graveled area. He stopped in front the blast-resistant door and used a remote device to open it and drove the Audi inside onto the gray epoxy concrete floor.

The warehouse didn't have windows, but with the video surveillance panels on all the interior walls he didn't need any. He was as safe inside as a man could be who wasn't hiding in a bomb shelter somewhere.

He took his black lambskin leather jacket off and sat down at his desk to call James Oliver and tell him he had his laptop.

"I have it. What do you want me to do with it?"

"Your place is safe. Keep it there for now."

"Are you going to have someone work on it?"

"Yes, the same man who helped me find out who had it."

"Will he come and get it?"

"I want him to work on it at your place."

"You know I work alone. I don't want someone I don't know wandering around in my shop."

"Then keep an eye on him and make sure he doesn't see anything you don't want him to see."

"You mean be his babysitter? I have other clients who need attention. I can't be tied down here all day."

"I retained you for three days. I'll extend it for another three if that will make you happy."

"Done. Have him call me."

Martinez leaned back and wondered what was so important about this laptop that was worth adding another three days at ten thousand dollars a day to his retainer. He'd have to find out as much as he could from Oliver's guy. Knowing as much as possible about Oliver's game was the best way to keep from becoming the scapegoat if things went wrong.

He'd worked for Oliver on three other occasions and those jobs had all been out of the country. The targets had all been Saudis who were financing terrorism. The U.S. had been reluctant to take them out because of the strategic alliance it had with the Kingdom of Saudi Arabia. Oliver had the proof from his cyber spying and acted on his own to arrange fatal accidents for them that couldn't be blamed on the CIA or the U.S. in any way.

This was different and it worried him. Oliver was using him at home for some reason. When he was trained by the FBI to be an assassin, he knew that with the FBI's jurisdiction technically restricted to the homeland he might be called on to eliminate a U.S. citizen involved in terrorism operating in the U.S. But that was when he was FBI.

In his line of work, your career ended when someone ended it for you. Oliver was smart and ruthless, and he'd always trusted him. But if Oliver was reckless enough to operate in the U.S, he was beginning to question the wisdom of continuing to do so.

Chapter Twenty

MARCO MORALES and Dan Norris sat quietly on stakeout a block away from an old warehouse. The tracking app on the smartphone Bill Nielsen had given the PSS team had led them from Ronald Reagan Washington National Airport to this industrial area in NE Washington, D.C. and to this warehouse.

Dan Norris, the former FBI HRT commander, was using a pair of Steiner Tactical 6508 binoculars to check out the warehouse.

"It doesn't look like much, but that place has state-of-the-art security. No one's getting in there with out being detected," Norris said.

"Any thoughts on who's in there?" Morales asked.

"It could be anyone. The agencies use places like this to keep the public from knowing what they're doing. Private contractors doing work for the agencies use them as well. I can't see satellite dishes or antennas, so I'm guessing it's non-government."

"If the laptop leaves the warehouse, we have all the ways out of here covered. But we're going to need more than the other team and us to watch the warehouse 24x7. We'd better give Drake a call and get another couple of PSS teams to Washington."

Norris turned his binoculars to track a motorcycle that pulled up to the front security gate of the warehouse compound. "We may not be here that long if the guy on the bike is here to take it somewhere."

Morales borrowed the binoculars and saw a lime-green Kawasaki Ninja ZX-14R and a rider dressed in black leathers and wearing a black helmet with the visor down. "If the laptop leaves on that bike, we'll never be able to follow it. That thing does two hundred miles an hour!"

"Do you ride?" Norris asked.

"Not a superbike but I am restoring a Triumph Bonneville."

Morales saw the rider lean down toward the security touch pad and straighten up as the security gate slid back. "Someone was expecting him."

The Kawasaki rolled forward across the gravel and stopped in front of an overhead door. When it rolled up, the motorcycle shot in and the overhead door closed.

Morales used his smartphone to call Drake. "The laptop is still in the warehouse, but someone in a very fast super bike just arrived. What do you want us to do?"

"Keep eyes on the warehouse. If you think the laptop is leaving on the motorcycle, keep one team there and the other follow it, if you can. With the GPS tracker on the laptop, we'll always know where it is."

"Copy that. Do we have any backup on the way? We're okay here for the long haul, if required, but those two SEALs in the other Yukon might need to pull back and get some sleep."

Drake and Norris laughed at the same time.

"I'll pass that along, Marco. I'm sure they'll appreciate you thinking about them. Mike is sending the Gulfstream back to Seattle tonight and it will return with four more men. They'll be here tomorrow morning, so make the best of it tonight," Drake said.

"How are Nielsen and his wife doing?" Norris asked.

"They stayed with the Senator and Mrs. Hazelton last night just to be safe. They're doing fine. Emma is very proud of her husband."

"Drake, this warehouse has state-of-the-art security. Are you thinking about going in and retrieving the laptop if this goes sideways? If you are, there are some things I'll need to get my hands on," Norris said.

"Ultimately I want to know what's on the laptop. Right now, I'd like to know who wants it so badly they'll kill to get it. Go ahead and let me know what you need. We can always take it with us if we don't need it. Keep me advised."

Morales ended the call and asked Norris what kind of things he wanted to get his hands on.

"If we're going in after the laptop, I need more information about the warehouse security. I used a tiny drone in HRT. If we had one of those, I could fly it around and get a closer look at everything. It's a tiny little thing that sits in the palm of your hand…"

"And it's called the Black Hornet," Morales finished for him. "I've flown one. We have the latest model, the Black Hornet 3, back in Seattle. We can have the new teams bring it with them when they come."

"I'm impressed," Norris said. "Do I want to know how you used it?"

"Nothing illegal, if that's what you're asking. We were watching a wealthy terrorist and his friends posing as students in Seattle. They were planning on using sarin nerve gas to attack the light rail system in Seattle, like the 1995 Tokyo attack. We stopped them."

"I thought an Israeli team assisted the transit police to stop the terrorists? We studied what they did in HRT."

Morales turned to Norris with a grin on his face. "We brought the Israelis in to help us. They had experience and knew how to spot terrorists before they acted. They insisted that the transit police take the credit, so they didn't have to stick around and be accused of racial profiling."

"Now I'm really impressed," Norris said. "Looks like there's a lot I don't know about Puget Sound Security."

"Casey's put together a team of men with experience, like you. You'll see plenty of action if you stick around."

"What's Drake's role in all of this?"

"Drake and Casey served together as a hunter/killer team in Delta Force. Casey runs the company and Drake's the company's lawyer, but he's more than that. He's our leader when we get involved in what they call our special projects."

"How often do those come around?"

"A couple of times a year. You need to stay in shape and keep your skill set sharp. You never know when a project like this comes along, and you never know how long you'll be involved in it. Like this one. I have a feeling this isn't anywhere close to being over."

Chapter Twenty-One

TONY YAMADA SAT on his Kawasaki Ninja and looked around at the immaculate workplace Martinez had built for himself. An area near an office with a long one-way window was set up as a gym with an Olympic barbell rack, a full set of dumbbells, a heavy bag and a treadmill. Across the way was a workbench with an eight-foot-long pegboard with hand tools hanging on it. At the far end of the warehouse was a two-lane indoor shooting range with a target-retrieval system.

When he turned back from admiring the shooting range, Vincente Martinez was standing ten feet away with a Glock pistol held loosely in his right hand.

Yamada took his helmet off and set it carefully on the gas tank in front of him.

"What's in the backpack?" Martinez asked.

Yamada slipped his arms out of his laptop backpack and held it out to Martinez. "Just my laptop and a few tools I need to work on Oliver's laptop. I'm not armed."

Martinez stepped forward and took the backpack and set it on the floor. "How long will you be here?"

"Not a minute more than I have to be. There are two black

SUVs parked at each end of the street out front. I'm guessing they followed you here. I don't want to be here when they come for you."

"They won't be coming for me and I wasn't followed. I had the laptop flown here by helicopter. I know when I'm being followed. Maybe they followed you."

"I wasn't followed. They probably have a tracking device on the laptop."

"They don't have the password for the laptop. How could they install GPS tracking software on it, smartass?"

"Then it's in the laptop case. You didn't think of that, did you, smartass?"

Martinez waved the Glock menacingly and pointed it toward the workbench. "I'll get the laptop. Show me a GPS transmitter or you won't be riding out of here on your bike."

Yamada got off his bike and picked up his backpack. "You always this paranoid?"

"Stand in front of the workbench where I can see you," Martinez said and walked over to a locker and opened it. Inside was a wall-mounted fireproof wall safe. Keeping an eye on Yamada, he spun the dial and opened the safe. Inside was an aluminum laptop case.

Martinez closed the safe, walked over, set the laptop case on the workbench and backed away. "Find a transmitter and keep me from shooting you."

Yamada calmly opened the laptop case and lifted a MacBook Pro out and then cut the foam at the northwest corner of the case. When he started to pull the foam from the wall, a thin wafer half the size of a credit card was exposed.

Yamada held it up to examine it. "I've never seen one this small. You have some very professional people tracking this laptop."

"Damn it, Oliver! What did you get me into this time?" Martinez asked. "Can you turn it off?"

"Probably not," Yamada said.

"What do we do with it?"

"WE don't do anything with it. YOU do something with it.

Oliver's paying me to find the password for this laptop, not stay here for a shootout with the guys in those SUVs."

Martinez turned and took ten steps toward Yamada's motorcycle then spun around and marched back. "We have to get the laptop to Oliver. I don't know what's on it and I don't want to know. I don't think you do either. What if we get the transmitter headed one way and you head the other way with the laptop? They'll never catch you on that bike of yours."

"Where would you take the transmitter without getting caught?"

"I have a way out of here. There's an old dry sewer line that runs underneath this place. I dug a tunnel to it. I can take the transmitter with me and dump it into the main line where the old line used to connect. The transmitter floats away and I escape to fight another day."

"That leaves me with the laptop and a motorcycle I love they can trace to me. How do I escape to fight another day?"

"They won't catch you. Hide the bike somewhere then sell it or whatever. You'll think of something. I'm sure Oliver will make it worth your while to get the laptop out of here to keep it safe."

Yamada took a deep breath and nodded. "When I'm ready to go, you'll need to raise the overhead and open the security gate at the same time. The Ninja does zero to one hundred kilometers per hour in 2.7 seconds. I don't want to crash into your gate if you're too slow."

Chapter Twenty-Two

DAN NORRIS WATCHED the warehouse with the binoculars in his lap when the overhead door rolled up and the green Kawasaki burst out. By the time he raised the binoculars to focus on the speeding motorcycle, it was racing toward the security gate that was rolling back.

Morales was on his smartphone checking on the ETA of the PSS Black Hornet 3 mini drone when he heard the scream of the accelerating Kawasaki. In mid-sentence, he dropped his smartphone and grabbed the smartphone with the tracking app in the console cup holder to check the location of the laptop.

"The laptop's still in the warehouse," he said. "Wonder why he's leaving in such a hurry."

"I can't believe how fast that bike is! Good thing we didn't have to follow him," Norris said.

Morales was staring at the screen of the smartphone as the red dot started moving south and coming toward them. "You see anything coming our way?" he asked.

"From the warehouse?"

Morales held the smartphone up so Norris could see its screen.

Norris opened his door and jumped out to look skyward. "It's not flying out over our heads."

The red dot on the screen moved steadily toward their Yukon. "Then it's moving underground."

"He must have a tunnel or something for an escape route," Norris said. "The good news is we can still follow the laptop's transmitter."

Morales started the engine and handed the smartphone to Norris. "You navigate and keep us as close to the moving red dot as possible. If we're lucky, we can be there when he comes topside. I'll let the other team know the laptop is on the move."

Norris waited until the moving red dot passed by them on a straight line ten yards east of them and told Morales to turn the SUV around and drive slowly down the street. "If it's a sewer line, there might a manhole cover that I can go down and follow him."

Morales drove down the street to the middle of the block until Norris raised his hand. "Something's wrong. The dot was moving south at a steady walking pace but now it's moving three times that fast, heading east."

Morales pulled to the curb. "What are the possibilities? He could have a bike or scooter down there he had to reach. Maybe he's running and just afraid of rats."

"Then he would have been running the whole way. There is another possibility that you're not going to want to hear. Maybe they found the transmitter and it's floating down a river of sewage."

"You're right. I don't like that possibility. We better let Drake know what's happened."

Drake answered on the first ring. "Yes, Marco."

"Boss, we have a situation. You're on speaker. We think they may have found the tracking transmitter."

Morales explained what had happened and waited while Drake thought about what he wanted them to do.

"The motorcycle arrived while you were watching the warehouse, so the man who had the laptop was there when it arrived. The motorcycle left and then the tracker started moving, correct?"

"Correct."

"The person who ultimately received the laptop from Nielsen might return to the warehouse. Keep eyes on the warehouse until replacements arrive from Seattle. We'll be able to follow the transmitter, even if it's floating somewhere in the sewer, and see where it goes. We have two objectives; find the people who are after the laptop and find out what's on it.

"Liz and I are going to visit the FBI and drop in on the man responsible for the FBI search of PSS headquarters. The search warrant may not have any connection to Nazir's laptop, but it might. If we can't turn up anything here in D.C., Senator Hazelton will try to identify the FBI agents who took custody of Nazir in Montana. When we know who they are, we'll find out where they took Nazir and who's behind this.

"For now, stay the course. Trade off with the other team at the warehouse and get something to eat. We'll evaluate the need for additional manpower, in light of the disappearing tracking transmitter, and get back to you."

Morales looked at Norris. "Are you hungry or should we let the other guys go first?"

Norris was staring out the window. "If they found the tracking transmitter, they didn't find it until the guy on the Kawasaki arrived. I got the license on his bike. He's someone who can get us closer to the people we're looking for. What if I call in a favor and have his plate run? We could look him up on our way to get something to eat."

Chapter Twenty-Three

NORRIS HAD the name and address of the Kawaski's owner twelve minutes after the screaming green Ninja raced out of the warehouse. Tony Yamada, DOB 02/02/1989, in Kalorama Heights.

"I know that area," Norris said as he entered the address in the GPS navigation system. "Expensive real estate. It'll be interesting to find out what our Kawasaki rider does for a living."

Morales pulled away from the curb and began following the map on the eight-inch touch screen display. "Why don't you call Drake and ask him to have someone at headquarters find out about this guy? Knowing our resident hacker as I do, he'll know everything about our man before we drive to his address."

Norris made the call. "I ran the plate on the motorcycle that left the warehouse and we thought we'd go see where he lives. His name is Tony Yamada, age twenty-nine. I have his address. Will you ask Kevin to see what he can find out about Mr. Yamada?"

"That's a good idea, but why don't you call Kevin? Liz and I are just leaving for FBI headquarters to see the man who requested the search warrant for our offices."

"What's the agent's name?"

"Thomas R. Danforth, III. Do you know him?"

"Everyone in the FBI knows him. He's the head of the counter-terrorism division and an arrogant SOB. Why would he want to search our offices?"

"They were looking for Nazir's laptop."

"Why would Danforth be looking for that? They already have the information Nazir sent to the FBI Tipline and they have Nazir. There's something else going on. Someone as high up the ladder as Danforth doesn't get involved in an evidentiary search for a laptop. The SAC in Hawaii or Seattle would handle that."

"That's what we intend to find out. Go ahead and call Kevin. I'll check with you later."

"Did you decide what you want us to do about the warehouse?" he asked Drake.

"Sorry, I should have told you. We're not going to bring in anyone else from Seattle. We'll keep eyes on the warehouse until midnight. Take breaks with the other team, as needed. We'll see if anyone returns and then regroup tomorrow."

Norris looked straight ahead, sitting in the Yukon with Morales, without saying anything for a long minute. "This isn't making any sense. I know Danforth. He's a big picture guy. He doesn't get involved in the minutiae of building a case for prosecution."

"How much do you know about what went down in Hawaii?" Morales asked.

"I know you made a citizen's arrest of this guy Nazir but not much else."

"We went there primarily to arrest a radical professor who was funneling money to the Antifa thugs trying to start a civil war. We found Nazir at the villa and flew him and his laptop back to the mainland where Drake arranged for Homeland Security investigators to question him.

"When Casey landed with Nazir in Montana, FBI agents were there instead of the HIS guys and took custody of Nazir. Casey kept Nazir's laptop and took it back to Seattle for Kevin to work on, but Nazir had an encrypted password for the laptop. We sent the laptop to Washington. You know the rest."

"Then the only hand the FBI had in all of this was taking custody of Nazir and searching for his laptop, correct?"

"Correct."

"So, Danforth could only be interested in Nazir as a terrorist. But someone else could be after the laptop. Danforth wouldn't go so far as to have a United States senator's staffer killed and then threaten to kill a guy's wife to get the laptop."

Morales shook his head to disagree. "I don't know Danforth, but I know some pretty nasty things get done in the name of national security."

The female voice from the navigation system warned them that their destination was just ahead.

Norris checked his smartphone for the address he'd been given for Tony Yamada and pointed to an old Victorian-styled building in the middle of the block. "That's it. Looks like they've converted the building into luxury condos."

"Give Kevin McRoberts a call. See what he can tell us about Yamada," Morales said. "First there's an old warehouse tricked out with state-of-the-art security and now an old brick Victorian converted into luxury condos Yamada's living in. Whatever these guys do for a living it looks like it pays well."

They drove around the block and saw there was covered parking available but no sign of the green Kawasaki Ninja.

"When we hear from Kevin about Yamada, let's come back and pay him a visit," Morales said. "I'm curious about what this millennial was doing at the warehouse."

"It's the warehouse that I'm curious about," Norris added. "There are a number of nondescript old buildings in D.C. the intelligence community uses. If this is one of them, we need to know it before we go poking around in their business."

Chapter Twenty-Four

DRAKE AND LIZ left their suite in the newly renovated Kimpton Glover Park Hotel in upper Georgetown to drive to the FBI headquarters on Pennsylvania Avenue Northwest.

Their plan was to catch Thomas R. Danforth, III by surprise, if they could talk their way in to see him. If they couldn't, they would ambush him at his home that evening.

"Has Danforth always been in the Counterterrorism Division?" Drake asked.

"He started out in Chicago," Liz said. "He was on a gang task force that took on the MS-13 gang and put a lot of them in jail, including its leader. Danforth wasn't the senior agent on the task force, but he found a way to get most of the credit. Danforth is a natural in front of a camera and became something of a crime-fighting hero in Chicago. He's climbed the FBI ladder faster than any agent I know of."

"Sounds like you're a fan."

"I can't stand the guy and he's aware of it. I embarrassed him once when he was giving a presentation at Homeland Security. I was there as Director Rawlings' executive assistant and corrected him in front of a room full of DHS agents. He cornered me afterwards and demanded an apology. I refused and was a little salty in the way I did it."

"This should be fun," Drake said, grinning. "Maybe I should see him by myself."

"No way."

They entered Dupont Circle and Liz told Drake to exit onto New Hampshire Avenue NW and then Pennsylvania Avenue NW when they reached it.

"Did your 'friend' Sam say anything about why Danforth wanted our offices searched?" Drake asked.

"You enjoy teasing me about him, don't you?"

"Sorry, I didn't mean to. I started to call him your 'boyfriend' and put a little more emphasis on 'friend' than I should have."

"Uh huh. No, he didn't have any idea why Danforth ordered our offices searched other than he knew it was about a laptop Danforth was looking for."

"If there's a legitimate reason Danforth wants the laptop, it would have to be because he thinks Nazir is more than just a hacker helping anarchists last summer. We know Nazir's a terrorist, but how would Danforth know he is?" Drake asked. "We didn't tell anyone in law enforcement everything we know about Nazir."

"That's Pennsylvania Avenue up ahead. You're looking for One Parking. It's a three-level underground parking a block away from FBI Headquarters. Maybe Danforth had intel about Nazir from some other source and this isn't connected to Hawaii at all."

Drake saw the entrance sign for the underground parking ahead and signaled that he was turning right. "Time to go find out what Thomas R. Danforth III knows about Nazir and his laptop."

Liz used her old DHS badge and identification wallet to get them into the J. Edgar Hoover Building and asked to see Assistant Director Danforth of the Counterterrorism Division. When she was asked why she wanted to see him, she said she had information concerning a laptop computer he was interested in locating.

After being told they would find out if Assistant Director Danforth was available and standing around for fifteen minutes, Liz and Drake were escorted into a small conference room with a table, four chairs and a picture of the president on one wall. They sat quietly and waited to find out if they were going to get to see Danforth.

Twenty-five minutes later, the door swung open and the assistant director of the Counterterrorism Division of the FBI walked in, alone.

"Elizabeth, what a surprise. I didn't know you were back with Homeland Security."

"I think you know that I'm not, Tom," Liz said and stood to shake his hand. "I apologize for the subterfuge, but we need to know why you're so interested in Zal Nazir's laptop."

Danforth eyes blinked but otherwise his face remained impassive.

Drake stood up and moved beside Liz. "I'm Adam Drake. You had my office searched looking for Nazir's laptop. Why did you think I had it?"

"I don't know what you're talking about, Mr. Drake. I don't know anything about a Nazir laptop, whatever that is. I'm afraid you're misinformed. If you'll excuse me, I need to get back to work."

"But you know about Nazir," Drake said. "You have him in custody. Where is he, by the way? We haven't been able to find out where he's being held since you snatched him away from the Homeland Security investigators in Montana."

Danforth glared at Drake. "It's time for you to leave before I have Liz arrested for impersonating a federal officer."

He opened the door and summoned a security guard to usher them out.

Drake stopped in front of Danforth at the door and said, "I will find out what you're up to, Danforth. I promise you that."

They walked out of FBI headquarters hand in hand and waited until they were out on the street before speaking.

"He knows where Nazir is," Drake said. "But there's more to it than that. Parading Nazir before the press and identifying him as a terrorist the FBI had arrested is what I would expect from someone like Danforth. Hiding him somewhere is what I would expect from the CIA, except the CIA doesn't have authority to do that to an American citizen."

"It's possible the CIA and the FBI are working together on this," Liz offered. "But I can't see them killing the senator's staffer and threatening Emma Nielsen to get the laptop. Maybe Senator Hazelton can find out what's going on. As the chairman of the Senate Intelligence Committee, he has the authority to question the two agencies.

"What do you want to do about Danforth?" Liz asked.

"Find out everything we can about him."

Chapter Twenty-Five

DANFORTH RETURNED to his office and shut the door. Why had they come to him asking about Nazir's laptop and the search of the PSS headquarters? The search warrant was supposed to have been linked to the Russian's villa in Hawaii as a further investigation of the events that had taken place there.

Someone was talking and that had to stop.

Danforth sent an encrypted text to James Oliver and read his response.

Do you have the laptop?

Yes. What do you want me to do with it?

Get it to me. I'll take it to the ranch. Just had someone asking where Nazir was being held. We need to guarantee the two agents that took him from HIS don't talk.

I can have someone from the ranch take care of it, if you want.

Do it. Meet me at Signature Flight Support at Reagan National

tomorrow. I'll tell you when after I have my flight arranged.

I'll take it to the ranch to get Nazir started on it.
See you then.

Danforth sat back and drummed his fingers on the top of his desk. He would need a couple of days of emergency leave to make the trip to his ranch with a detour to the federal prison in Colorado. There was someone there who owed him a favor.

––––––

JAMES OLIVER SLAMMED his fist down on the desk. If Danforth was starting to tie up loose ends, it was time for him to do the same. The only two people who could link him to Danforth were the two who helped him get the laptop; Yamada and Martinez.

Yamada wasn't a problem. He could have Martinez go to Yamada's condo tonight to get the laptop and make sure he didn't talk.

Martinez was the problem. Martinez was a CIA trained assassin and paranoid as hell. The good news was he wasn't about to talk to anyone, with the number of kills he had to account for. Of course, if he was ever arrested for any of them, Oliver would be a big chip to bargain with. He'd have to think about Martinez later.

The immediate problem was getting the laptop in time to meet Danforth at the airport tomorrow. He used his iPhone with its encrypted communication app to message Martinez.

I have another job for you.
Anyone I know?
He has the laptop. Bring it to me.
What about him?
Do what you do best.

––––––

TONY YAMADA LOVED his two-story luxury condo in Kalorama Heights. Working from home, there were only two places outside of it that he regularly visited; His Brazilian Jiu Jitsu school in Tyson's Corner and a nearby whisky bar that served the best BBQ in the city. Fresh meats and vegetables were delivered to his house by

Whole Foods Grocery delivery service and a maid cleaned the condo and took his clothes to and from the dry cleaners.

It was an expensive lifestyle but one he could afford. With the things he'd learned working for the NSA and the hacking skills he'd developed long before that employment, he was able to charge a premium fee for his work. Most of the work he did was legitimate and legal. The work that wasn't was only performed for intelligence agencies, with the understanding that he'd be protected from prosecution if he was ever caught.

The new work for James Oliver was different and made him nervous. The senate staffer whose name and address he'd given the CIA man had been killed and he had a strong feeling the man at the warehouse was responsible. Oliver was the one who sent him there and that could only mean that Oliver was also responsible for the kid's death.

While he had the laptop, he was in jeopardy, no question. He was getting himself deeply involved in the very thing he'd tried to avoid, working for the dark side in Washington. He couldn't allow this to get any worse. For now, he would make sure he recorded every contact he had with Oliver or the man at the warehouse, for insurance.

He'd installed IP camera security surveillance in his "smart home" condo when he bought it. The system included motion detection software and face recognition software that automatically sent an alert whenever one of the networked cameras zoomed in on a face that wasn't recognized. Anything that happened in his home was recorded and stored on an off-site cloud that he could access from anywhere. The IP cameras also had microSD slots that allowed him to physically pull the video from a single camera and check it.

He wasn't worried about failing to record a conversation in his home or when he was away from it either. He'd developed an audio app for his smartphone that recognized his voice and recorded any conversation he was having and automatically transmitted it to the same off-site cloud that stored all the data from his condo.

With his martial arts training and his security system, he was as safe as any person could be who lived in a city with a violent crime rate that was three times higher than the national average.

What he was worried about was being a loose end in some scheme Oliver was involved in. The CIA wasn't known for the loyalty it had for the contractors it used for things it didn't want the world to know about. He'd seen the fire storm that raged after a squad of Blackwater contractors killed seventeen civilians in Bagdad in 2007. Embarrassing the government here at home would be ten times worse.

For the foreseeable future, he would have to be very, very careful if he wanted to keep from being connected to the killing of a senior senator's staffer.

Chapter Twenty-Six

THE PSS TEAM met to compare notes at the Smoke & Barrel, a beer, BBQ and bourbon restaurant in Georgetown. Mike Casey had promised the two SEALs some good barbeque while they were in Washington and had eagerly made the reservation for the seven of them.

After a round of beer, bourbon and a margarita for Liz, Casey asked Drake sitting across from him about the meeting with Danforth.

"He denied knowing anything about the laptop or Nazir. Got a little prickly when I asked him where they'd taken Nazir after they snatched him from Homeland Security. He called security to show us out."

"Do you think he has the laptop?" Casey asked.

"I don't know if he has it, but I know he's looking for it."

They pulled two tables together so that everyone was included in the conversation. After their orders had been taken, Drake asked Morales and Norris what they thought happened with the laptop.

"Something spooked them," Morales said. "It wasn't long after the motorcycle arrived and left again that the tracking transmitter started moving. It had to have been underground because it passed right under where we were parked."

"The warehouse has state-of-the-art security," Norris added. "By the way they handled the exfil of the Kawasaki I'd say these guys are pros. They knew they were being watched when they found the tracking transmitter."

"What about the guy on the Kawasaki? Could he have left with the laptop?" Liz asked.

"Hard to tell," Norris said. "If we're right about the tracking transmitter being put in the sewer to throw us off, the laptop could still be in the warehouse or with the guy on the Kawasaki."

"What do we know about the guy on the Kawasaki?" Casey asked.

"Dan got the license number on his bike and called in a favor. We know his name, Tony Yamada, and where he lives, but that's all," Morales said.

"I called Kevin back in Seattle and asked him to do some digging. I haven't heard back from Kevin yet," Norris said.

Their food arrived, platters of smoked pork ribs, brisket and chicken and sides of baked beans, coleslaw and corn bread.

Drake smiled as he watched his friend Casey attack the platter of ribs. "I'm going to ask Senator Hazelton and his friends to find out what Danforth is up to and where he's holding Nazir. In the meantime, what do you think we should do about the warehouse and the guy on the Kawasaki? I can't ask you to keep four of our guys here indefinitely."

Casey finished a rib and took another from the platter. Let's finish the week here. I've got a couple of meetings with potential new clients and I need to pay a visit to the law firm we use for our federal contracts. If we haven't made any progress by the weekend, we'll fly back to Seattle together."

"Let's keep Borden and Manning watching the warehouse for another day or so, if that's all right, and have Morales and Norris see what they can find out about Yamada," Drake said. "Senator Hazelton has invited us for dinner tomorrow night at his favorite Italian restaurant and you're included."

"Sounds good," Casey said. "What will you be doing all day?"

"I thought I'd see what a day in the life of Thomas R. Danforth, III is like."

"You mean follow him around and see if he has a mistress or something?"

Drake shrugged his shoulders. "I don't know if he's that kind of guy. There's something about him that doesn't ring true. I'm not sure what it is, just a hunch, but I intend to find out."

Dan Norris's smartphone started playing a catchy jazz ringtone and he got up and left the table to take the call. When he returned two minutes later and sat down, he had a worried look on his face.

"Kevin's heard of Tony Yamada," Norris reported to the others. "He's a well-known hacker who worked for the NSA and is a hacker-for-hire. Kevin says he was the NSA's go-to guy for decrypting top-secret enemy transmissions when he worked there and was probably brought in to get around Nazir's encrypted password."

"Does Kevin know who he might be working for now?" Liz asked.

"He doesn't, but Yamada's been heard to claim at hacker conventions that it's incredibly easy to hack foreign governments and their embassies. Kevin thinks he does work for the intelligence community when they don't want the hacking traced back to them."

"That would explain why Yamada was at the warehouse, trying to decrypt Nazir's password," Drake said. "How would you and Marco feel about visiting Yamada after dinner and asking him about the laptop?"

"Nothing I'd like better," Norris said. "What about you, Marco?"

"A little recon of the enemy's lair is what I was trained for. You bet. Maybe he'll let me ride his Kawasaki Ninja if I ask politely."

Drake looked down the table to Bordon and Manning. "You two okay with watching the warehouse for another day?"

"Sure, if that's all you want," Don Bordon said. "We could do a little more than that if you need us to. My sidekick used his tablet to find maps of sewer lines in the city. He found one that runs right under the warehouse on the same path the moving tracker transmitter took. We know where the sewer main covers are… We could get a look inside the warehouse, if you want."

"If this warehouse has the state-of-the-art security I think it has, you'd be wasting your time," Norris said. "The IP cameras would send an alert out as soon as they detected your presence. You'd be trapped inside before you had a chance to look around. If we need to, we can use the Black Hornet micro drone to try to get a peek inside."

"All right then," Drake said. "We have our assignments. Let's find out where the laptop is and who's looking for it before Mike takes us back to Seattle Saturday. I, for one, don't want to leave until we have some answers."

Chapter Twenty-Seven

VINCENTE MARTINEZ PARKED his white Audi A4 quattro in the alley behind Yamada's condo in Kalorama Heights and made sure there was no one around before he got out of the car. Yamada was expecting him.

He'd seemed relieved to hand over the laptop and said he was happy to be finished with whatever James Oliver was up to. Martinez had to keep from laughing when he'd said that, knowing how far out of it he would be after tonight.

Martinez wasn't surprised to see Yamada open the back door of his condo as he started up the steps. There was an IP camera above the door.

"Nice place," Martinez said. "How long have you lived here?"

"I've had it for a year, but I just finished renovating it. Come in have a look around if you'd like."

Martinez followed Yamada inside and admired the kid's taste. A galley kitchen stretched ahead of them with white marble counter-tops, a fancy stove with a hood and a commercial refrigerator. Beyond the kitchen was a living area with hardwood floors, modern leather furniture and an eighty-two-inch flat screen on one wall. On the opposite wall, black metal railing ran along stairs to a second level. The walls were all painted white.

A quick survey of the interior of the condo as he walked through the kitchen ahead of Yamada revealed six IP cameras strategically placed in the corners of the living area and high on the walls of the kitchen. He walked to the middle of the living area and turned slowly around taking it all in.

When he faced Yamada again, he recognized a Kimber K6 DCR revolver with its rosewood grips in a leather paddle on Yamada's right hip. It had been concealed by a loose-fitting cream-colored guayabera shirt that was pulled back by Yamada's hand on the grips of the revolver.

"Is that really necessary?" Martinez asked.

"You tell me."

"I'm just here for the laptop. Oliver said he needs it tonight and told me to come and get it."

"He had you kill that senate staffer I identified for him, didn't he? I can connect him and you to the murder. Ergo, I'm a loose end and you're an assassin."

"Look kid, I don't know where you got the idea that I'm an assassin or that I killed someone. Give me the laptop and I'll leave."

Yamada looked to the right toward a coffee table…

Martinez shook a throwing knife loose from its sheath on his right forearm and threw it before Yamada's eyes looked back to him.

The knife pierced Yamada's neck and sliced through the cartilage of his larynx.

Yamada's hands grabbed for the knife and his eyes flew open and stared at his killer.

"Sorry kid, you were right. I am an assassin."

Martinez watched Yamada's final struggle to live on the white tiled floor of his kitchen. When it was over, he quickly started searching for the digital video recorder that received the data transmission from the condo's IP cameras.

He found the DVR upstairs in Yamada's office on the shelf of a LAN rack with other computer components. Returning downstairs with the DVR under his arm, he picked up the laptop on the coffee table and walked around Yamada's body, stepping carefully to avoid leaving a footprint in the pool of blood.

With one last look around, he walked through the kitchen to the back door and left the condo.

————

DAN NORRIS VEERED RIGHT onto Columbia Road NW from Connecticut Avenue NW in their black Yukon while Marco Morales googled the 1900 Victorian where Yamada lived.

Morales whistled when he saw the listing of the condo that was still on the internet and how much the hacker-for-hire had bought the place for. "One point seven million for a fifteen-hundred-square-foot flat! Wow! Drive on past Kalorama Road NW and turn down the alley behind his condo. Let's see if his Kawasaki's there."

Norris slowed and turned right into the alley. In the middle of the block behind the old brick Victorian a white Audi was parked beside Yamada's back door.

"Looks like he also drives an Audi," Norris said and stopped.

A man was coming down the steps carrying something under each arm.

"That's not Yamada," Morales said. "Yamada's maybe five foot six. That guy is five ten or so. I wonder who he is."

Norris took out his smartphone and took a picture of the Audi's license plate. "We'll find out later. Does that look like a laptop under his left arm?"

"Could be. If Yamada is a computer geek, I'm not surprised someone he knows has his laptop with him."

They watched the man open the trunk of the Audi to store the two things he was carrying and closed the trunk. As he walked around to the driver's door, he looked back over his right shoulder and saw the Yukon in the alley.

He paused for a moment and then quickly opened the door and got in. Three seconds later, the Audi drove down the alley, turned left and was out of sight.

"Did you notice anything?" Norris asked.

"The lights didn't come on when he opened the door," Morales said. "Maybe the guy is one of the spooks Yamada does work for."

"Let's go ask him." Norris drove forward and stopped where the Audi had parked behind Yamada's back door.

Morales got out, walked up the short flight of steps and looked up at the IP camera above the door. "He knows we're here," he said over his shoulder.

The solid wood oak door didn't have a doorbell and Morales knocked three times.

After a minute, he knocked three more times and waited. When no one came to the door, he tried the door knob and it turned in his hand.

Morales looked to Norris at the bottom of the steps. "Shall we see if Yamada's here?"

Chapterr 28

Morales led the way and stopped ten feet inside the condo, raising a closed fist. There was a smell he recognized.

Both men pulled their PSS-issued Glock 19s and listened for any sounds in the condo. Hearing none, they moved forward toward a body on the floor at the other end of the kitchen.

Morales leaned down to find a pulse and saw the paracord-wrapped handle of a throwing knife that was lodged in Yamada's throat. He moved to the other side of the body and shook his head.

When they were sure they were alone on the ground floor, they moved up the stairs to the second floor and found no one there either. Before they went back downstairs, Norris went back to Yamada's office.

"Those IP cameras use a DVR to store the data," he said to Morales standing in the hallway. "I don't see one in here. Let's see if there's one downstairs."

They didn't find one, but Norris did see something that made him grin. The IP cameras had microSD card slots that allowed the SD cards to be physically removed. He looked for the one that had the best view of the area where Yamada lay and removed it.

"What do you think?" he asked Morales. "Do we call the police or leave and make an anonymous call?"

"If the DVR was one of the things the guy in the Audi took with him and we didn't find one, there's nothing to prove we were ever here. I say we leave and call it in. There's too much going on that we can't explain to anyone right now."

Morales agreed with a nod of his head and led them back through the kitchen to the back door. "There's another camera above the door outside. Do you want to get that SD card?"

Norris stepped out to the landing and looked up at the IP camera. "No, let's go," he said softly. "It's an outdoor camera and doesn't have a card slot."

They got in their Yukon and drove down the alley, turning right onto Eighteenth Street NW to return to their hotel.

"What do we need to see what's on the SD card?" Morales asked.

"We can buy a card reader for a laptop at Walmart for ten bucks. Find the closest Walmart and we'll get one before we get back to the hotel."

"What about the guy in the Audi?"

Norris saw the time on the Yukon's dashboard and shook his head. "It will have to wait until tomorrow. My friend at Metro PD has already left for the day."

They drove on for five minutes without any further conversation, each of them thinking about the murder of the hacker-for-hire.

"Is it always like this, working for PSS?" Norris asked Morales.

"Only when you're picked for one of Drake's special projects. The rest of the time it's mostly routine security stuff. Close protection work, security and risk assessments and investigations for corporate clients dealing with industrial espionage and such."

"Have you worked any kidnappings?"

"Not that I know about. I'm guessing that might be why Casey brought you on board," Morales said. "It's only a matter of time before one of our wealthy clients has a ransom demand for someone who's been kidnapped."

"Casey said the same thing. He hinted that he might hire a couple more people to deal with kidnappings and hostage situations.

Apparently, he and Drake have been talking about restructuring PSS to provide a broader range of services for its clients."

Morales found the closest Walmart on his smartphone and set it on the console when he called Drake so Norris could hear their directions.

"Boss, we have a situation and we need advice."

"Did you see our hacker-for-hire?"

"We did but he didn't have anything to say."

"How's that? You were your usually polite self, weren't you?"

"He didn't say anything because he couldn't."

Drake thought about what Morales was trying to tell him.

'We'll show you what I mean as soon as we get there. Norris needs to get something here first."

"I'm having a drink with Liz and Mike on the patio bar. Call me when you get here, and we'll go to one of our rooms to see what you have."

"Copy that. See you soon."

Norris walked into Walmart and came back carrying a small sack and popped something in his mouth. When he opened the door and got in, he tossed a bag of chocolate-covered M&Ms to Morales.

"I have a sweet tooth and we didn't have dessert. Hope you like M&Ms."

"Doesn't everyone? Did you get a card reader? I called Drake and he wants to see what we have."

"What we have is a very professional killer throwing a knife so fast his hand is just a blur. I used one of the display laptops to make sure there was something on the SD card. I've never seen anything like it. It even has a conversation recorded and we have a new player we need to identify, some guy named Oliver."

"And the thot plickens," Morales joked. "Anything on the card that will help us identify the killer?"

"We'll have to study it more thoroughly than I was able to at the electronics counter. But Yamada was clearly murdered for the laptop for someone who wanted it tonight."

"And the guy in the Audi has the laptop and is going to take it to him?"

"That's what the killer said he was told to do."

"Then we need to find him before he has a chance to deliver it. Do you know anyone else other than your Metro PD friend who can run the Audi's plate?"

Norris thought for a moment. "There is someone, but I'll owe her big time."

"Make the call, amigo, whatever it costs you."

Chapter Twenty-Eight

VINCENTE MARTINEZ WAITED for James Oliver in the green short-term parking garage at Washington Dulles International Airport to come and get the laptop. He'd gotten it twice for Oliver and wasn't going to hand it over again until he knew why the thing was so important.

In his line of business, you didn't always know why your employer wanted a person killed. When his employer was the government, he really didn't care. He wasn't naïve enough to believe that every person he killed was an enemy of the country or a traitor. Those decisions were made at a higher level by someone with more information about the target than he had. Knowing that information gave you the opportunity to agree or disagree with the decision and made it harder to do your job.

It wasn't difficult to understand why Yamada had to be killed, however. He'd been seen leaving the warehouse by whoever had put the tracking transmitter in the laptop case. He didn't try to hide his identity or what he did for a living and was known in the intelligence community. If he was caught, there was no reason for him to conceal why he had the laptop or who he was working for.

That wasn't the case for Martinez. He needed to know why

Senator Hazelton had the laptop in the first place and why Oliver had taken it from him. If Oliver was being investigated by the Senate Intelligence Committee, he needed to know about it. Working for the government provided him with a limited degree of liability for his actions. Working against the government provided him with none.

Martinez watched Oliver's silver Mercedes GLE turn down his row in the parking garage and tapped his brakes three times. The SUV pulled into the empty space to the right of Martinez's white Audi and Oliver rolled down his window.

When Martinez rolled down the passenger's window in the Audi, Oliver said, "Bring the laptop over, I'm in a hurry."

"We need to talk first. Get in," Martinez said and waved for him to come over.

"I don't have time for this, Martinez. Give me the laptop."

"Make time, James. It will only take a minute."

Oliver said something under his breath that Martinez didn't catch and then got out and slid into the passenger seat of the Audi.

"What's on this laptop?" Martinez asked. "Why did you have me kill two people?"

"What is this, Martinez? You never wanted to know before."

"Something tells me this time it's different. This isn't something for the CIA, is it?"

"Why would you think that?"

"Because you're too smart to have me kill a senator's staffer on behalf of the CIA. You're off the reservation on this one, aren't you?"

"Why does it matter?"

"Don't play games with me, Oliver. Why did Senator Hazelton have the laptop? Is there something on it that implicates you? Is he investigating you?"

Oliver sighed and shook his head. "You really don't want to do this."

"Is that a threat, Oliver? Are you forgetting who I am?"

"Forget about Senator Hazelton. Elected politicians don't run this country, we do. You are a tool we use but that doesn't mean you have to understand why. There's a bigger picture that you wouldn't understand. Leave this alone and be thankful for the money we pay you."

"Well, you see that's part of the problem, Oliver. I had a lot invested in my warehouse sanctuary and now it's lost to me. The tracking transmitter in the laptop you had me get for you let someone know that I was involved. I have to start over and find a new place and you haven't paid me enough to do that."

"That's your fault, not ours. You should have found the transmitter before you took it back to your warehouse."

"I need half a million, Oliver. I know you can get it for me. When you do, the laptop's yours."

Oliver sighed and said, "I'll get the money for you, but I have to get the laptop tonight. You know who I am and where I live. You know I'll get you the money if I say I will. Now, is the laptop here?"

Martinez smiled. "That's more like it, Oliver. The laptop is in the trunk, I'll get it for you."

Oliver turned with a Glock 36 in his right hand and fired two rounds into Martinez's back as he started to get out of the car to get the laptop.

"That's all right, I'll get it for myself," Oliver said and reached over to pick up the key fob that had fallen to the floor.

He wiped his fingerprints from the inside and outside door handles as he got out and quickly retrieved the laptop from the trunk of the Audi. With the laptop in hand, Oliver jumped into his SUV, backed out and drove down three floors and out of the parking garage.

He knew why Thomas R. Danforth, III wanted the laptop, to erase anything that connected Danforth to the Russian oligarch. He also knew that Danforth thought he wanted the laptop so that the CIA could identify all of the members of Nazir's group of hackers and use them as double agents to provide false information to their Iranian sponsors. But that wasn't all that he wanted the laptop and Nazir for.

He wanted Nazir and his hackers to launch a cyberwar attack on the biggest banks in America that would be blamed on Iran.

Then the president would be forced to declare war on Iran and its allies, including Russia.

America should already be at war with Russia because of its unrelenting social media war. He understood Russia's chaos theory of political warfare based on what they called the Gerasimov Doctrine. The aim was to destabilize an adversary from within, by getting an enemy's population to question its institutions, fragmenting its culture and polarizing its people and their beliefs.

Russia didn't want to become stronger than America. It was using psychological warfare to depress the population and get it to stop believing in its government and its traditional values. One analyst's conclusion that had been circulated opined that Russia wasn't aiming to become stronger than America but to weaken America until the two countries were equivalent.

He believed that was what Russia was doing, based on what he saw every day, and he wasn't going to allow Russia's cyberwarfare to continue unopposed. Even if it meant crippling America's banking system to do it.

Chapter Twenty-Nine

DRAKE, Liz and Casey were in Drake's suite at the Kimpton Glover Park Hotel when Morales and Norris arrived.

"What happened?" Drake asked as soon as the door closed behind the two men.

"Let me use a laptop and I'll show you," Norris said.

"Mine's next to the TV," Liz said.

Norris put her laptop on the small table near the window and inserted the card reader with the SD card. "This is an SD card from one of the IP cameras in Yamada's condo. This happened just before we got there."

They watched silently as Yamada met a man at the back of his condo and then followed him through the kitchen. They saw Yamada pull his shirt back to rest his hand on the grips of a revolver, listened to the exchange of words between the two men and then watched the blur of motion as the killer threw a knife that lodged in Yamada's throat.

Liz gasped loudly. "Sorry, I didn't expect that."

"Yamada didn't either," Casey said.

They continued watching as the killer left the room to go

upstairs and saw him return with a DVR and leave with it and the laptop.

"When we got to Yamada's place, there was a white Audi parked at the rear of the condo. We saw the killer come out, get in it and drive away," Morales said. "We got the Audi's license plate. Dan has someone who might be able to run the plate for us tonight."

Drake asked Norris to play the video again. "Why does the video and audio start when the killer enters the condo? Wouldn't it be recording all the time?"

"Some of the IP camera security systems have facial recognition software that only starts recording when the camera sees a face it doesn't recognize," Norris explained. "I'm guessing that's why it wasn't running before the killer got there."

"When the killer took the DVR, would these SD cards keep recording?" Drake asked.

"I believe so, why?" Norris asked.

"Because if they do, your presence in the condo after the murder has been recorded," Drake said. "When Yamada's body is discovered, the police will pull the other SD cards, like you did, and want to know why you two were there."

"Getting the police involved before we know who's looking for the laptop was what we were trying to avoid," Casey said. "I don't see a way around it now."

"Neither do I," Drake said. "We'll have to get this SD card to someone in law enforcement we can trust before Yamada's body is discovered."

"Dan, is the person you think might be able to run the Audi's plate someone in law enforcement we can trust?" Liz asked.

"She's an FBI agent and I trust her," Norris said. "If we give her the SD card, I'm sure she'll want to run the plate and try to catch this guy."

Drake let out a sigh. "I'm not sure giving the SD card to the FBI is the right thing to do."

"Why?" Liz asked.

"Danforth is most likely the person in the FBI looking for the laptop. We know that because he's the one who dialed up the search warrant for our offices. We also know that he knows we had the laptop and that we're interested in finding out why he wants it because we told him so. Investigating us to find out why we were in Yamada's condo would tie us up, get us out of his way and give him a way to find out just how much we know."

"Why would he care how much we know about the laptop? The FBI has already concluded that whatever Nazir sent to their Tipline wasn't credible," Liz said, challenging Drake's answer.

"Okay, how about this? I just don't trust the guy."

"What if the agent I know agrees that she will look at the SD card and not say where she got it until she has to?" Norris asked. "We'll have to explain why we were at Yamada's condo when they pull the other SD cards. Maybe by that time she will have discovered things we won't be able to by ourselves."

"Do you trust this agent that much?" Casey asked. "Withholding information about where she got the SD card is a good way to end a career."

"Yes, I do trust her that much," Norris said. "I almost asked her to marry me."

"May I ask why you didn't ask her?" Liz asked.

"Marrying me, after I was blamed for the failed hostage situation at HRT, would have ruined her career. I couldn't do that to her."

"What's her name? Liz continued. "Maybe I know her."

"Special Agent Kate Perkins."

Drake and Liz looked at each other and said together, "We know her."

"Kate Perkins was the one we worked with when we discovered the president's closest advisor in the White House was an agent of influence for the Muslim Brotherhood," Drake explained.

"She's the only person I know in the FBI that I would trust to have our back if Danforth plays dirty," Liz said.

"I agree," Drake added.

"Do you want me to call her?" Norris asked.

"It's okay with me," Drake said.

"It's fine with me as well," Liz said.

Norris took out his smartphone and walked over to the window, keeping his back to the others while he made the call.

"Small world," Casey observed. "Kate Perkins was just doing her job, but I'm not fondly remembering that long night we spent at FBI headquarters, convincing her and her superiors that you shot the president's adviser's lover in self-defense."

"It could have been worse, if she hadn't been on our side," Drake said.

Norris turned around and walked back from the window smiling. "She's willing to meet us tonight in the bar downstairs. I had to promise to take her to dinner before I leave."

"Oh, you poor man, having to take a beautiful woman to dinner," Liz teased.

"Just trying to do my job, ma'am," Norris said and laughed.

Chapter Thirty

IT WAS ten o'clock in the evening by the time Special Agent Kate Perkins walked into the bar of the Casolare Ristorante in the Kimpton Glover Park Hotel.

Drake, Liz and Casey watched from their table as Dan Norris went to greet her with a hug and bring her back to meet them.

Drake and Casey stood up to welcome her and Liz waved from her seat.

"Hello Kate," Liz said. "Surprised to see us again?"

"Even more surprised to see this guy with you," she said. "I knew Dan left HRT, but I didn't know he moved to Seattle to work with you all."

Norris pulled out her chair and Drake asked if she'd like something to drink.

"Remembering what you three got me into the last time you were here? Make it a double dirty martini, please."

Drake motioned to the waitress and said, "We appreciate you offering to run a license number for Dan, Kate, but there's more to it than that. I'll try to give you as much information as I can, but I need you to agree to something first."

Kate wrinkled her brow. "Agree to what?"

"Agree to investigate something without getting us involved until it's absolutely necessary."

"That will depend on what you want me to investigate."

"A murder that's recorded on an SD card that we have."

"Are you involved in this murder in any way?" she asked. "If you are, you know I can't agree to what you're asking of me.

"Our only involvement is discovering the murder and procuring the evidence that's on the SD card," Drake said.

"How am I supposed to investigate a murder without explaining how I found out about it?"

"By saying you were given the SD card anonymously," Norris offered. "When it's necessary to disclose my identity, I'll come forward and explain how I obtained the SD card."

"By doing that, will it mean you'll be charged with something?" Kate asked.

"It shouldn't," Norris said. "If it does, it's something I'm willing to risk."

"Kate, we trust you to use your best judgment and handle this without getting yourself in trouble," Liz said. "The only thing we're asking is to keep us out of it as long as you can."

"Why is that important?" she asked.

Liz looked to Drake, who nodded for her to explain.

"We think this is connected to something we're looking into that may involve someone in the FBI."

"Who?"

"Thomas R. Danforth, III."

Kate turned to Norris and said, "I suppose I don't want to know how Danforth's involved, do I?"

"It's best if you don't until we're sure that he is," Norris answered.

Special Agent Perkins took a deep breath and looked around the table until she was looking directly across at Drake. "Okay, I agree. Where's the SD card?"

Norris took the SD card and card reader out of his pocket and handed it to her.

"The man you'll see killed a man named Tony Yamada. He left

Yamada's condo just as we arrived. I have the license plate on his white Audi A4. It shouldn't be hard to find him."

"Who is Tony Yamada?" Kate asked.

"The head of my IT department tells us that he's known as a hacker-for-hire who used to work for the NSA," Casey said. "I'm afraid that's all we know about him."

"Am I going to wind up investigating someone in the intelligence community?" she asked.

"I don't know," Drake said.

"But you think I might wind up investigating one of the most powerful men in the FBI?"

"It's possible. We don't know yet."

"Just so we're clear, you just want me to investigate a murder. If it leads to something else, I'm to use my best judgment on how to proceed."

"That's correct," Drake said. "Of course, we'd appreciate it if you would share with us whatever you learn in the course of your investigation."

"I will, if I can. I can't promise that."

"Understood."

Kate turned to Casey and asked, "If I wind up losing my job because I helped you guys, will there be a place for me at Puget Sound Security?"

"We've hired discredited FBI agents before," Casey said and winked at Norris, "we could probably do it again."

Special Agent Perkins held up her martini and said, "Then I guess I'd better finish this and go catch a killer."

When she did, Norris offered to walk her out to her car.

Liz watched the two of them leave. "How in the world could he walk away from that? She's beautiful and smart and he obviously still cares for her."

"Maybe this will give them a second chance," Casey said. "She told him that she was prepared to move to Seattle if she lost her job. That tells me he's still in the picture if he wants to be."

Drake was quiet, listening to his best friend and the woman he loved talk about what Kate would do if she lost her job. It was a possibility he didn't want to think about. Following a hunch, like the one he had now about someone in the government aiding and abetting a plot to start a civil war in America, had caused trouble for and endangered most of the people he cared for over the last couple of years.

He didn't want Special Agent Kate Perkins to be added to that list.

Chapter Thirty-One

THOMAS R. Danforth, III waited patiently in the passenger lounge of Signature Flight Support at Ronald Reagan Washington National Airport for James Oliver to arrive. His chartered Learjet 75 would wait outside to fly him to Denver for as long as necessary, he knew, but he wasn't leaving without the laptop. Oliver was late and would have to be reminded that was not acceptable.

But the man had managed to find the laptop, as he had promised. That was more important than schooling him today for the lack of respect he was demonstrating by being late.

Men like Oliver were effective tools to be used when necessary. He had to remind himself that the CIA man and the contractors Oliver provided to care for Nazir at the ranch were still needed. Once he was confident there was nothing on the laptop to connect him to the Russian oligarch, however, he would find a way to erase any connection to Oliver and his men.

For the time being, there were things he needed to accomplish to ensure his safety. If it required camaraderie and a smile, so be it, he thought as he stood and waved to Oliver when he walked into the lounge with the laptop.

"Sorry I'm late," Oliver said. "Traffic was bad."

"Isn't it always? Did things go smoothly?"

"There were complications, but Yamada was taken care of and we have the laptop."

"What complications?"

"The man I used to get the laptop had to be taken care of as well."

"How did you accomplish that?"

Oliver's steely blue eyes gave Danforth his answer. "I see."

"I will call the men I have at your ranch and let them know you're coming," Oliver said. "I wouldn't want you to surprise them. What time do you think you'll be there?"

"I have to make a detour to a federal prison in Colorado to see someone. I should be at the ranch by dark."

"Who's at the supermax prison in Colorado you need to see?"

"Not in the supermax but the same facility. He's the MS-13 gang leader I busted when I was on the gang taskforce in Chicago. We wanted him to know how close he came to a hole in hell for the rest of his life, so he's in the Florence Federal Correctional Institution nearby. He's cooperating so that he stays out of the supermax."

"Is he providing you information on a new case?"

"He's going to take care of something for me."

"Something or someone?"

It was Danforth's turn for a steely-eyed answer.

"Anyone I know?"

"When are you planning on getting to the ranch?"

"A week before Halloween."

"How are you going to get Nazir to use his network of hackers? From what you've told me, he's refusing to cooperate."

"That won't be a problem." Oliver smiled. "I've been watching him for a while and I know the names of all the hackers he put together in his Islamic Revolutionary Council of America. I know where they all live. He won't sacrifice them if I tell him what I'll do to them if he doesn't cooperate."

"I hope you get the result you want."

"I will and then some."

Oliver looked at his watch. "Is there anything else we need to discuss before you leave?"

Danforth pointed to the laptop case next to Oliver's chair. "Not that I can think of."

Oliver slid the case across to Danforth and got up to leave. "Have a nice flight then."

Danforth picked up the laptop case, opened it to make sure there was a laptop in it and left the lounge to walk out to his chartered Learjet.

His first destination after landing in Colorado before going to his ranch was the federal prison one hundred and seventeen miles south of Denver. The man he'd arranged to talk with was the leader of the Chicago unit of La Mara Salvatrucha, known as MS-13. With twenty thousand documented gang members in the U.S., MS-13 had its satanic claws in every major city in the country, including Washington, D.C.

Angel Torres Garcia had a younger sister who was in jail in Chicago, awaiting trial for chopping a rival gang member to pieces with a machete, along with other gang members.

Danforth was aware that a key witness was in the federal witness protection program and he knew where the FBI was keeping her. He also knew that the witness had a drug record that was being kept from Garcia's sister's defense attorney.

If Angel Torres Garcia was willing to do him a favor, Danforth was willing to reciprocate and give him the information about the witness's drug record and where the witness was staying.

The favor he wanted Garcia to do for him was to pass along the names of Adam Drake and Elizabeth Strobel to members of MS-13 in Chicago and have them take care of the two in Washington, D.C. He never wanted to be bothered by them again.

Chapter Thirty-Two

SPECIAL AGENT KATE PERKINS called Adam Drake at seven thirty Friday morning with news about the man who murdered Tony Yamada. He was eating breakfast with Liz and Casey in the hotel restaurant.

"I'm not sure what you're involved in, counselor," she said, "but it looks like you're dealing with some nasty people. The man who murdered Tony Yamada is a man named Vincente Martinez. He's former CIA and was trained as an assassin after 9/11. That program was cancelled in 2009 and we think he's been freelancing since then."

"Do you have him in custody?" Drake asked.

"Not yet, we don't know where he lives. We're looking for his white Audi, but he doesn't have an address or post office box that we can find."

"Did you find any connection between Martinez and Yamada?"

"Your guess is as good as mine. You said Yamada was a hacker-for-hire and Martinez appears to be an assassin-for-hire. If there's a connection, it might be who they worked for."

"How are you going to find that out?"

"By finding out where they got their money. Yamada was apparently very well paid. He bought his condo for one point six million."

"Did you turn up anything at Yamada's place?"

"We've been working the crime scene all night and we have his computer from the condo. I'll let you know if we find anything that leads us to Martinez or his employer."

"I'll do the same if we come up with anything."

"Perkins says the killer was a former CIA assassin with no known address. They don't know where to start looking for him," Drake told the others.

Casey poured himself another cup of coffee from the carafe on their table and stared into the dark swirling brew as he added cream. "We know Yamada and Martinez were working together to get the laptop to some unknown person. We also know Yamada was at the warehouse where the laptop was for a time. The warehouse could belong to Martinez. We should check it out before we leave for Seattle tomorrow."

"Norris said the warehouse has a good security system. It's unlikely they're going to be invited in peacefully if Martinez is there," Drake cautioned.

"It's also likely that whoever's there would use the same escape route that was used last time," Liz added.

"It's still worth finding out if that's Martinez's lair," Casey said. "I'll send Norris and Morales to check it out. What are you two planning on doing the rest of the day before dinner with the senator tonight?"

"I asked the senator to see what he could dig up on Thomas Danforth. Liz suggested we drop by his senate office and see what they were able to come up with. What about you?"

"They have some things for me to sign at our law firm and then I thought I'd do some sightseeing. I haven't seen the World War Two Memorial."

"Meet back here for a drink before dinner, say six o'clock?" Drake asked.

"Done," Casey said and got up to leave. "See you then."

"Is it too early to go to the senator's office?" Drake asked.

"I'm sure there will be some of the eager-beaver staffers there. Give me five minutes and I'll be ready to go. I need to go back to our room and get my purse. You need anything?"

Drake patted his right hip where his Kimber Ultra Carry .45 was holstered. "I'm good. You might want to do the same."

He signaled for their check and, before it arrived, his phone buzzed in his pocket.

"We just found Martinez," Special Agent Perkins said. "Someone shot him in his car. His Audi is parked in the green short-term parking garage at Dulles. The whole garage is cordoned off, but I'll have Metro PD escort you up if you want to come over."

"We'll head your way. Any idea who shot him?"

"We'll have the CCTV video to look at, but a lot of cars have been in and out of here since last night. It looks like he's been dead for ten to twelve hours."

"Thanks for the call," Drake said. "See you in a few."

He called Casey. "Agent Perkins just called. They found our assassin-for-hire. Someone shot him in his car. I'm going to go there with Liz. Let Norris and Morales know that Martinez is dead and there might not be anyone home when they get to the warehouse, if it's his."

"The bodies of people involved with that laptop are starting to pile up. Someone's making sure we don't find out who's got it now."

"There's only one person we know who's looking for it, Danforth and the FBI."

"I don't think the FBI is killing people to get the laptop. They already have whatever Nazir sent them on their Tipline. You don't start killing people just to verify what Nazir himself can verify for them. He's in their custody."

"Do we know that? Didn't you ask the senator to see if he could find out where they have him? Has he gotten back to you?"

"No, he hasn't."

"There are two FBI agents who will know, the two who met me in Montana when I flew him back to the mainland from Hawaii. I stayed in the plane and didn't get their names. Maybe we can track them down and find out where they took him."

"If the FBI isn't saying where Nazir is, it's unlikely they'll give us the names of those two agents."

"There were also two investigators from DHS there. They were the ones who were supposed to take custody of Nazir. I'll bet they didn't let the FBI take him without verifying their identity."

"Good point," Drake said. "I'll ask Senator Hazelton to call Secretary Rawlings and see if he'll find out for us."

"I don't want to think we have targets on our backs, Adam, but we just might. Be extra careful from here on."

"Just like old times, Mike."

Drake ended the call and saw Liz enter the restaurant.

"Are you ready to go to the senator's office?" she asked.

"Change of plans. Perkins called. They found Martinez shot dead in his car. She invited us to join her at the crime scene."

"Why would she do that?"

"She might think we had something to do with it."

Chapter Thirty-Three

THEY WERE MET at the entrance to the green short-term parking garage at Washington Dulles National Airport by two Metro police officers standing in front of their patrol cars with LED light bars flashing blocking traffic into the parking garage.

Drake rolled down the window of the SUV and asked to see Special Agent Perkins.

The officer who came to his window backed away to speak into his shoulder mic while the other officer motioned for him to pull the SUV next to the patrol car on the right and stay there.

Drake took his concealed carry permit out of his wallet and Liz did the same. "Let's see how well-respected Special Agent Perkins is when we tell these two we're armed."

The first officer keyed his mic and nodded his head before approaching the SUV again. When he got closer to the open window and saw what they were holding up, he backed away again to ask for clarification.

It took longer this time before he walked back and collected their permits. "Special Agent Perkins says you're cleared to enter. Leave the keys to your SUV in the ignition and take the stairs to the third floor. She'll meet you there."

Drake thanked the officer and walked Liz between the two patrol cars and into the parking garage. When they reached the third floor, Kate Perkins was waiting for them with her hands on her hips.

"You're not making my day any easier by coming here carrying," she said. "Are either of your weapons a .45 caliber pistol?"

"Yes, mine is a .45 Kimber," Drake said.

"Terrific! Let me have it, please," she said. "Martinez was shot with a .45. I'll need a statement about where you were last night and have this tested before I can give it back to you."

"You know I didn't kill Martinez and then give you that SD card that identified him, Agent Perkins," Drake said.

"I might know that, but my superiors don't. I have enough trouble explaining why I was looking for Martinez without having to explain why I didn't rule you out as his killer when Martinez turns up dead."

"What do you need from me to help you with that?"

"I need to know how you came to know about Yamada in the first place. Why you think Danforth might be involved. Why you're here in Washington. That would be nice for starters."

Liz stepped closer to Special Agent Perkins and said, "Kate, that's somewhat complicated and will take longer than you might have right now. Take my word, as a former FBI agent, that you will understand when you hear it all. Can we meet you somewhere else and talk?"

Special Agent Perkins looked back at the swarm of forensic techs going over the white Audi. "I'll be here for another hour or so and then I have a report to write. Where will you be this afternoon?"

"We're going to Senator Hazelton's senate office and then wherever you want us to meet you," Liz said.

"Let's meet at your hotel," she said. "Here, take your .45 back for now, Drake. I don't want to explain why I wanted it just yet. Will you be back at the hotel by two o'clock?"

"We will be, if that's when you want to meet," Drake said.

"It is. Be ready to tell me everything because I need some answers."

They took the stairs down to their SUV and got in with a wave to the two officers as they backed up and drove away.

"How are we going to tell her everything?" Liz asked.

"We aren't. We'd have to go all the way back to when we knew Nazir was involved in the attacks on the Catholic churches in Portland. Then we'd have to explain about how we knew he was involved with Volkov and Professor Bradley trying to start a civil war in America and why we went to Hawaii to make a citizen's arrest of the professor. All of that, even before we found out about the laptop and brought it back to the mainland and didn't hand it over to the FBI."

"I don't see how we can get away with only telling her a little of the story."

"We'll have to think of something or none of us will be flying back to Seattle tomorrow. Let's go to Senator Hazelton's office and see if we can't get a few answers before we meet Kate."

Drake followed her directions to the parking garage she used when she worked as the senator's advisor on intelligence matters for the Senate Select Committee on Intelligence. They were almost there when Casey called.

"The warehouse belongs to Martinez. Morales got in without setting off any alarms by using the sewer line the tracking transmitter moved through They found a well-stocked armory, a shooting range, knife-throwing target and his office. They want to know what we want them to do."

"Have they found anything that might help us identify who Martinez was working for?" Drake asked.

"There's a computer in his office but no file cabinets or other records."

"Tell them to make sure no one will know they were there. We're meeting with Special Agent Perkins at the hotel at two o'clock. She wants to know everything we've learned or suspect. We'll let her know about the warehouse and the FBI can tear it apart."

"Copy that. See you at two."

"The warehouse belongs to Martinez," Drake said. "He must have sent the laptop out with Yamada on his Kawasaki and then gone back to get it when he killed him."

"Who has the laptop now, the guy who killed Martinez?" Liz asked.

"That's what I'm thinking."

Chapter Thirty-Four

EMMA NIELSEN, wife of the cyber security expert who had the laptop before being forced to give it up to protect her, met Liz and Drake in front of the reception desk in Senator Hazelton's senate office.

Liz gave Emma a big hug and Drake did as well.

"Let's use the small conference room," she said and led the way with a file under her arm.

The conference room was elegant, with mahogany wood paneling hung with historic paintings of the Revolutionary War and its heroes. Four hand-crafted wooden chairs with dark blue seat cushions surrounded a round inlaid mahogany table.

"How are you and Bill doing?" Liz asked.

"Bill thought it was a great adventure delivering the laptop to the helicopter, he's fine. I get sick every time I think about it," Emma said.

"How are you and the rest of the staff dealing with the death of Riley Garrett?" Drake asked. "That has to have been quite a blow, even with all the murders in this city."

He knew the murder rate per capita in the capital was three

times the national average and wondered how the young staffers dealt with the fact.

"You read about murders all the time, but it's sobering when it happens to someone you work with. We're all pretty sad about losing Riley," Emma said.

"I can only imagine," Drake said and asked to change the subject. "What can you tell us about Thomas R. Danforth, III?"

"Before I forget it, Senator Hazelton wanted me to tell you the FBI denies having Mr. Nazir in their custody. They admit they received something on their Tipline that purported to come from someone named Nazir, but they were unable to verify the information or find the man who sent it to them."

Drake looked to Liz and ever so slightly shook his head. There was no need to get Emma involved by telling her what they knew about Nazir and the FBI taking him when Casey landed in Montana. One member of the senator's staff had already paid the price for knowing something about the laptop or the man who owned it.

"Thank you, Emma. Now, about Danforth," Drake said.

"Everything I could dig up about him is in this file. You probably want to read it for yourself. He's made quite a name for himself at the FBI. He's from a prominent family in Chicago and appears to be quite wealthy. Reading between the lines, I'd say he's not well liked by the rank and file at the FBI. According to one secretary I know over there, he has a bit of a god complex when it comes to counterintelligence. He thinks he knows everything that's going on in the world."

"That's the Danforth I know," Liz said. "May we take your file with us or do you want us to look at it here?"

"Senator Hazelton asked me to prepare it for you, it's yours. If there's anything you want me to follow up on, just let me know."

Liz stood and picked up the file. "Thank you for doing this for us, Emma. You've been a big help."

"It's the least I can do, Liz. It's so good to see you back in this office. We all wish you were still here, but we understand why you left," she said and smiled at Drake as she walked past him holding the door open for the ladies.

After making the rounds and greeting all the staff she knew from before, Liz caught up with Drake waiting for her out in the hall.

"If the FBI officially says they don't have Nazir in custody, who does?" she asked.

"The Homeland Security Investigators Secretary Rawlings had there in Montana to interrogate Nazir wouldn't have turned him over to someone claiming to be FBI without verifying their credentials," Drake said as they walked down the hall to the elevator.

"Maybe Danforth was telling the truth when he said he didn't know anything about Nazir. You said it sounded like something the CIA would do, taking someone to a black site to interrogate them, maybe it is."

"No, Danforth knows," Drake said shaking his head as the elevator door opened and they walked into an empty elevator. "He didn't say he didn't know about Nazir, he said he didn't know anything about a Nazir laptop. If the FBI is telling a powerful U.S. senator that it doesn't have Nazir in custody, then Danforth is operating on his own or working with the CIA on something. I just don't understand why he would do either of those two things."

"With the laptop who knows where it is right now and with both Yamada and Martinez dead, where does that leave us?" Liz asked. "Danforth is the only person we think might be involved in all of this and he isn't going to tell us anything."

"I know. I can't ask Mike to keep picking up the tab and keep us here without a good reason. Right now, I don't have one."

They left the building and walked outside arm-in-arm and felt the crisp fall edge in the air of a bright fall day.

"What are we going to tell Kate Perkins this afternoon?" Liz asked.

"We're going to give her an abbreviated account of what we've done since we came into possession of Nazir's laptop. Just enough to satisfy her and keep us from getting any further involved in this mess. Let her pursue the murders of the senator's staffer, Riley Garrett, Tony Yamada and Vincente Martinez because they're all related somehow. She's better equipped to put it all together than we are anyway."

Liz turned her head to look up at Drake. "That doesn't sound like you, letting someone else finish something you started. Don't you still want to find out who tipped off Volkov? That's connected to this somehow. That's what we came here to find out."

"I will never stop looking for the person or persons who helped the Antifa anarchists get those AK-47s or stop trying to find out why Danforth wants Nazir's laptop. I don't know what else I can do here in Washington."

"You'll think of something. You always do."

Chapter Thirty-Five

SPECIAL AGENT KATE PERKINS sat on a bench at a table on The Deck, the outdoor patio at the Kimpton Glover Park Hotel, looking over a menu when Liz and Drake found her.

"I hope you don't mind me eating while we talk," she said. "It took me longer to get out of the office than I expected. Nice idea, Liz, meeting out here."

"I like to enjoy the fall for as long as I can," Liz said.

The patio waiter came over and she ordered a chicken BLT and iced tea before asking them, "Do you guys want anything?"

They both joined her and ordered two iced teas.

"Learn anything new about Yamada or Martinez?" Drake asked.

Agent Perkins folded her hands on the table and leaned forward. "You first, Adam Drake, Oregon lawyer-cum-citizen-soldier or maybe vigilante. Why is it I keep running into you when you're hunting bad guys or terrorists?"

Drake smiled and deflected. "Is that what you think I am, a vigilante?"

"Why don't you tell me? I searched our files and saw that you were in Hawaii and caused some trouble at a Russian oligarch's villa guarded by ex-Spetsnaz soldiers. We found a dead radical professor there who'd been tortured. Did you have a hand in that?"

"No, I didn't. Professor Bradley was dead when we got there. His torturers were those Spetsnaz soldiers you mentioned."

"Why were you there in the first place?" she asked.

Drake took a deep breath and glanced at Liz. An abbreviated account of things didn't appear to be in the works. It certainly couldn't include any information about his father-in-law and former elected leaders that called themselves the "committee, small 'c'" asking him to investigate wealthy elite progressives who were funding the anarchist violence of the last summer.

"I'm not at liberty to tell you everything, Agent Perkins, but I was there because I had been asked to investigate the Antifa violence in Portland and find out where Antifa was getting its money. We found out it was being funded and sponsored by a few wealthy elite Americans and a Russian oligarch. Mikhail Volkov was the oligarch who owned the villa and I went there to make a citizen's arrest of Professor Bradley who we thought was involved with Volkov."

"Why did you want to arrest Bradley?"

"Because our investigation learned that the professor and the student organization he founded was the conduit Volkov was using to get his millions to the anarchists."

"You want me to believe that you decided to do this on your own, instead of turning your information over to the FBI and letting us handle it? Why did you decide to do that?"

"If you read the FBI files about me that should be obvious. The FBI and I aren't on the best terms."

"That's the only reason?" Agent Perkins asked incredulously. "I worked with you before. Agent Williams was working with you when he was killed. Is it all of us or just a few FBI agents you aren't on good terms with?"

Drake mirrored Agent Perkins' posture and leaned forward and put his folded hands on the table. "I didn't go to the FBI because someone in the government was aiding and abetting Volkov and Bradley, that's why. I think it might be someone in the FBI."

Agent Perkins leaned back and studied Drake when the waiter came toward them to deliver their sandwiches and iced teas. When he left, she said, "Someone like Thomas Danforth, you mean."

"I don't know, but maybe."

"This isn't the whole story, is it?"

Drake picked up his glass of iced tea and said to Liz, "Why don't you tell her why we're here in Washington?"

Liz nodded. "Kate, we came back from Hawaii with a laptop that we thought might show us who in the government was helping Volkov and Bradley. We sent the laptop here to have it investigated. Since then, one of Senator Hazelton's young staffers who had the laptop briefly was killed. Tony Yamada and Vincente Martinez have been killed after they got their hands on the laptop that was mentioned on the SD card we gave you. The person we think is after the laptop could be the same person who helped Volkov and Bradley."

Agent Perkins' squinted eyes made Drake think of Clint Eastwood in the movie *The Good, the Bad and the Ugly*.

"You knew all of this when you asked me to run the license plate on the white Audi. Why didn't you tell me all of this then?"

"Because I didn't want all of this included in your FBI report at the time. I still don't," Drake answered.

"You two are putting me in a hell of a spot. What am I supposed to do with what you've just told me?"

"Continue to investigate these murders with what we've told you in the back of your mind. We'll stay out of your way and help in any way we can. We're returning to Seattle tomorrow, but we'll be available to make formal statements if you need them."

Agent Perkins sighed and shook her head. "I don't think it's going to be that easy. We took a peek at Yamada's finances and found several payments he received from someone in the CIA. The CIA uses outside contractors with special skills all the time. Yamada could have been doing something on the up and up for him, but now I'm going to have to find out what it was. I'm going to have to investigate someone in the damn CIA."

"Could we do that for you," Drake asked, "and keep you out of it?"

"I'll have to think about that. Anything else I need to know?"

"There's a warehouse we believe that belongs to Martinez. You might want to have a look at it. Dan Norris has the address."

"I'm beginning to regret answering his call the other night."

Drake winked at Liz and said, "You never know, this could have a happy ending. You have a shot at solving three murders, maybe uncovering a traitor in the government and having dinner with Dan."

Liz flashed him a look that said loud and clear, "Leave it alone."

Drake smiled at her, shrugging his shoulders and answering with a silent, "What?"

Chapter Thirty-Six

SENATOR HAZELTON HAD RESERVED a table at his favorite Italian restaurant, the Ristorante Piccolo in historic Georgetown, for dinner with Drake, Liz and Casey. He and his wife, Meredith, were already seated at a table for six next to a golden wall that reminded Drake of fields of wheat in eastern Oregon.

The table's centerpiece with two burning candles reflecting their flames off the water glasses was a warm invitation to a romantic evening.

Drake put a hand on Casey's shoulder as they walked behind Liz to their table. "I wish Megan was here to enjoy this."

"If the food is as good as this place looks, I'll bring her with me next time," Casey said. "She loves going out to dinner. I just don't take her out often enough."

Senator Hazelton stood and greeted Liz with a kiss on the cheek while Drake leaned down to kiss his mother-in-law.

"You look beautiful, Mom," he told her.

"You clean up pretty well yourself, Adam."

"Mike, I'm glad you could join us," Senator Hazelton said. "I know you enjoy a good meal and I can promise you that you'll have one tonight."

"Thank you, senator. I'm sure I'll enjoy it."

When they were seated, Senator Hazelton nodded his head in the direction of the sommelier, who walked to them with a bottle of prosecco.

When their champagne flutes were filled, the senator proposed a toast. "Here's to good wine and two beautiful women."

"Here, here," Drake and Casey each said and raised their flutes together.

"Liz, I understand you stopped by the office today," Senator Hazelton said. "Was the information Emma put together helpful?"

"I'm sure it will be. We haven't had time to go through it yet."

"Robert, let them enjoy their evening," Meredith chastened. "You can talk about that later."

The senator smiled and nodded his head graciously. "Of course. Let's talk about something more entertaining. Have you heard about Senator Hutchins' bill to ban baggy pants in America?"

That round of laughter was the first of many, as the five of them traded stories while enjoying Ristorante Piccolo's delicious fare.

While the women excused themselves for a quiet conversation away from the men later in the evening, Drake summarized what they had learned that week and where they were now on the night before they returned to Seattle.

"There are two men we don't know much about but think they may be involved; Thomas Danforth and a man named Oliver who's with the CIA. I believe Danforth knows where Nazir's being held, and Oliver's paid a hacker-for-hire two large sums in the last week before he was killed."

"I couldn't get anything out of the FBI about Nazir being in their custody, but I can find out about Oliver at the CIA," Senator Hazelton said.

"There's another way we can find out where Nazir is, senator," Casey said. "When I landed in Montana to turn Nazir over to the investigators from DHS, the two FBI men were there to intercept him. Secretary Rawlings will know who the two DHS men are and can ask them who were the FBI agents they let take custody of Nazir. We can take it from there."

"I'll call Secretary Rawlings. Anything else?"

"Not that I can think of," Drake said.

When the women returned, the men stood and sat back down with them.

"Would anyone care for another glass of prosecco?" Senator Hazelton asked.

"I'm fine," Drake said. "Liz?"

"It's been a wonderful evening, thank you, senator, but I would like to get a good night's sleep and go for a run on one of my favorite trails here tomorrow before we leave."

"That's fine with me, Liz," the senator said. "I keep Meredith out late too many nights as it is."

While Senator Hazelton paid for their dinners, Drake and Casey escorted Meredith and Liz outside to wait for him on the sidewalk.

Drake casually looked up and down the street, as he always did to be aware of his environment, when he saw them. Two young men sitting in an old gold Cadillac lowrider were watching them.

Drake moved over to stand next to Casey.

"I see them," Casey said. "What do you want to do?"

"They could be here waiting to pick off easier prey later in the evening," Drake said.

"The restaurant closes at eleven. We might be the easy prey."

"Let's share a ride back to our hotel with the senator and Meredith. We can come back for the Yukon tomorrow. If they follow us, we'll decide what to do then. Go inside and let the maître d know he's got a couple of gang bangers out here. He can call the Metro police to come and roust them."

Drake kept an eye on the lowrider and its occupants until the senator and Casey came out.

"Senator," Drake said, "we'd like to share a ride back to our hotel, if you don't mind."

"Is something wrong?"

Drake looked down the street toward the lowrider. "We just want to get everyone home safely."

Chapter Thirty-Seven

DRAKE AND CASEY stood beside Senator Hazelton until the senator's driver pulled up in a black Escalade.

Drake opened the rear passenger side door of the SUV and said, "Why don't we let Casey and Liz sit in the way back and I'll ride shotgun up front? The senator and Meredith can sit together in the second row."

Liz shot Drake a questioning look, just before Casey took her hand and helped her up into the SUV.

"That works for us," Casey said.

When they were seated back in the third row, Drake helped Meredith and Senator Hazelton into the second row of seats before he got in next to the driver.

Drake reached across to shake hands with the driver. "I'm Adam Drake, the senator's son-in-law. He's offered to give us a ride to our hotel, the Kimpton Glover Park over on Wisconsin Avenue."

"He's told me a lot about you, Mr. Drake. My name is Lewis. I'll have you there in no time."

As they drove past the lowrider, Drake noticed the tattoos up the arm and on the neck of the driver. He was wearing a black bandana on his shaved head and a blue and white Dallas Cowboys game jersey. Blue and white was the color of the El Salvadorian flag and the favorite colors of La Mara Salvatrucha, MS-13.

Drake turned in his seat to see if the lowrider pulled away from the curb and turned around to follow them.

When it did, Casey, who had been watching the lowrider too, turned his head back and nodded at Drake. They were being followed.

Drake leaned closer to Lewis and said softly, "Are you also the senator's bodyguard?"

"I'm not his primary, but I do serve in that capacity when I'm needed. Why?"

"We've got a couple of MS-13 gang bangers following us. Are you armed?"

"There's a revolver in the center console."

"If we make it to the hotel without an incident, take it and get Senator Hazelton and his wife inside the hotel until we know what's going on."

"What about the other woman in the back?"

"She's former FBI. I'll try to get her to go inside with you, but that's a battle I'll probably lose."

Drake turned around and leaned between the two bucket seats to talk with Senator Hazelton. "When we get to our hotel, I would like you and Mom to go inside with Lewis until we know it's safe. We have a couple of gang bangers following us."

Senator Hazelton reached over to hold his wife's hand. "I thought it might be something like that when I saw you watching the old Cadillac. Do you want me to call the police?"

"No, we're almost to our hotel. We'll be there before the police could arrive. We'll be all right."

He wasn't sure of that but had no way of knowing if it was true.

The lowrider stayed with one car between the Escalade all the way to the hotel.

"Lewis, swing around in front of the valet parking stand so you're facing back out to the street. As soon as we're stopped, open the door for Mrs. Hazelton and rush her and the senator inside. Liz, you and Mike follow them out and cover me until I join you."

As soon as Lewis turned off the street and swung around in front of the valet parking stand, the senator and his wife were rushed inside. Casey and Liz started to lower a seat down to follow them when Drake saw the lowrider drive on past the hotel, with the passenger leaning out and flashing the MS-13 hand sign, the "devil's head".

"False alarm, they drove on by," Drake said.

He opened his door and started to get out when he saw gang members walking four abreast toward them to his right. Two of them held what looked to him like modified and shortened AR-15s. The other two held handguns loosely at their sides.

"Get around here, Adam," Liz shouted. "There are four more of them coming from the left."

Before his feet hit the ground, the two men with the AR-15s on his right started firing point and spray on full auto, shooting out the windows above his head as he crouched and ran around the back of the SUV. One round hit him in the left arm before he could reach Liz and Casey.

Liz and Casey were crouched behind the Escalade with their Glocks out. Casey was returning fire to slow the gang bangers down.

Drake moved next to Liz and returned fire as well.

Casey stood and fired over the top of the left front fender of the SUV at the gang bangers advancing forward. He hit the two gang members firing on full auto center mass, putting them on the ground. The other two on the left kept coming from their positions twenty-five yards away. They were firing one round with each step they took, holding their pistols horizontally in front of them, gang-style without aiming. Casey let them advance another five yards before he put them down with head shots.

Drake popped around the back of the Escalade and shot the man coming toward him with a shaved head and firing a .50 caliber Desert Eagle pistol in his right hand and holding a machete in his left hand.

Seeing machete man fall, the remaining three gang bangers spread out along the sidewalk and continued firing into the side of the Escalade.

In the distance, they heard sirens racing toward the hotel.

Drake shouted over the sound of the AR-15s firing into the side of the Escalade. "Let 'em live or take them down?"

Casey shouted back, "They're just wasting ammunition, but I'd like to find out who sent them. Let's put them on crutches for now."

Casey moved to the rear of the Escalade next to Drake and looked to him to start shooting. Drake nodded and stepped out and put two of the men on the ground, grabbing their legs and crying out in pain. Casey moved around him and shot the only gang banger still standing in the knee, dropping him to the ground as well.

Chapter Thirty-Eight

THEY WAITED until the Metro police arrived and cuffed the three gang bangers before they laid their guns down and walked out from behind the senator's Escalade with their hands raised. District Commander Emerson walked forward and told them to lower their hands; Senator Hazelton had called and explained the situation.

After they had each identified themselves to the commander, he told them Senator Hazelton was lucky to have them in his vehicle when they'd been attacked.

"How bad is the arm?" he asked Drake.

Liz had run inside the hotel to get a towel and wrapped it around Drake's left arm before the police arrived, but blood was soaking through and dripping onto the ground.

"It hurts like hell, but the bullet missed the bone. I'll be fine."

"Any idea why they came after the senator?" the commander asked.

"No idea, commander," Drake answered quickly. "Any idea who they are?"

"They're MS-13; I know that from their tattoos and blue jerseys. Our gang taskforce should be able to identify them; we keep a close watch on the gangs. I haven't seen them use this much firepower before though."

"Commander, would you mind if I had a look at their weapons?" Casey asked. "I've heard they're manufacturing their own 'ghost guns', I think you're calling them, weapons that can't be traced. I have a security firm in Seattle, and I need to know what we might have to deal with."

Casey left to stand over one of the modified AR-15s and study it.

"The senator's SUV is pretty well shot up," Commander Emerson said. "Would you like us to take Senator Hazelton and his wife home and get you to the hospital? We can get your statements tomorrow, if you like?"

"Commander, if you don't mind, we have four men from Puget Sound Security here in town with us," Drake said. They're on their way to escort the senator and his wife home after we've had a word with them."

"No problem," the commander said and handed Drake a business card. "Come down to the station tomorrow whenever it's convenient for your statements. We might have these guys identified by then."

"We appreciate the courtesy, commander," Drake said and shook the man's hand.

"I didn't know Morales and the guys were called to come and get us," Liz said.

"They weren't, I'll go do that now," Drake said. "They've collected our guns to run ballistics. Until we get them back, I'll feel better when we have our guys here to protect us. The senator wasn't the target, we were. That's why eight MS-13 members were waiting here at our hotel."

Casey came back from studying the firepower the gang members brought with them. "Ghost guns, no serial numbers on them. They've used components you can buy online to put together a modified AR-15 that has a two-and-a-quarter-inch barrel and a collapsible butt stock and fires on full auto, like a military assault rifle. That's sophisticated, for a street gang."

Liz took hold of Drake's right arm and pulled him toward the hotel entrance. "Go talk to your in-laws while Mike and I call the guys and get our rides over here. I want you to get to hospital sometime tonight."

"You just want to see me squirm when they fix me up."

Liz made a pouty face. "Why would you say something like that? I didn't think a big tough guy like you ever squirmed."

"Oh, he squirms all right," Casey said with a chuckle. "He doesn't like needles either."

"That's it," Drake said and walked off. "Can't a guy get any sympathy when he's been shot?"

Liz and Casey said, "No," in unison and followed him into the hotel lobby.

A crowd of onlookers from the hotel parted to let Drake enter the lobby and walk over to where Senator Hazelton and Meredith stood with their driver.

His mother-in-law kissed him on the cheek with a tear in her eye. "That's the second time you've kept us safe. Thank you, Adam."

"It wasn't all me, Mom, Liz and Mike did more than I did. I'm just sorry we put you in a situation where you had to be protected."

"You think this was about the laptop?" Senator Hazelton asked.

"They were waiting for us here at our hotel. It has to be about the laptop. But MS-13 being involved doesn't make any sense. But because they are, I'd like to have a couple of PSS guys stay with you tonight, in case they want revenge for the guys they lost."

"Certainly, Son, if you think it's necessary."

"Liz," Drake said, "why don't you take Mom and Dad into the bar and order them a night cap while Mike and I make arrangements to keep them safe? Order me a double bourbon while you're at it."

Casey took out his smartphone to call Morales to bring the two rented SUVs over when Special Agent Perkins entered the lobby and walked over.

"I heard about the shootout. What happened?" she asked.

"We were followed by a lowrider when we left from the restaurant. Eight MS-13 came at us from two directions. We were lucky."

"I'm not sure luck had a lot do with it. I heard that was some good shooting that took those guys down, including the three leg shots. How did they know you were at the restaurant for dinner, I wonder."

"I wonder about that, too, Kate. We didn't make the reservation, Senator Hazelton did."

"I said you were involved with some dangerous people, now it seems that you're involved with some powerful people as well."

"You mean like intelligence community types?" Casey asked. "The kind that like to use contract hackers and contract assassins and eavesdrop on civilians?"

"Yes, and aren't afraid to use street gangs as well," Drake added. "You know anybody like that, Kate? Maybe someone in law enforcement?"

"I hope you're not thinking about Thomas Danforth."

"Why, didn't I read that he's credited with putting away a leader of MS-13 in Chicago?"

"Do you think these guys are MS-13 from Chicago?"

"It would certainly be an interesting coincidence if they are, wouldn't it?"

"I hope you're wrong, Drake, for all our sakes. That would make Danforth an enemy I don't want to have."

Chapter Thirty-Nine

THOMAS R. Danforth, III was tired when he turned off Colorado Highway 179 in northern Colorado onto the county road that led to his ranch.

By the time he'd driven from Denver to the federal prison in Florence, Colorado, for his brief meeting with Angel Torres Garcia, the leader of the Chicago branch of MS-13, and back to Denver, it was four o'clock in the afternoon. That left him with a three-hour drive to his nine-hundred-acre ranch southwest of Steamboat Springs.

Garcia had jumped at the chance to keep his little sister from going to jail in exchange for sending some of his gang members to Washington to silence Adam Drake and Liz Strobel. The information about the informant's drug record that the prosecutor was keeping from his sister's defense counsel was enough to guarantee a not guilty verdict. He had a strong suspicion, however, that Garcia would send his men to the informant's safe house to make sure he never testified.

He didn't feel remorseful at putting the lives of the U.S. marshals guarding the informant at risk. If the witness protection program couldn't do its job, that was on them. If they were able to keep the informant safe, at least he would have achieved what he wanted from Garcia when Drake and Strobel were dead, even if the informant made it to the sister's trial.

When his five-bedroom, five-bathroom seven-thousand-square foot home came into view in the distance, he felt an immense sense of pride at what he had created. The house he had designed was located on the top of a small ridge that provided a three-hundred-sixty-degree view of the surrounding land and the creek that meandered through below it. The trout fishing was superb in the summer and in the winter racing a snowmobile through the deep powder was a thrill he looked forward to all year long.

Keeping Nazir on the ranch was a no-brainer. The nearest neighbor was three miles away and a landing strip allowed him to come and go, weather permitting, with ease. He had chosen to drive to the ranch this time because he didn't want any record of his visit.

When he reached the private drive and turned off the county road, he stopped and called the leader of the security contractors James Oliver had hired.

"Fourteen, twenty-nine, eleven," he said, repeating the numbers Oliver had sent him to gain access to the ranch.

"Twelve, twenty-seven, nine," was the coded message that told him it was safe for him to drive on.

Ten men Oliver had used before provided round-the-clock protection for the young terrorist named Nazir they were babysitting. His interrogation had been far from "enhanced" but thorough enough to convince him that he was risking a transfer to a black site somewhere if he didn't cooperate.

Oliver's plan was to use Nazir and his Islamic Revolutionary Council of America to launch a cyberattack, similar to a cyberattack in 2012 by a group calling itself Izz al-Din al Qassam Cyber Fighters. Due its sophistication, the U.S. believed the group was a front for Iran seeking retribution for cyberattacks it attributed to America.

The attack hadn't been nearly as devastating as the one Oliver planned and there hadn't been indisputable evidence, at the time, that Iran was to blame. This time, however, the cyberattack Oliver designed would leave plenty of evidence behind that Iran was to blame. When the president was forced to retaliate, the main source of terrorism in the world would get what it deserved.

Danforth didn't know the particulars of what Oliver had in mind, but he didn't need to. That was Oliver's area of expertise. His area of expertise was counterintelligence and he knew that the current president's disengagement around the world was a threat to the security of the country. Old enemies were rattling their sabers more loudly than at any time he could remember.

Oliver was playing a long game, he knew. His game was more immediate. All he needed was to make sure there was no evidence of his dealing with the Russian on Nazir's laptop. The file that Nazir sent to the FBI Tipline did not mention his name or that he'd provided information to the Russian, but he couldn't take a chance that there was other information on it that would eventually lead someone back to him.

That's why he'd gone to such lengths to recover the laptop and bring it to its owner who had the password. With that, he'd be able to examine the laptop for himself.

He parked his rental car at the rear of the house and was met by the leader of the security contractors, a man named Landers.

"I need to get back to Denver tonight," Danforth said. "Where is he?"

"We're keeping him in a storage room in the basement."

"How is he?"

"Scared. The weapon for his jihad was his computer. I don't think he's done a violent thing in his life, judging by the way he reacts to the things I've promised we'll do to him if he doesn't cooperate."

Landers led the way down the stairs to the basement and opened the door to the storage room.

"I need a moment alone with him," Danforth said.

Nazir was shackled and sitting on a metal framed cot, wearing an orange jump suit. He hadn't been allowed to shave and his jet-black hair was unkempt. He watched Danforth nervously as he placed Nazir's laptop on the metal writing table pushed against the far wall of the storage room.

"It has taken me a considerable effort and expense to retrieve your laptop, Mr. Nazir. Your encrypted password has kept it locked. You will open it for me to examine it or every member of your Islamic Revolutionary Council of America and their families will be killed. If you cooperate with us, you will remain here and be given more liberties than you enjoy now. Do you have any questions for me before I leave?"

"Who are you and why am I here?"

"Who do you think I am?"

"You're not the FBI. I would have been arrested and be in jail. You're probably CIA."

"To answer the second part of your question, you are here because you are a terrorist who has received support from an enemy of the U.S. You are here because you worked with Mikhail Volkov and Professor Bradley and tried to start a second civil war in this country. You forfeited your rights to live freely as a citizen of this country when you betrayed it. You will be allowed to live in exchange for doing what we ask of you. Is there anything else, Mr. Nazir?"

Nazir stared silently and shook his head.

"Excellent," Danforth said and took the laptop with him as he left the storage room.

Chapter Forty

DRAKE, Liz and Casey met for breakfast Saturday morning in the hotel's restaurant. Drake's arm had been patched up in the ER late the night before and was in a dark blue sling.

They were waiting for Special Agent Perkins to join them with the news about the MS-13 gang members killed or captured last night.

"Do you two really think Danforth is using MS-13 to do his dirty work?" Casey asked. "How would we prove it if he is?"

"I don't know, Mike," Drake said. "I know he knows where Nazir is, but I don't know why he would come after us. I saw a flash of anger in his eyes when we visited his office that was out of place. Everything seems to be related to Nazir's laptop."

Special Agent Perkins entered the restaurant and walked over to their table. She was wearing the same tan slacks and blue blouse under her FBI jacket that she wore the night before. It was her blood-shot eyes, however, that said that she'd been in the FBI field office all night.

"We ordered a Bloody Mary, Kate," Liz said. "You look like you could use one too."

"I think I will, thanks. How's the arm?" she asked Drake.

"No serious damage done, it's fine."

"Have you been working all night, Kate?" Liz asked.

"I had to wait for the medics to take care of their leg wounds before I could talk to them. They're not saying much. They asked for attorneys right away. They're in the system, so it wasn't hard to identify them. They're all from the Chicago branch of MS-13."

Drake looked at Liz but didn't say anything.

"What were they doing in D.C.? Casey asked.

"We don't know that yet. We do know they drove straight here yesterday, from gas receipts we found in two of their cars that were parked not far from your hotel."

"They didn't look like new recruits," Drake observed. "They looked pretty seasoned. Do you think someone even more senior ordered them to come here?"

Special Agent Perkins looked at Drake for a long moment. "Are you suggesting they came here just to attack you?"

"I think that's pretty obvious, don't you? We were followed from the restaurant and as soon as the lowrider left, we were hit from two sides. The only thing they didn't do was have someone in the hotel to hit us from the rear."

"I considered that and asked the Chicago field office to check with their informants to see if this was a hit. But if it was, do you have any idea why someone wants you dead?"

Drake waited for their four Bloody Marys to be handed out before answering. "At first, I thought it was all about the laptop we had that somebody else wanted. We don't have it anymore, so it must be something we know or something someone wants to keep us from finding out. That's the only thing I can come up with."

"What is it that you know that's worth killing for?" she asked.

Drake saw the slightest movement of Casey's head and knew what he was signaling; don't say anything about someone in the government aiding and abetting the enemy.

He looked her straight in the eyes and said truthfully, "If I knew that I'd know who to go after."

"If you find out what it is, you come to me first and let me take care of it, all right? That's my job, not yours."

"What were you able to learn about the CIA guy, Oliver?" Casey asked.

"I know that James T. Oliver is the associate director of the CIA's Directorate of Digital Innovation and that he lives in the Watergate West. He's involved in cyber defense of the government's secrets and in cyber tradecraft."

"Is cyber tradecraft what I think it is? Casey asked.

"It is if you're thinking it's cyber espionage," Perkins said.

"Kate, did you find anything that would explain the money Vincente Martinez received from Oliver?" Liz asked her.

"I only have the financials for Martinez, and it shows that Oliver has paid him ten thousand dollars a number of times. Given what Oliver does for the CIA and how many things the CIA is known to outsource, I don't think Oliver's paying him is anything I can get anyone interested in investigating."

"What about a link between Oliver and Danforth?" Drake asked.

"I haven't looked for one."

"What would you do if we found one?"

"I would investigate it, of course. Why do you ask?"

"I know we'd be asking a lot to ask you to investigate an associate director of the CIA, but it's something we could do."

"Do I want to know how you would do that?" she asked with a slight grimace.

"Probably not, but it wouldn't be anything that would come back to haunt you."

"If you go down that road, you're on your own, but let me know if you come up with anything," she said. "Are you guys going to order something for breakfast? Because I'm hungry."

Chapter Forty-One

BY THE TIME they finished breakfast, an agreement had been reached on the best way to proceed.

Drake and company would investigate James T. Oliver and Special Agent Perkins would give them his bank account that showed the ten-thousand-dollar payments to Tony Yamada, hacker-for-hire. They would also continue to search for the person or persons who had Nazir's laptop.

Special Agent Perkins would continue her investigation of the murders of Senator Hazelton's young staffer, Tony Yamada, Vincente Martinez and the MS-13 gang members from Chicago.

"How long will you be in Washington?" Perkins asked Drake.

"We're staying until Senator Hazelton has additional security for himself and his wife in place, probably tonight or tomorrow," Drake said.

"Do you all fly back in the company jet?" she asked.

Drake smiled broadly. "There's room for all of us. Why do you ask?"

He knew the answer but wanted to see if she would admit it.

There was a trace of color bloom on her cheeks. "Dan owes me dinner, that's all."

Liz jumped in to prevent Drake from making Perkins any more uncomfortable than she already was. "If we decide to leave tonight, he'll find a way to keep his promise, Kate. I'm sure the company would be happy to reimburse him for a ticket, if he has to fly back commercially tomorrow, wouldn't it, gentlemen?"

Casey nodded in agreement. "Of course, it would. You've been a big help, Kate, and we appreciate it."

Agent Perkins finished her second cup of coffee and got up to leave. "I'll send Liz the information about Oliver's bank account; then I'm going home to shower and take a nap. Let me know when you're leaving and thank you for my breakfast."

Liz got up and walked Kate out of the restaurant.

"You're going to get an earful for teasing Agent Perkins, my friend."

"No doubt, but you have to admit it was fun seeing an FBI Special Agent blush. She's tough, she can take it."

"Does your father-in-law have someone in mind for additional security?" Casey asked.

"I don't know if he does, but I do."

"Borden and Manning?"

"What better than a couple of SEALs who just happen to work for us," Drake said. "I'll call him right now."

Liz gave him the look as she came back into the restaurant and passed Drake walking out. Casey was right; he was going to get an earful when they were alone.

"Hello Adam, how's the arm?" Senator Hazelton asked when he answered Drake's call.

"It's fine, just sore. How's Mom dealing with last night?"

"She was frightened, but she's okay. She's worried about you, but she saw the way you and Liz and Casey handled the situation."

"We're probably going to fly back to Seattle tonight or tomorrow. I would like to see you beef up your security until we have a better understanding of what we're dealing with. Is that something you're willing to do?"

"If you think it's necessary, certainly. Who should I call?"

"You're talking to him. We have two SEALs with us and they're available to augment your security. They'll stay with you until we feel it's safe for them to return to Seattle."

"That might be a while. Secretary Rawlings called me this morning. He didn't get in touch with the two DHS investigators he had waiting to take custody of Nazir in Montana. They're both dead. He got ahold of the report they filed that identified the two FBI agents they handed Nazir off to and those two agents are dead as well. One heart attack, one suicide and two car accidents. All four deaths are under investigation."

Drake was stunned. "I assumed Nazir was being held by the FBI or CIA. Maybe it's not them at all. Who's handling the investigations?"

"The FBI is investigating the death of their two agents and DHS is investigating their two investigators. Secretary Rawlings believes the FBI isn't investigating the deaths of the two DHS because the FBI agents didn't make a report or, if they did, there was no mention of DHS involvement."

Drake was silent for a moment, thinking. "If the FBI or CIA doesn't have Nazir and there's someone else involved, there's no reason for them to kill the two DHS investigators. The FBI agents, maybe, because they could identify whoever snatched Nazir. This doesn't make any sense, but it does eliminate the last lead we had to find Nazir."

"What about his laptop?" Senator Hazelton asked. "We couldn't get past the encrypted password, but Nazir would be able to. Wouldn't they want to get the laptop to him? Do we have any way to find the laptop?"

"Not without a tracker transmitter on it or it accesses the internet and we knew its IP address, which we don't."

"Something will turn up, Adam. It seems you've done all you can for now."

"You may be right. I'll send our two SEALs over to meet you. Introduce them to the head of your security detail and let me know if they will fit in."

"All right, Adam. Thanks for taking care of this for me."

"You're welcome, senator."

Drake stayed in the hotel lobby to digest the news about the dead agents and what the senator said about finding Nazir's laptop. There was a way they might be able to find it.

When Kevin McRoberts, their hacker extraordinaire, was trying to find out who was trying to hack the IT system of one their clients, he traced the phishing attempts to a server at the Intel Corporation in Portland. The person using the server was communicating with other hackers. That person was Zal Nazir. If Kevin knew the IP address of Nazir's laptop, they might be able to locate it and Nazir, but only if he was using the laptop to access the internet.

Drake left the lobby and returned to the restaurant, where Liz and Casey were both on their smartphones.

Without looking up, Liz said, "Kate sent me Oliver's account information and I sent it to Kevin to work on. Kevin just called to say that he hacked Oliver's account and saw that he's purchased a plane ticket to fly to Denver tomorrow on Frontier Airlines. We're trying to buy tickets for Dan Norris and Marco Morales to follow him and see where he's going."

"That might be the break we need," Drake said. "But you better let Norris know he's leaving tomorrow. He'll need to make a dinner reservation for tonight to keep his promise to Kate."

Liz looked up and pointed a finger at Drake. "We'll talk about Kate and Dan later. You call Dan and tell him to call Kate. He has a promise to keep."

Chapter Forty-Two

DAN NORRIS and Marco Morales were dropped off at Terminal A at Ronald Reagan Washington National Airport in separate black SUVs driven by Drake and Casey for an early flight to Denver, Colorado. If James Oliver was checking to see if he was being followed, the two men couldn't be seen together.

Norris found a seat at Gate 5 and opened his iPad to read the *Washington Post*. He also had a photo of James Oliver on it that Kate Perkins had given him the night before to identify the man he would be following to Denver.

Marco Morales stopped at a news stand and looked for a paperback to read on the flight, keeping an eye on passengers walking by. He had a photo of Oliver on his iPhone as well, but he'd studied it for so long on the way to the airport that he didn't need to look at it again. Oliver wasn't a handsome man, but his thinning gray hair that was almost white and the round John Lennon glasses made him an easy person to spot.

One hour before departure, Oliver walked past the news stand pulling a black Tumi four-wheel carryon, wearing jeans, a white cable knit sweater and a black wool Ivy cap. He also had a laptop carrying case slung from his shoulder.

Morales watched him as he walked on past Gate 5 to the last of the Frontier gates and then turn around and walk back to the men's room nearest to Gate 5. Ten minutes later, Oliver came out of the men's room and sat down three seats to the right of Norris.

Morales waited until the seating around Gate 5 started to fill up half an hour before departure and then found a seat facing Oliver two rows over. As soon as he sat down, he took out his iPhone and started playing solitaire, being careful not to look at Oliver.

Their flight was on time and the passengers boarded the plane quietly, as passengers do when it's seven o'clock in the morning. The traveling business men and women took out their laptops to prepare for the presentation they were flying to Denver or beyond to give. Several of the young men closed their eyes and tried to sleep during the flight safety video while the rest of the passengers ignored the video altogether.

Oliver was seated near the front of the plane on the left with Norris seated two rows behind him across the aisle. Morales was seated in the middle of the plane and would go straight to the Hertz counter to get his rental car, where Oliver had also rented a car. Norris would follow Oliver and get in line at Hertz behind him for his Hertz rental. With only two cars, they would have to be careful and maintain a loose tail on Oliver, but they had the training and experience to do it successfully.

Two hours and nine minutes after talking off, their Airbus A391 touched down in Colorado at Denver International Airport. Forty-five minutes later, three Hertz rental cars had cleared the congestion of Denver and were traveling west on I-70.

Norris pushed the push-to-talk button on his two-way radio. "How far behind him are you?"

"Two hundred yards or so," Morales said.

"Let's trade places when we intersect E-470."

"Copy that. Wish I had a cup of coffee, we're headed west to who knows where."

"The energy bars Liz got for us will have to do for now. What do you want to do if he stops somewhere?"

"You sat close to him at the airport. I'll stop with him and you continue on to the next exit that GPS shows you can get back on behind me when we pass."

"Copy that. Enjoy the scenery."

Oliver's gray Range Rover Evoque passed Gray's Peak and turned north at Silverhome onto Colorado-9 toward Steamboat Springs.

Morales pushed the PTT button on his radio to call Norris. "It's a little early in the year to go skiing, where's he going?"

"Maybe he has a place here."

"Do CIA guys make that kind of money?"

"Not the ones I've run into. Want to trade places again?"

"Yeah, I'm getting tired of looking at the rear of your black Yukon. You'll have an easier time following my white Jeep."

Three hours after leaving Denver, Oliver was approaching Steamboat Springs on Co-40 when he turned off onto a county road and slowed down.

Morales radioed Norris. "He turned onto the county road coming up and is driving west at a slow rate of speed. He's checking to see if he's being followed. I'll drive on and you hang back and then follow him. I'll turn around and follow you."

"Copy that. I see his taillights."

Norris waited until Oliver's vehicle disappeared around a corner on the county road and then accelerated to follow him. When he was a hundred yards behind the gray Range Rover, he kept pace with it and radioed Morales.

"I don't think he knows I'm following him, but catch up as soon as you can. If he slows down or turns off, I'll drive on and you see where he's going."

"Copy that. I'm pulling off onto the county road now."

Oliver drove on for fifteen minutes at the speed limit and then Norris saw his brake lights go on as he slowed and stopped in front of the gate of a ranch. The gate had a keypad on the left with an IP camera above it and on the right was a large orange sign.

Norris saw as he drove by that it was a sign warning that the ranch had guard dogs and they would attack.

"He's stopped at the gate of a ranch with a large orange sign and a keypad," he radioed to Morales. "I'll drive on and then come back to join you."

"Copy that. I'll hold back until he's out of sight and then approach the gate."

Norris drove back and parked his Yukon on the road opposite Morales, who was out of his Jeep taking a picture of the warning sign with his iPhone.

"There's no call box and yet it says to notify the owner before entering," Morales said. "How do you do that if you don't know who the owner is?"

Norris stood beside Morales and saw the taillights of Oliver's SUV a good quarter of a mile away on the ranch road. "Whoever he is, he owns quite a spread, judging by the split rail fence that bordered the county road for the last mile or so."

"What now?"

"Not much we can do tonight. Let's drive on to Steamboat Springs and find a place to stay. I'll call Drake on the way and see if he can find out who owns this place. If we know who the owner is, we could always contact him and make up an excuse to go in and find out what Oliver's doing there."

"That's the only way I'm going in there," Morales said. "I'm not a big fan of guard dogs, free to attack anyone who doesn't have the owner's permission before entering."

"You don't even know if there really are guard dogs."

"And I'm sure not going to find out the hard way. Go call Drake and let's find somewhere to stay. Oliver will still be here tomorrow."

Chapter Forty-Three

CARL LANDERS, the head of security at the ranch, was waiting for Oliver when he parked his Range Rover behind Danforth's Colorado hideaway and got out.

"Two guys were snooping around at the gate after you called me to let you in," Landers said. "Were you followed?"

"I don't think so, but find out who they are. How's Nazir? Did Danforth get him to unlock his laptop?"

"He didn't try. He wanted you to be the one to watch him do it, in case he tries something."

"It's late, I'll go introduce myself. When I return, find me something to eat. I didn't stop for anything on my way here from Denver."

Oliver followed Landers to the basement store room to meet the man he'd been watching as Nazir put together his band of Muslim hackers.

Nazir was resting on his cot when Oliver knocked on the door and entered the storeroom.

"I've been wanting to meet you for some time, Mr. Nazir. I followed you as you recruited hackers for your Islamic Revolutionary Council of America. It's a shame you chose to work with Professor Bradley on his fool's errand trying to start a civil war here. If you'd kept waging cyber jihad as you'd planned, instead of listening to your Iranian sponsor, you could have hurt us quite badly."

Nazir sat up slowly and hung his head. "Who are you and what do you want? If you know all that, why am I here instead of in prison or some dark site being tortured?"

"Is that what you would prefer? That can still be arranged."

Nazir swung his head from side to side and sighed. "The man who has my laptop threatened the members of my Council and their families if I don't cooperate. Now you're saying I'll be in prison or tortured somewhere. You must be the good cop. What is it you want, Mr. good cop?"

"We'll get to that tomorrow. It's late and I haven't eaten anything today, so I'll leave you to work out what I want from you. Good night, Mr. Nazir. We'll get started in the morning."

Oliver left the room smiling. Nazir wasn't going to believe what they wanted him to do.

He found Landers upstairs in the kitchen seasoning a steak and drinking a glass of red wine. "How do you like your steak and eggs?"

"The steak rare and the eggs over easy. Has Nazir been fed? He looks a little pale."

"We give a ham sandwich and water at lunch. If he's hungry, he'll eat. So far, he hasn't."

"That's cute. Ask him what he wants tomorrow and give it to him. I need him alert and focused when we start. Have you found out who the men at the gate were?"

"Not the men but who they work for. The SUVs they were driving were rented from Hertz. I paid a friend in Denver to go to the Hertz counter with their license plates claiming they were seen leaving the scene of an accident and he wanted to get the information to the police. Both SUVs were rented by Puget Sound Security in Seattle. That mean anything?"

"Unfortunately, it does. They're probably staying in Steamboat Springs tonight. See if you can find out where and send one of your men there to keep an eye on them until I decide what to do about them."

Oliver poured himself a glass of wine and went out to the flagstone rear deck to have a smoke as he waited for the nicotine to calm his anger and clear his head. The security firm and its attorney just kept coming. They couldn't know what was on the laptop because he had it and it hadn't been unlocked yet. They couldn't know that he was the one who had taken it back from them because he hadn't left anyone alive who could tell them.

How had they known to follow him to Colorado? Danforth's ranch was owned by one of his shell companies. Even if they suspected somehow that Danforth was involved, they wouldn't know this ranch was his.

Before he went ahead with his plan for Nazir, he had to know what the two men from PSS knew and why they were following him.

Oliver dropped his cigarette and ground it out on the flagstone before returning to the kitchen.

Landers had a large Buffalo steak resting on a cutting board and was frying eggs in the cast iron skillet he used for the steak when Oliver sat down on a bar stool at the kitchen island across from him.

"I need to know why the two men at the gate are here. When you find them, bring them here and we'll find out."

Landers cut the steak into strips and added them and the eggs onto a plate and slid it over to Oliver.

"What if they don't want to come willingly?"

"I don't care how you get them here. Ask them why they were taking pictures at the gate. Ask them if they know the owner and are here to speak with him. You'll think of something."

"Will they be leaving the ranch after you've finished talking with them?"

"That depends, but probably not. Leave their SUVs in town where Hertz can find them once they disappear."

Landers left to give his men their instructions while Oliver poured himself another glass of an excellent California cabernet from the Midnight Rose winery. He made a note to get a case of the wine, learn about its winemaker and the story behind the winery's name.

Chapter Forty-Four

AFTER CHECKING into the iconic Rabbit Ears Motel in downtown Steamboat Springs, Norris and Morales walked to the nearby 8th Street Steakhouse that had been recommended by the night clerk. By the time they walked up the steps to the front door of the restaurant with the temperature in the mid-twenties, they were both hungry and cold.

Drake had asked them to stay in Steamboat Springs for the night, while he and Kevin McRoberts back at PSS headquarters worked to find out about the ranch that James Oliver was visiting.

When they were seated at their table and had ordered their adult beverage of choice, bourbon for Norris and tequila for Morales, they walked to the meat counter to select the steaks they were going to cook by themselves.

"Are you as hungry as I am?" Morales asked, choosing an eighteen-ounce bone-in ribeye steak for his dinner.

"We'll see," Norris said, pointing to another eighteen-ounce bone-in ribeye steak for himself.

After standing at the long lava rock grill with their drinks in hand and laughing with other patrons cooking their own steaks and shrimp skewers and sautéed veggies, they returned to their table to enjoy their first real meal of the day.

As soon as they sat down, Morales' iPhone pinged with a text message from Drake.

Stay another night and reserve rooms for two more. We'll join you tomorrow. A shell company owns the ranch and Kevin thinks it's Danforth's.

Morales turned his phone around so that Norris could read the message.

"Huh, Drake's hunch that the FBI and the CIA could be working together on something seems be right on the money," Norris said.

"If they are, they're both way off their reservations."

"It wouldn't be the first time for the CIA, but I'm having a hard time thinking the FBI might be involved."

Morales cut into his steak and grinned as he savored his first bite, pointing to his steak with his fork. "This is really good."

Norris sat staring at his steak and shaking his head. "Why would a guy like Danforth do something like this?"

"You know him?" Morales asked with a mouthful of loaded baked potato.

"Not directly. He's counterintelligence and one of the FBI's golden boys."

"You never know when someone takes a wrong turn."

"I suppose," Norris said and waved to the waitress with a raised and empty bourbon tumbler.

Norris and Morales ate without talking until their plates were empty and the waitress returned to ask if they wanted dessert or an after-dinner coffee.

They declined and asked for two black coffees and their check. When the check arrived, Morales used his PSS American Express card to pay for dinner.

"Does everyone get one of those?" Norris asked.

"You're still a newbie. You'll get one for expenses when your probation's over."

"What probation?"

Morales grinned like a Cheshire cat. "You don't have a credit card, do you?"

"Right, and you can get the rooms for Drake and Liz while I use the hot tub and then hit the sack."

"Touché. You ready to go?" Morales asked.

"Ready if you are."

The temperature was closer to twenty degrees when they left the restaurant and began the half-mile walk back to their motel.

Ski season was a month or two away and there weren't many tourists on the streets. When they were a block away from the parking lot of the Rabbit Ear Motel, however, they saw four men standing around their two SUVs.

Morales stepped aside and pulled Norris into an alley next to them. "What do you think that's all about?"

"They're all wearing the same black parkas and watch caps. Local law enforcement?"

"Maybe private security for the town, but why are they interested in our two Hertz rentals?"

Two men wearing the same black parkas and watch caps came out of the motel's office and joined the four men standing around their SUVs. They couldn't hear what was being said, but one of the men turned around and pointed down the street toward the 8th Street Steakhouse a half mile away.

"Are you thinking what I'm thinking?" Morales asked.

"I'm thinking they're looking for us. Let's wait until they leave and get prepared to have a word with them when they return."

"Have you had time to get your PSS armed security guard permit?"

"No, but I have a concealed carry permit for Maryland where I'm still registered to vote. Colorado recognizes permits from other states, so we're good if it comes to that."

"How do you want to do this?" Morales asked.

"Why don't I wait for them in my car and when you see them coming back, get behind them. I'll find out what they want with my phone on so you can hear what's being said."

"There are six of them. We can't shoot it out in the street if we don't like what they say."

"We might not have a choice," Norris said. "The other option is to leave and see if they follow us."

"I'd rather find out why they're interested in us tonight. I'm not keen on being chased when I'm not familiar with the lay of the land."

"That's it, then. Let me know where you'll be. I'll duck into the motel office and find out what they wanted and then wait in my car."

Norris jogged to the motel office and went inside.

Morales ran across the street and entered a park next to the motel with a clear view of the Rabbit Ears Motel parking lot.

Norris came out of the motel office and walked to his SUV in the parking lot and got in.

Morales called to tell him he was in the park nearby.

"They told the night clerk we were seen trespassing on their ranch and they wanted to have a word with us," Norris reported.

"If this is some CIA operation on the ranch, Dan, we might be stepping into something tonight we don't want to be stepping into. Maybe we should leave town and wait for Drake to get here tomorrow."

"Too late for that, I see them coming down the street."

Chapter Forty-Five

NORRIS STAYED in his SUV until the six men from the ranch got within twenty yards before he got out and stood behind the open driver-side door.

"I understand you wanted to talk with me," he said. "Who are you and what is it you want?"

One of the men stepped forward and said, "The owner of the ranch is a very private person. He wants to know why you were snooping around his property."

"I'm afraid you were misinformed," Norris said calmly." We weren't snooping around anyone's property. What property are you talking about and who's this owner? For that matter, who are you? Do you guys work for this owner, whoever he is?"

"Where's the guy you were with?"

"He's around here somewhere, why?"

"Because both of you need to come with us. The owner wants to talk with you."

"I'm afraid that's not going to happen. We're not going anywhere tonight."

The leader, who appeared to be in his mid-thirties with the head of snake visible on the left side of his neck, turned to look at the others and then opened his parka to let Norris see his holstered Glock on his right hip. Norris also saw an AN/PRC-148 Multiband Team Radio on his left hip.

"Let me guess, you guys are CIA, right?" Norris asked.

The leader's eyes blinked and then narrowed to slits. "What the hell are you talking about?"

Norris pointed to the Glock and then the radio. "Glock 19, a favorite of CIA operatives, and your AN/PRC radio, that's why."

"I'll ask you just one more time, who are you?" the leader said as he pulled his Glock and pointed it at Norris's chest.

"Weren't you taught never to point a gun at someone unless you plan on shooting them?" Norris asked loudly to make sure Morales heard him.

"Who says I'm not going to shoot you, wise guy?"

"That would be me," Morales shouted as he walked out of the park behind the six men with his pistol held at eye level and pointed at the leader's head. "You boys might want to run back to your ranch, the police are on their way."

Five men spun around, drawing their weapons as the first sound of sirens racing to the Rabbit Ears Motel reached them.

The leader lowered his weapon and backed away. "This isn't over," he said, turning and running to the far end of the parking lot where two white Ford Excursions were parked. The Ford's engines started as the men ran to their SUVs. They pulled out of the parking lot before two patrol cars arrived.

Morales stood beside Norris as two Steamboat Springs patrol cars screeched to a stop and their drivers jumped out and stood behind their car doors with guns drawn.

"Show us your hands," one officer shouted.

Norris and Morales complied with the command, but Morales couldn't resist saying, "They went that way, sheriff."

"Very funny," Norris said softly.

"I always wanted to say that," Morales whispered. "Officers, I'm the person who called 911."

"Sir, why did you call 911?" the officer asked.

"We were coming back from dinner at the 8th Street Steakhouse when six men tried to kidnap my friend at gunpoint," Morales explained. "They raced off when they heard your sirens."

"Keep your hands where we can see them and come forward."

Norris and Morales did as they were told. The lead officer came out from behind the door of his car and holstered his weapon, while the other officers kept their weapons covering them.

"Show me your ID."

"Officer, we're armed and have concealed carry permits. We work for Puget Sound Security in Seattle," Morales said.

"Slowly show me your weapons and then your IDs," the officer said.

Norris and Morales opened their jackets to display their holstered Glocks and then took out their wallets open to show their driver's licenses.

After looking at them briefly, the officer asked, "Maryland and Washington, why are you here in Colorado?"

Morales looked to Norris before answering. "We followed a man from Washington, D.C. who may have committed a crime there."

"Isn't that a matter for law enforcement to deal with?"

Norris answered before Morales could think of what to say. "We're assisting Special Agent Kate Perkins of the FBI in the matter. That's all we're at liberty to say."

"I assume she'll corroborate that?"

"She will."

"Okay, follow us to the station for your statements about this attempted kidnapping. I will also need the number for this FBI agent."

"Certainly officer," Norris said. "Lead the way."

As they walked back to Norris's SUV he told Morales to drive. "I need to call Kate before she gets a call from this guy and tell her about Oliver and the ranch."

Morales held out his hand for the keys and said, "You think she'll be willing to say that we're assisting her with her murder investigation?"

"I may have to promise to take her to dinner again. I think she will, especially when I tell her Oliver is in Colorado on Danforth's ranch."

Chapter Forty-Six

CARL LANDERS WAITED until Oliver came into the kitchen for coffee in the morning to tell him that his men had failed to bring the two men snooping at the gate back to the ranch.

"How many of your men did you send?" Oliver asked calmly while pouring himself a cup of coffee.

"Six of my best men."

Oliver leaned back against the kitchen island to face Landers. "How good could they be, Carl, when six of them couldn't do what they were asked to do? If they can't get the job done, find me men who will."

"Sir, I don't think it was their fault. The police showed up unexpectedly and they had to leave or explain what they were doing."

"Carl, I need another day or two to work with our guest. I don't want to worry about someone interfering with that. Can you think of a way to find out why they were at the gate without bringing them here and risk getting the police involved?"

"We could take them somewhere else and find out what you want to know, I suppose?"

"Excellent plan, Carl. Take them somewhere, do what you need to do to get them to talk and make sure I won't have to spend another minute worrying about them. Can you do that for me?"

Landers started to say something…

"CAN YOU DO THAT FOR ME, CARL?" Oliver shouted.

Landers glared at Oliver before looking away and nodding. "Sure, I can do that, but don't ever shout at me like that again. I think you're forgetting who I am."

Oliver set his cup of coffee down and moved forward into Landers's personal space. "I think you're forgetting who I am, Carl. Get the job done and there won't be a need for me to shout at you. Now, make sure Nazir has breakfast and a shower before we begin with him. I have a lot of work to do today."

Oliver dismissed his head of security with a wave of his hand and loaded a plate with scrambled eggs, bacon and a croissant and went into the breakfast nook. He sat looking out the window with a view of the creek below that meandered across the nine hundred plus acres of the ranch. In the distance he could see an air sock on a pole at the end of the ranch's airstrip.

The only thing he could think of that would explain why two men were snooping around the ranch was that Danforth had screwed up in some way. Tony Yamada and Vincente Martinez were dead and didn't know anything about Nazir or the ranch before they died. Martinez found the tracking transmitter that had been on the laptop case and there was no way the laptop had been followed to the ranch.

Someone had to be on to Danforth and if they were on to him, they might know about his ranch. He had traveled to the ranch with the laptop, maybe he had been followed. And if that was the case, there was no way he could allow himself to be found here with an American citizen in custody, even if he was a terrorist, because the CIA wasn't supposed to operate on home soil. It did, of course, but you just didn't want to be caught doing it.

He finished his breakfast and called Danforth with the encrypted iPhone they both used.

"Someone's been snooping around the ranch. Is it possible that you were followed when you came here?"

"No, I flew to Denver in that chartered jet and drove there from Denver."

"And you're sure you weren't followed when you drove to the ranch?"

"I know how to spot a tail, James. Do you know who's been snooping around?"

"They're driving Hertz SUVs rented on a credit card issued to Puget Sound Security, but I don't know who's driving them."

"How do they even know about the ranch? There's no way they can find out it's mine. My shell company has too many layers of ownership for them ever to know it's mine."

"Why would Puget Sound Security be looking into the owner-ship of the ranch? Is there something you're not telling me?"

"Their attorney will know the FBI took custody of Nazir when they flew him back from Hawaii and he will know that I was looking for Nazir's laptop. You know that. That's all he can know, unless he's found out that you got the laptop back for us."

"But he can't know Nazir is here. The two FBI agents and the two DHS investigators who knew about Nazir are dead. We've come too far to screw this up now. How do you want to handle this?"

"How much more time do you need with Nazir?"

"Just long enough to get him to send my malware to the members of his council to launch the cyberattack on the banks, a day, maybe two."

"Will you be able to take out the two snooping around for the security company before you're finished with Nazir?"

"The head of my security detail assures me that he can, why?"

"As soon as you launch the cyberattack, we'll fly you and Nazir out of there. The airstrip is long enough for a jet and your security can sanitize the place when you leave. There won't be anything to tie us to anything if you and Nazir and his laptop are no longer there."

"Whatever you arrange to fly us out can never be traced to you or this ranch. Do you have somebody who can make sure of that?"

"I'll find someone."

"That's not good enough. I know people, I'll handle it."

"Do you have the funds to do that or do you need something from me?"

"Transfer a couple hundred thousand to me from your offshore account. That should cover it."

"Don't screw this up, James, or we'll both spend the rest of our lives in jail."

Oliver ended the call and let fly with a string of expletives.

I'm not going to let you live long enough, Danforth, to risk that happening! As soon as I take down the banks and force the president to deal with Iran, I will kill you myself.

Chapter Forty-Seven

AFTER A LONG NIGHT at the Steamboat Springs police station giving their statements about the attempted kidnapping and a short night's sleep, Norris left Morales finishing a free continental breakfast with a coffee to drive to the airport. The PSS Gulfstream G650 was arriving at nine o'clock that morning.

While the sergeant who took their statements did most of the talking, Norris was able to learn a lot about the nine-hundred-acre Double R ranch. It had recently been purchased by a corporation to host clients who liked to ski. As far as the sergeant knew, no one had seen any of these clients in the last year, but an occasional plane was seen landing on the airstrip. The ranch had a manager who lived there, but employees who worked there lived at home in and around Steamboat.

There had been reports of security personnel on the ranch whenever a plane was tied down on the airstrip. The airstrip could be seen from the county road and the sergeant drove by the ranch every day on his way to work and said there was no plane there now.

If the men who confronted Norris and Morales were security

personnel from the ranch, it was something new without a visitor being in residence.

If Kevin McRoberts was right and the ranch belonged to the FBI's Thomas Danforth and the CIA's James Oliver was there, it was a dangerous game they were playing.

The FBI HRT was one of three "Tier 1" U.S. counterterrorism commando teams, along with Combat Operations Group (Delta) and DevGru (SEAL Team 6). He'd trained with Delta operatives and SEALs and knew hard men when he saw them. The six men he'd met last night were hard men.

Norris drove west for twenty-five miles to Atlantic Aviation, the general aviation FBO at the Yampa Valley Regional Airport in Hayden, Colorado. Adam Drake, Liz Strobel and Kevin McRoberts and were waiting for him when he arrived at eight fifty-five Monday morning.

They were all pulling rolling carryon luggage and Drake was carrying a large, black range duffel bag in his right hand when they greeted him in the Atlantic Aviation terminal.

"Welcome to Colorado," Norris said in greeting. "Here, let me carry that duffel bag, Drake. I imagine it's heavy, if it has what I think it has inside."

"Thanks," Drake said and let him have the duffel bag. "Morales called about last night. That was a pretty aggressive reaction."

"That was just from our stopping at the front gate. You can imagine how they'd react to someone entering the ranch without permission."

Drake smiled and said, "Oh, I can imagine. That's why I brought Morales his favorite toy, a Black Hornet drone. We'll fly it in today and have a look around."

Norris led them out to his Hertz SUV and helped them stow their luggage. When they were seated and driving out of the parking lot, he asked if they'd learned anything more about Danforth.

"Liz got a call from Kate Perkins last night," Drake said. "Danforth took a day off the day before we were attacked at the hotel and two days after we visited him in his office. With the MS-13 gang members being from Chicago, I asked her if, by any chance, Danforth had been in Chicago recently. He hadn't, but she remembered that the leader of MS-13 in Chicago that he was instrumental in putting away was in prison here in Colorado. She said she'd check and see if he's had any contact with him. It's a long shot, but it's too much of a coincidence that MS-13 from Chicago came after us in D.C."

"Drake," Norris said, "it's also too much of a coincidence that the six men who came for us last night all looked like special operators. You know the look and they all had it."

"Why would Oliver need men like that to protect him on this ranch? He traveled here alone, so why now?" Liz asked.

"Maybe they're not here to protect Oliver," Drake suggested. "Maybe they're here to protect someone else or maybe something else."

"Like Nazir or Nazir's laptop?" Liz asked.

"Or both," Drake said. "Kevin, I've been trying to think of some other way to locate Nazir's laptop and I had a thought. When you were trying to find out who was trying to hack the IT system at Caelus Research, Nazir was communicating with other people using that proxy server at Intel in Hillsboro. If Nazir had his laptop back then and was using it now to communicate again with those people, would you be able to locate the laptop?"

"Sure, if he's on the internet, I can track his IP address to a region and city or town," McRoberts said.

"When you get settled in at the motel, see if he's using his laptop. I'd like to know where it is," Drake said.

Liz turned back to enjoying the scenery on the way to Steamboat Springs. "I'd like to come here and ski sometime."

"We can do that," Drake said. "Don't forget that I promised you a ski weekend in Oregon."

"I haven't forgotten, but if we come here, we'd have to be away from the office for more than a couple of days. Our time in Hawaii spoiled me."

They were entering Steamboat Springs when Liz saw the sign for the Rabbit Ears Motel up ahead and laughed. "Is that where we're staying?"

"Don't laugh," Norris said. "It's old but it's one of the better ones in town. You'll like it, pink sign and big bunny ears and all."

Norris parked in front of the office and got out to help them unload their bags. "I'll call Morales to come down and give you the keys to your rooms. You're already checked in."

He left them to park the Yukon in the parking lot and called Morales. When the call went to voice mail, he tried again with the same result.

He must be in the hot tub or something. He's sure making the most of his time here.

Norris walked back to the motel office and shrugged his shoulders as he walked past Drake and went to the front desk.

"My friend isn't answering his phone and he's got two room keys for these three. They're all charged to Puget Sound Security. Could I get two more keys, please?"

The woman at the front desk looked puzzled. "He just left here not five minutes ago with three men. Are you sure he's not out in the parking lot?"

Chapter Forty-Eight

NORRIS WALKED BACK and motioned for everyone to follow him outside.

"Morales left with three men five minutes ago. He's in trouble."

"Were they the police with more questions from last night?" Liz asked.

"I didn't ask, I'll be right back," Norris said.

Drake turned to Kevin McRoberts. "Take your laptop and find out where Morales is."

McRoberts nodded and went back into the motel lobby to get his laptop.

Norris walked quickly back. "They weren't the police. They're dressed like the men last night, black parkas and watch caps."

"They can't be too far away," Drake said. "We'll find him."

"How?" Norris asked.

"All PSS employees have microchip implants," Liz explained. "You don't have yours yet, but you'll be glad when you do. It saved Carol Sanchez last year when she was being held by terrorists in a cabin in the Oregon coast range."

"There's a program on Kevin's laptop that will track the microchip. Bring your SUV around and we'll catch up with these guys," Drake said and went back into the motel lobby to get his duffel bag and ask the desk clerk to secure their luggage until they returned.

McRoberts' fingers were flying over the keyboard of his laptop when Drake walked up to the chair he was sitting in.

"They're on Fish Creek Falls Road about five miles east of here, Mr. Drake."

"Good work, Kevin. Bring your laptop and guide us to them."

Norris was waiting outside with the Yukon idling when Drake jogged out with McRoberts in tow. "Kevin, sit up front and give Dan directions."

Drake jumped in back with his duffel bag and sat beside Liz.

"They're headed east about five miles ahead of us," he said and opened his duffel bag and took out her Glock and his Kimber .45. "Are you carrying, Dan?"

"Sure am," Norris said. "How do you want to handle this when we catch up with them?"

"They'll recognize your Yukon, so they'll know were coming for Morales. We defend ourselves and do whatever it takes to get Morales back."

Norris drove up Third Street to Oak Street, per McRobert's directions, and then accelerated onto Fish Creek Falls heading east and then southeast out of town.

"Any idea where they're going?" Norris asked.

"There's not much on this road except Fish Creek Falls way ahead, but they could turn off anywhere," McRoberts said, staring at the screen of his laptop. "When Fish Creek Falls Road becomes Highway 32, there aren't many houses around that I can see on Google Maps."

"What do you think they want, Dan?" Liz asked.

"Probably the same thing they wanted last night, to find out why we're interested in the ranch. I don't think they know we followed Oliver there."

"They're on Highway 32 now," McRoberts said.

Drake took out three soft modular body armor vests and handed one to Liz and laid one ahead on the center console for Norris.

"These are the latest from the SHOT show in Las Vegas this year. Let's hope we won't need them."

Liz saw the look in his eyes and knew they probably would, unless the men who had Morales flew a white flag as soon as they saw who they were.

"They just turned off Highway 32 and headed up into the hills," McRoberts said.

Norris saw the turnoff up ahead and slowed down. "What does the road they took look like from where it turns off the highway?" he asked McRoberts.

"It runs fairly straight paralleling the highway for three hundred yards or so and then makes a hard left up to what looks like maybe a rock quarry. They've stopped just inside the quarry or whatever it is."

Drake looked up the road and saw that it had a stand of quaking aspens on both sides. "Dan, let me out as soon as you start up the road. Drive slowly to give me time to get up to the quarry. Liz, trade places with Kevin. Get within sight of them and then stop. They'll wonder what you're planning while I figure out the best way to get Morales out of there. I'll use my iPhone and let you know what we're going to do."

Norris turned off onto the road and stopped just long enough for Drake to jump out.

The slope up to the quarry was shimmering leafy gold from the aspen leaves rustling in the breeze. Drake ran dodging between the trees for fifty yards before he found an aspen tunnel that opened up through the trees and allowed him to sprint ahead like he was racing his German Shepherd Lancer up the road at his old stone farmhouse in Oregon.

When he reached the end of the tunnel, he slowed at the sound of voices coming through the trees. He moved forward until he had a clear view of three men surrounding Morales who was on his knees in front of them.

The man standing behind Morales shoved him forward with his foot, knocking him to the ground.

When two of the men pulled him back up onto his knees, the man behind him said, "This is your last chance, amigo. Tell us why you were snooping around at the ranch or we'll leave you here with a bullet in the back of your head."

Drake called Norris. "Dan, race up there as fast as you can and stop at the entrance to the quarry."

At the sound of the Yukon throwing gravel and roaring up the road, the three men turned around to see who was coming.

Drake ran to the edge of the open area at the bottom of the quarry and walked out into the open with his .45 aimed at the back of the man doing the talking.

"Turn around slowly and I can tell you, amigo," Drake shouted as he closed the distance to the three men.

At the same time, Liz and Norris jumped out of their SUV with their pistols also aimed at the men.

"Keep your hands where we can see them, or you'll be the ones with bullets in the back of your heads. My friends won't miss at that distance."

Seeing that there were weapons covering them from both directions, each of the men raised their hands away from their bodies to shoulder height and stood silently.

"All you all right, Marco?" Drake asked.

"I'm better than these three are going to be in a minute. Mind if I use your .45 for a little payback?"

"Now wait a minute. You can't shoot us in cold blood," the man who kicked Morales to the ground said.

"Sure, we can," Drake said as he walked forward and helped Morales to his feet. "That's what you were going to do."

"I was just trying to scare him, that's all."

"How did that work out for you?" Drake said, "Dan, call 911 and tell them to get up here and arrest these three for kidnapping, attempted kidnapping and being stupid enough to take on you and Morales last night. Maybe when their boss comes to bail them out, we'll find out what's going on at their ranch. If he doesn't come, then we'll just go out there and find out for ourselves."

"That would be a big mistake, mister," the man said.

"Not as big a mistake as you men made when you decided to work for a James Oliver and Thomas Danforth."

Chapter Forty-Nine

BEFORE NORRIS COULD CALL 911, Drake changed his mind.

"Dan, forget 911. Take their weapons, their phones and shoes and we'll let them walk back to the ranch."

Norris came forward and handed Morales his pistol while he began relieving the three men of their belongings. When they were shoeless and down on their knees, Drake asked Liz to disable the Excursion the men were driving before they left.

"When you get back to the ranch," Drake told the three men, "tell Oliver I know he's in there. Tell him I'm willing to meet with him face-to-face any time he wants. But if he's sends anyone else after me or any of the people with me, I'm coming for him myself and I don't think he wants that."

Drake waited until Norris and Morales had their weapons and other belongings loaded in the SUV before telling the three men not to turn around or get up until they'd left the quarry.

When they reached the highway, Drake asked Morales what had happened.

"Not long after Dan left for the airport to pick you up, the front desk called and said they needed to talk with me. When I got there, one of them came up behind me from out of the continental breakfast area and stuck a gun in my back. There were people in the lobby, so I let them walk me out to that Excursion and they drove me to the quarry. That's pretty much it until you guys got there."

"Did you learn anything about what's going on at the ranch?" Liz asked.

"The one guy did all the talking, but I heard one of them say to the other they shouldn't have to cover their four-hour shift because they were out dealing with me. I took that to mean there are probably twelve of them providing security."

"That's a lot of men just to protect Oliver while he's here," Norris observed.

"I agree," Drake said. "Marco, do you feel like taking the Black Hornet out for a look-see at the ranch? It's in my duffel bag. Let's find out what's going on at the Double R Ranch."

"I think I can handle that, boss. I love flying that little drone."

"Did either of you see a good place to park and fly the drone from?" he asked Norris and Morales.

"South of the gate a split-rail fence borders the ranch with a stand of aspen behind it," Morales said. "We can pull off the road and not be seen from anywhere on the ranch."

"Any idea how far away the house is?"

"You see it in the distance at the front gate," Norris said. "It sits on top of a rise about a half mile away."

"Kevin, use your laptop and give Liz directions to the ranch and let's go have a look."

Liz drove the distance to the ranch in fifteen minutes and did a U-turn to park beside the spit-rail fence on the north side of the road. Norris got out and pretended to be fixing a flat tire while Morales got the Black Hornet UAV brown canvas base station out of Drake's duffel bag and hung it around his neck.

The nano drone resembled a helicopter small enough to sit in the palm of your hand and weighed a mere eighteen ounces. It had three cameras and transmitted live video and HD still images back to a seven-inch screen on the operator's base station for situational awareness. With a range of up to one mile and flying at a speed of twenty miles an hour, its nearly silent approach would allow Morales to fly around the ranch or hover overhead and see what was going on below.

Remaining in the SUV in the seat behind Drake riding shotgun ahead of him, Morales handed the Black Hornet out to Norris, who held it in the palm of his hand for launch. Controlling the little drone with its one-hand controller, Morales flew it up over the aspens and toward the ranch house.

Morales scooted to the middle of the second row of seats in the GMC Yukon, so Liz and Drake could see the base station screen.

They saw a small creek meandering through grazing land and a large dark brown house on the top of a ridge in the distance.

"I don't see any cattle," Liz said, "but there's sure a lot of grazing land down there."

On a gravel road running from the main gate to the ranch house they saw a four-wheel ATV with a cloud of dust trailing behind it racing up the ridge.

"Close in on the ATV," Drake said. "Let's see what the security looks like."

Morales flew the Black Hornet ahead of the ATV and turned it around to hover above, so they could get a good look at the two men riding in it.

"The one on the left has an M24 sniper rifle across his lap and the driver has a Heckler and Koch MP5 on a sling across his chest," Morales said. "That's a lot of firepower."

"Especially if you're right and there are twelve of them and they're all equipped like that," Drake said in agreement. "Fly around and let's see how many more of them we can see."

Morales spun the drone around and flew it above the road toward the house on the rise. The house was configured in a V, with a high vaulted roofline for the main entrance at the intersection of the two wings. In front of the main entrance was a large, circular open area with a waterfall and a putting green.

"There's a guard at each end of the house carrying M4 carbines and three more ATVs parked over in front of that four-bay garage," Morales called out and flew around to the back side of the house where they saw two more guards with a view of the creek and a hundred acres of grazing land.

"With a three-hundred-sixty-degree view from the top of that rise," Drake said, "there's no way to get to the house without being seen, unless you parachute in."

"You're not thinking of doing that, surely?" Liz said.

"No, but we'll have to come up with something if we want to find out what Oliver's doing here in Steamboat Springs," Drake said.

Norris was standing outside the SUV, waiting for the Black Hornet to fly back and land in his hand, when he leaned in through the open window next to Morales, and said, "I might have an idea."

Chapter Fifty

JAMES OLIVER HAD Nazir brought up from the basement store room to the study where he'd prepared a work station for him to start working on the cyberattack on U.S. banks.

"You look better than the last time I saw you," Oliver said in greeting. "Did you have something to eat?"

"A ham sandwich," Nazir said. "Your man Landers thought he was being cute."

"Yes, he is a little crude, isn't he?"

"Why am I here and not down in your dungeon?"

"The storeroom isn't a dungeon, but I'll admit it's not as nice as this study. You'll be allowed to work here from now on."

"Work on what, exactly?" Nazir asked.

"I want you to launch an ATM 'cash-out' strike on big banks. I've already created the malware for you. All you have to do is get it out to the members of your council for synchronized fraudulent withdrawals to drain bank accounts."

"Whose big banks?"

"Our big banks, of course. You wanted a cyber jihad strike against America and that's what I'm giving you."

"Why would you want me to attack America? I don't understand."

"You don't need to understand. All you need to know is that you're saving the lives of the members of your council and their families by doing what I'm asking you to do. They won't know you're doing it for me. They'll think you've come up with a brilliant plan to strike at America."

"Aren't you concerned about the damage you'll be doing to your own country?"

"It's for the greater good, trust me."

"What if I refuse to help you with this?"

"Then you'll die along with your friends and their families, and I'll find someone else to do it for me. Either way, it will happen. It's just easier for me using your group because they're already dedicated to the very thing you'll be asking them to do."

Nazir walked over to the workstation Oliver had set up for him. "You really went all out for me, I see. A sheet of plywood atop two saw horses."

"At least the chair's comfortable," Oliver said and pointed to his laptop. "When you unlock your computer, I'll install monitoring software so I can see everything you're doing. If you try to sabotage my plan or try something cute in any way, Landers will put a bullet in your head. There are four IP cameras in this study and I will also be able to see everything you do. Go ahead and use your encrypted password and let's get to work, shall we?"

Nazir looked around the room to locate the four IP cameras, shrugged and sat down in the chair in front of the workstation.

Oliver turned around when he heard Landers come into the study and motioned for him to the back of the room.

"I sent one of my men out when the three I sent to bring the snoopers back here weren't answering their phones. He hasn't found them yet."

"And you have no idea what's happened to them, is that what you're telling me?"

"Yes, sir, that's what I'm telling you."

Oliver leaned closer to Landers and hissed, "I warned you not to fail me again, Landers. What do you suggest I do now?"

Landers held his ground and said, "I think you were followed by some people who are more of a problem than we thought. I suggest you leave and let us do what we do best, secure this ranch and protect your man over there until you no longer need him."

"First, I wasn't followed. Second, if these people are as big a problem as you think they are, how do I leave? They could be out there waiting for me to do just that."

"There's an airstrip at the north end of the ranch by the ranch manager's place. Hire a plane to fly in and pick you up."

"If I do that, do you think you can protect my asset until he finishes his work or do I need to get someone else in here to get the job done?"

"I have nine of the best men you can hire for something like this and we have the high ground here. I'll get it done."

"I hope you're right about that, Landers. Go find me a plane so I can get out of here."

Before he left, Oliver walked across the study to look out a picture window, lined with solar film to block the heat from a southwest sun. The study had a bank of wall-mounted flat screens and a trading desk with two monitors Danforth used for managing his stock portfolio. A red-headed turkey vulture was circling over something down near the creek.

Danforth's ranch had seemed to be the perfect place to hide Nazir and make use of the members of his Islamic Revolutionary Council of America. Danforth had promised him that no one knew about the ranch or that he owned it, but clearly someone did.

He had to find a way to distance himself from Danforth and yet go forward with his plan. Nazir's Iranian-backed jihadi group would take the fall for the cyberattack on the banks. No one knew the plan was his idea, but someone knew about Danforth.

And they may have learned that he was holding Nazir on Danforth's ranch.

When he was safely back in Washington, he would have to make sure there was nothing that would lead anyone back to him.

Chapter Fifty-One

ON THE SHORT drive back to the Rabbit Ears Motel from the ranch, Norris explained his idea for finding out what Oliver was up to on the ranch.

"Before I left HRT, we were asked to evaluate a new light-based personnel immobilization device the army was testing. It used a Xenon-based searchlight pulsed with a unique strobe modulation that was mounted on a small unmanned UAV. Anyone within the beam of the searchlight was disoriented to the point of being immobilized by the dazzling light. If we get our hands on one of these special searchlights mounted on a quadcopter drone, we could get on the ranch without having to deal with the security guards."

"I read about that project for the Army," Kevin McRoberts said, "but after the initial testing, the reporting went dark when the Army classified the information. How would we get one?"

"I was in charge of the evaluation," Norris said. "I know the person at the company that headed up the project. I can find out if they're commercially available."

"That might work," Drake said, "if we had a good reason for storming the ranch and taking out private security. All we know now is one of the CIA's top guys is on a ranch that we think belongs to one of the FBI's top guys. The fallout, let alone the criminal charges, that would result from doing something like that would land us all in jail."

"Not to mention how it would impact PSS," Liz added. "We would need a good reason to justify an action like that."

"Liz is right," Drake said, "unless we thought we were preventing the threat of imminent death or great bodily harm to someone on the ranch. That could justify the use of deadly force, in case we have to defend ourselves against armed security."

"It was just a thought," Norris said.

"And a good one, Dan, if we had a better reason for using something like that. I'll mention it to Casey the next time I talk with him. PSS could use a device like that to protect our clients from anarchist mobs like we had running around this last year."

When they got back to their motel, Liz asked if anyone was hungry, even before they got out of the SUV, because she said she was starved.

McRoberts did a quick internet search with his smartphone and suggested they try the nearby Creekside Café & Grill. "It says they have great hamburgers. If you go there, would you bring me back a bacon burger and fries?"

"Aren't you going with us?" Drake asked.

"I thought I'd see if Nazir is using his laptop. You asked me to find the laptop and I haven't had time to do it since we got here. Besides, there's a little grocery store just a block away and I don't think the Creekside Café & Grill will have the energy drink I need right now."

"A bacon burger and fries it is then," Liz said. "Stay in the car and we'll drop you off at the grocery store."

Liz pulled back onto the street and drove north a block and let Kevin out. "He lives on energy drinks, doesn't he?"

"Pretty much 24/7," Morales said, "Whatever it takes, I guess, to keep that mind of his working."

Liz parked in front of the small restaurant that prided itself in serving breakfast and lunch all day and was the first one through the door, with three men hurrying to catch up.

When she was asked if her party wanted to be seated outside on the patio, she made the decision for all of them and followed their host out onto a patio. A small creek ran next to the patio that was lined with pink and white potted flowers.

"I could live here," she said to Drake when they were seated.

"It's pretty all right, but I want to see if the food is a good as the ambiance."

Norris and Morales were trying to decide if they wanted to order breakfast or lunch when Drake's iPhone pinged with a text message from McRoberts.

His laptop is on the internet and you won't believe where his IP address says he is. Right here in Steamboat Springs!

Drake showed Liz the text message. "It's gotta be on the ranch! That must be why Oliver is here."

"What's on the ranch," Morales said, laying his menu down, "Nazir's laptop? If his laptop is there and it's being used, then Nazir there's as well. They need his encrypted password to unlock the laptop."

"Oliver could have gotten Nazir's password somewhere else and brought it here with the laptop," Norris said.

"Why would he do that?" Drake asked. "If Oliver has the laptop and the encrypted password, why bring the laptop to Colorado to use it? He could do that anywhere."

"Unless Nazir is on the ranch and Oliver brought the laptop to him," Liz said. "We know Nazir was in Montana when the FBI took custody of him, that's not far from here. We know the laptop was in Washington before people started dying. Oliver must have gotten the laptop from Vincente Martinez before he killed him."

"Boss, what do we do if she's right? We'll have the reason you said we needed to go see if Nazir is there," Morales said. "If they're using his laptop, they have no reason to keep him alive any longer."

"Let's slow down and think this through," Drake said. "If it was something on the laptop that was important enough to kill people for, why start using it? Oliver would know its IP address could be traced as soon as it was on the internet."

And then the light went on for Drake. "But Oliver wouldn't know that we knew Nazir was using a proxy server at Intel to communicate with his people. That must be the way Kevin knew Nazir's laptop was on the internet; he was watching to see if Nazir was communicating again with those same people as before."

"What do we do, boss?" Morales asked again.

"Oliver must be using Nazir and his laptop for something we haven't thought about. You guys go ahead and order something to eat. I need to call Casey."

Chapter Fifty-Two

DRAKE WALKED to the end of the patio and leaned down, putting both hands on the wrought iron railing and looking down into the clear water of Soda Creek flowing by.

Zal Nazir was a terrorist. He'd crossed paths with the man earlier in the year when he'd found him in Hawaii in an ocean-side villa owned by a Russian oligarch, Mikhail Volkov. When Nazir had been flown to the mainland in the PSS Gulfstream and the FBI had taken custody of him in Montana, he thought he'd never have to worry about the man again.

Now it was possible that Nazir was here in Steamboat Springs on the ranch of Thomas Danforth, who shouldn't have any interest in his laptop, and in the presence of James Oliver, who may have been involved in three murders.

Whatever was on the laptop, it had to involve both men in some way. But was finding out what the connection was important enough to trespass on private property and risk someone being killed to find out?

Drake searched for an answer a little longer, staring into the rippling water of the creek below, before taking a deep breath and calling his best friend in Seattle.

"How's Colorado?" Mike Casey asked.

"Confusing, actually, that's why I'm calling."

Drake heard the door in Casey's office close before he was asked to explain.

"Norris and Morales followed James Oliver to Steamboat Springs to a ranch we believe belongs to Thomas Danforth."

"Okay, what's the connection between Oliver and Danforth?"

"The only connection I can see is their interest in the laptop."

"And we don't know what's on the laptop."

"Correct."

"But we do know that someone in the government knew about the laptop because they came looking for it when we came back from Hawaii."

"And they knew we sent it to Washington because someone attacked Kevin in his apartment and he told them," Drake added.

"None of this sounds like the way the FBI handles things. I'm not so sure about the CIA, but they're not supposed to operate at home unless they're involved in some terrorist plot they know something about."

"Like a foreign government, say Russia, getting involved in domestic matters and funding a civil war."

"If they knew about Mikhail Volkov and Professor Bradley, why didn't they do something about it instead of letting us get involved?"

Drake didn't answer right away. "Because they didn't care if whatever Volkov and Bradley were up to was successful. We know someone in the government warned Volkov."

"Which brings us back, my friend, to what connects Oliver and Danforth. If they're the ones who aided and abetted Volkov and Professor Bradley, maybe they're just trying to cover it up."

"Mike, if that's possibly true, we have to do everything we can to prove it. The government's not going to do it for us when it involves two bureaucrats as high up the ladder as Oliver and Danforth."

"By doing what exactly?"

"By getting on that ranch and finding out what Oliver's doing there. Dan Norris has an idea that might allow us to accomplish that without anyone getting hurt, if he can get his hands on something the Army was testing when he was with HRT."

"What kind of thing that the Army was testing?"

"A strobing searchlight mounted on a small UAV, like a quad-copter drone, that immobilizes people."

Casey laughed. "You mean the device that one of our clients developed for the Army eight or nine years ago? They make them for the Army, but the technology was initially classified. Do you want me to see if I can get us one?"

"Absolutely."

"Answer something for me first. Are you planning on getting onto the ranch with or without one of these searchlights?"

"I'll have to, Mike. I can't let these guys get away with treason."

"That's what I thought. Let me see what I can do, but promise me you won't do anything until you hear back from me."

"I promise."

Chapter Fifty-Three

CASEY CALLED Drake back later that afternoon to say that their client was willing to loan them one of its immobilizing searchlights, ostensibly to see if it was something PSS might be interested in purchasing. He had to agree to indemnify them for any damage to the searchlight or any injury suffered by anyone if it was being tested somewhere.

"To make sure we're not indemnifying anyone, I'm coming along with the searchlight to make sure it's used properly," Casey said.

"Is that what you're telling your wife to explain why you're flying to Colorado on short notice?"

"Of course it is. Do you think Megan would let me come if she knew I planned on going with you when the searchlight's used at the ranch?"

"We both know the answer to that."

"How much reconnaissance have you done?"

"Morales wants to go in by himself tonight but I'm not sure that's necessary. Danforth bought the ranch recently and the realtor's internet ad for the ranch is still online. It features a drone flyover of most of the nine hundred acres."

"How are we getting onto the ranch?"

"We're still working on that," Drake said. "The ranch manager's house is on the north end of the ranch near an airstrip. The road to his house isn't gated like the gate to the main house and doesn't have a keypad. It does have an IP camera, but we can take care of that."

"How heavily armed is the ranch security?"

"H&K MP5s, M4s and one M24 sniper rifle that we've seen. If the searchlight is as effective as Norris says it is, we shouldn't have to worry about the weapons they have."

"I'll bring some things along just in case it isn't."

"When will you get here?"

"First thing tomorrow. I'll call you when we're wheels up."

Drake finished talking with Casey and called the others and told them to meet him and Liz in the parking lot in ten minutes to go for a little drive.

Liz was sitting on the end of their bed in their room at the hotel, using her laptop to find a store that sold the type of drone they needed.

"Do you know how much this searchlight weighs?" she asked.

"If they are anything like the handheld Xenon handheld searchlights the U.S. Army or the Coast Guard and Border Patrol use, they can't weigh more than ten pounds."

"Does PSS use drones?"

"Yes, for surveillance work, why?"

"You'll need to ask Mike how heavy a load they can handle. From what I'm seeing,

hexacopter drones that can carry ten pounds are pretty expensive."

"How expensive?" he asked.

"Here's a Freefly ALTA 8 for $11,995."

"I'll call Mike and see what our drones can carry before we spend that kind of money. We'd better get going; the others will be waiting for us."

Norris, Morales and McRoberts were stamping their feet to keep warm when they reached the parking lot.

Norris held out the keys to the Yukon to Drake. "Do you want to drive?"

"You go ahead, you know the way to the ranch. I'll explain what we're planning and what we need to think about before Casey joins us tomorrow."

"Why is he coming to Colorado?" Morales asked.

"He's bringing us one of the immobilizing searchlights you wanted."

Drake sat up front with Norris. When they were out of the parking lot and driving south on the highway toward the Double R Ranch, he explained what he thought they needed to do before Casey arrived.

"We need to find a way to get on the ranch and be close to the main house when we turn on the searchlight and then find a way to get out quickly. Any thoughts on how we do that?"

"How long can the strobing searchlight incapacitate someone?" Morales asked.

"Dan, do you know the answer?" Drake asked.

"When we tested it at HRT, they didn't give us a limit on how long we could keep it on once it was activated."

"From your experience, then, we could incapacitate the security guards, find a way to get past the main gate and drive up to the main house during the time they remain incapacitated and drive back out again."

"As far as I know, yes."

"If we don't want to go in through the main gate, we could go in from the north and use the road into the ranch manager's place," Morales suggested.

"Do we know anything about the ranch manager?" Drake asked. "As far as we know, he's an innocent and not involved in whatever Oliver and Danforth are doing."

"Couldn't we incapacitate him along with the security guards?"

"We would need two drones and two searchlights to do that, as far away as it is from the main house to the ranch manager's place," Drake said. "Casey only mentioned one searchlight."

"You guys could always just hike in and be in place when the searchlight is turned on," McRoberts said.

Norris elbowed McRoberts in the ribs and said, "You sound like you're not offering to hike across a big ranch at night with us, Kevin."

"I just figured…"

"It's okay, Kevin," Drake said. "We need you or Liz to fly the drone and she's never flown one. It looks like it's your job, if you have any experience flying a drone."

"I do, Mr. Drake. I own one and fly it whenever I get the opportunity to be out of the city and restricted airspace."

They were getting close to the ranch when Norris asked, "Do we want to take a look at the north end of the ranch and check out the road into the ranch manager's place?"

"We'll need to sometime; now's as good a time as any," Drake said. "I'd like to have a plan that we think will work before Casey gets here and right now I don't see how we're going to pull this off."

It took Norris another twenty minutes to reach the cattle crossing and dirt road that led to the ranch manager's place. There wasn't a gate, but there was a cattle guard with barbed wire fencing on both sides. An IP camera on a pole on the left end of the cattle guard monitored the road. On the other side was a sign offering hay for sale and a phone number to call.

"It looks like we just found our way in," Norris said.

Chapter Fifty-Four

THE PSS GULFSTREAM G650 landed at ten o'clock that night at the regional airport in Hayden, Colorado, bringing Mike Casey and the equipment he thought they might need for the infiltration of the ranch.

Drake and Liz were there to greet him and load the equipment in their SUV.

"Two black storage totes, three tactical range duffel bags and one hard shell long rifle case," Drake said as they were carrying the equipment from the Gulfstream to the SUV. "Where's your luggage?"

"It's in one of the totes with the searchlight and one of our surveillance drones. Don't worry; I still know how to load a kit for these adventures you keep getting us into. How's your arm?"

"It's fine."

"He won't change the dressing unless I make him," Liz said, "and I don't believe him when he says he's fine, but what can you do when a man's afraid to admit something hurts?"

"I'm fine, Mike. She's enjoying being my Nurse Ratched."

"Glad to see you two are getting along so well. How's Morales?"

"He has a few bruises but seems to be okay. He's looking forward to having a go at these security thugs," Drake said.

Liz let Casey ride shotgun up front and sat in the middle of the second row of seats, leaning forward with her head between the shoulders of the two men. "I know you two used to do this kind of thing when you were Delta operators, but I'm not used to winging it. Have either of you thought about what we're going to do with the security guards when they're no longer immobilized and come after us?"

"We'll make sure they can't come after us," Drake said. "We all wear balaclavas and use zip ties to make sure they stay put for a while."

"How long is 'for a while'?"

"Long enough for us to get off the ranch."

"What are we going to do with Oliver or Nazir if he's there?" she continued. "We could make a citizen's arrest of Nazir and take him with us, but that's not going to work for Oliver. We have our suspicions about him, but that's not enough to arrest a high-ranking CIA official."

"We can always be honest and say we're assisting the FBI to investigate three murders in D.C.," Casey said.

"Okay, one more thing. What do we tell the ranch manager when he sees we're not there to buy hay?"

"Why are we going to be there to buy hay?" Casey asked.

"There's a sign at the road to the ranch manager's place that reads, 'Hay for Sale,' and a phone number. Norris suggested that we call to say we want to buy some hay and just drive in," Drake explained.

"Is the ranch manager's road our exfil route?" Casey asked.

"The road to the main house is closer to the road, but we don't know if the gate opens automatically when you leave."

"I think Liz is right, we have some fine-tuning to do before we invade Danforth's ranch," Casey admitted. "When are we thinking of doing this?"

"It's too late to do anything tonight, but as soon as we can get it together," Drake said. "We don't know how long Oliver is going to be there."

———

JAMES OLIVER WATCHED the sun come up in the east as he waited for his plane with Landers in a Double R Ranch pickup at the end north end of the airstrip.

"Keep someone in the room with Nazir at all times when he's using his laptop," Oliver instructed. "I can watch what he's doing, but if he starts to try something cute, he has to be stopped immediately. Don't kill him; just make sure he knows how stupid it would be to try something like that again."

"How long do you think he'll need to complete the work you gave him?" Landers asked.

"A week at most. When I'm sure he's done what I asked him to do, I'll let you know. He's not to leave the ranch. Dispose of his body and then leave the ranch, a couple of your men at a time. The ranch manager doesn't know anything about you, other than that you are security for one of the owner's important guests. I don't want him to be able to tell anyone exactly when you leave."

"When do I get the final payment?"

"When you've taken care of Nazir and cleared off the ranch. What happened with the three men who didn't come back when you sent them after the men snooping around the main gate?"

"They never returned. They knew what would happen to them if they did."

"Then you'll get the rest of the money we agreed upon when you find them and silence them. They won't be around to get their share. I don't want them to think they can barter their silence for the money they think I owe them."

"That wasn't a part of our deal. There will be expenses incurred to track them down. I'll need another hundred thousand to handle it."

Oliver took off his glasses and held them up to see if they needed to be cleaned. "Our deal required that you provide twelve men for security that could be trusted. You only have nine men here doing that. I can reduce the money we agreed on by a quarter, or you can do what I'm telling you to do and get the full amount. It's up to you."

Oliver thought he heard Lander's teeth grinding and smiled. "You don't have to give me an answer now, but I'll need it before you leave the ranch."

The two men sat quietly for ten minutes until Landers pointed to the sky and said, "Your plane is here. Call me when you're finished with Nazir."

He got out and lifted Oliver's carryon out from the back of the ranch pickup and walked around to wait for Oliver to get out.

Oliver waited until the red-and-white Beechcraft Baron taxied to a stop in front of the pickup before he got out and walked toward the plane, leaving Landers to bring his luggage.

Chapter Fifty-Five

LIZ STROBEL APOLOGIZED AGAIN for being late. She'd stopped at the cattle guard on the road to the ranch manager's place driving a pickup and towing a flatbed trailer. She'd promised to get there before dark to take delivery of the one hundred bales of mixed grass and alfalfa hay she'd ordered, but she explained that she'd had engine trouble on the way.

It was eight minutes before seven o'clock and the end of twilight for the day. Two white GMC Yukons followed her up the road to the ranch manager's place with two men in each to help her load the hay onto her trailer.

The ranch manager and two black-and-white Australian sheep dogs met her pickup and walked on ahead of it to a covered storage building with bales of hay stacked up all the way to a corrugated metal roof above.

Liz got out and gave him one hundred and twenty-five dollars in cash for the hay and apologized again for being so late.

"I hope I'm not keeping you from your dinner," she said and waved toward the two SUVs. "They're here to help me load the hay, so it shouldn't take very long."

"Take your time, miss. There's no need to hurry. I'll be in my house if you need me."

When the ranch manager turned around and whistled for his dogs to follow him, Liz's four helpers got out to help load the hay. They started loading a few hay bales on the trailer until Liz signaled that he was back in his house and it was safe to proceed.

She left the pickup lights on, pointed to the storage building, as if to help the men see what they were doing, and joined Kevin McRoberts in one of the SUVs.

The hexacopter drone Casey brought from Seattle with the rail-mounted Xenon strobing searchlight attached was in the cargo area at the rear of the SUV. McRoberts had spent the morning at the rock quarry where they'd rescued Morales flying the drone until he was confident that he could fly it.

The drone had a duo camera for day/night vision and thermal imaging that would not only allow it to be flown to the main house at night but also give them the location of the security guards.

Liz got in the first SUV and slipped on one of the two FLIR NyX-7 Pro night vision goggles that Casey brought for all of them.

"Are you ready to do some immobilizing?" she asked McRoberts.

"Yes ma'am, been waiting all day."

Morales had returned to the ranch that afternoon with the Black Hornet drone to map the dirt road from the ranch manager's place to the main house, so they would know where the road was at night.

Liz flipped her night vision goggles down and drove past the other SUV that pulled in behind her with the headlights off. Drake, Casey, Norris and Morales were in the other SUV pulling on black tactical hoods and putting on bulletproof vests and their own night vision goggles.

"Kevin, remember to tell them the location of the security guards when you spot them on approach," she reminded him. "They'll also need to know where they are when they're immobilized, to put zip ties on them."

"Copy that," he said, mimicking the lingo of the men in the other SUV.

"You gentlemen ready to rock and roll?" Liz asked after hitting her PTT button on the Motorola combat radio on her belt.

"Lead the way," she heard Drake say in her tactical headset.

The main house was a mile and a quarter from the ranch manager's place. Liz drove at a slow and steady speed until she was three hundred yards from the four-stall garage at the back of the main house.

Drake was driving the other SUV and pulled alongside her.

Morales jumped out to help McRoberts get the forty-pound hexacopter drone out of the back of Liz's SUV and ready to fly.

They set the drone gently on the ground and McRoberts switched on the flight controls to start the six rotors spinning. Stepping away, he powered up the drone and flew it up vertically to a height of twenty feet above them.

He spun the drone around and nodded to Drake that he was ready.

The four men flipped their night vision goggles down and jogged down the road toward the main house with the drone flying above them to lead the way.

"No guards next hundred yards," McRoberts radioed.

Drake, Casey, Norris and Morales jogged ahead trusting their spotter.

"Clear for another hundred yards. Wait ahead as planned."

McRoberts flew the drone to an altitude of a hundred and fifty feet and searched the area around the main house.

The drone's thermal imaging lens picked up the orange glow of four men and their rifles slung across their chests at the corners of the reddish glow of the main house.

Beyond the main house he saw the bright yellowish white of a fire and five men sitting on a half wall surrounding a sunken fire pit. The men did not have rifles, but they all had pistols in drop-leg holsters.

"One guard posted at each of the four corners of the main house with rifles," McRoberts radioed. "Directly ahead of you at the rear of the main house is a sunken fire pit. Five men seated around the fire, each with a drop-leg holstered pistol."

"Copy that," Drake responded. "What about the house?"

"Two men in a room off the west wing; one sitting using a laptop and the other standing behind him."

"Stay above the house and report all movement," Drake ordered. "On my order, activate searchlight

"Copy that."

Chapter Fifty-Six

DRAKE MOTIONED for the others to come closer.

"Dan and Marco, take the two guards on the west wing front. Mike and I will take the two on the east end. When those four are down, we'll move to the five at the fire pit. Unless this turns into a firefight, we'll move in on the house when we're sure the nine outside aren't going anywhere.

"Kevin will have the searchlight on flood to cover them all, but if you see one of them not reacting like the others, tell him to focus the beam on that individual to incapacitate him. When we get within thirty yards, get off night vision. We'll be able to see without it. Any questions?"

There were none.

"We're here to make a citizen's arrest. We have the right to protect ourselves, but it's best if we go in and get out with Nazir without firing a shot. Let's finish this once and for all. Kevin, light 'em up."

When the strobing searchlight lit up the house and the area immediately around it, Drake took off running down the left side of the road with Casey next to him. Norris and Morales ran beside them on the right side of the road.

The two teams veered to the left and right of the four-stall garage and sprinted to their targets when Kevin saw that the guards were incapacitated and turned the strobing searchlight off.

Drake's guard was staggering around like a drunk trying to get to his car without falling after last call at his favorite tavern. He went down hard when Drake tackled him from behind and pulled his arms behind his back to restrain them with cable ties. He did the same with his legs at the ankles and rolled him over to slap a strip of duct tape over his mouth. He almost felt sorry looking down at the wide-eyed man wondering what in the world had just happened.

Casey stood up from his guard at the other end of the east wing a second later and gave Drake a thumbs up.

Norris radioed that the guards on the other wing of the house were down and restrained.

"See you at the fire pit," Drake radioed back.

Drake and Casey met at the wall along the east wing and ran along it toward the fire pit. Peaking around the corner, they saw two of the men stumbling around and three more on their knees shaking their heads and crawling away from the fire. From the looks of the empty beer bottles littering the floor around the fire pit, they'd all been drinking.

Drake stepped away from the wall of the house and signaled for Norris and Morales to move in on the five guards. In two minutes, five more men were restrained and staring up at the billions of twinkling stars in the night sky.

"Kevin, where are the two men in the house?" Drake asked.

"Off the covered patio above the fire pit is a large room with what looks like a sliding glass door. Enter there and go down the hallway on the left. The first door on the left is the room with the two men. They don't seem to be aware of what's going on outside."

"Let's go see if Nazir's in there," Drake told Casey. "Dan and Marco can keep an eye on things out here."

Drake led the way up the flagstone steps from the fire pit and across the patio to the opening side of the sliding glass door and took out his Kimber .45. Casey moved to the other side to cover with his Glock 17M Duty Pistol as Drake quietly pulled the door back and stepped inside.

The room was a great room with a towering river rock fireplace on one side that rose up to a peaked pine wood ceiling with massive black beams. A massive one-hundred-ten-inch flat screen TV was mounted on the opposite wall with a large white leather sectional in front of it large enough to seat at least a dozen people. An onyx bar was next to the entertainment area with six stools facing a mirrored wall with shelves lined with rows of top-end bottles of Danforth's favorite alcoholic beverages.

Drake crossed the room and looked back to Casey who mouthed, "Nice."

They moved together to each side of the west wing hallway and poked their heads around to see if it was clear. The first door on the left was forty-five feet away.

Drake stepped around the corner and slid along the wall on his side while Casey did the same on the other side. When they reached the door, Casey crossed the hall and took up position on the right side of the door opposite Drake.

They leaned their heads closer to the door and heard no voices coming from the other side.

With their pistols held out in front of them, Casey reached down with his left hand and slowly turned the door handle to open the door for Drake.

Drake nodded for him to go and jumped in behind the door as it swung open.

The man standing behind the person in the chair using the laptop spun around and reached for his pistol.

"Don't do it," Drake said calmly.

Carl Landers saw two men with pistols aimed at him and moved his hand away from the pistol in his drop-leg holster.

"How did you get past my men?" he asked.

"Don't worry, they're outside unharmed."

Nazir sat still, listening to the conversation, and turned around when he recognized Drake's voice.

"I was hoping we'd find you here," Drake said to Nazir. "We have things to talk about."

Chapter Fifty-Seven

THEY LEFT the ranch by the main gate at eight o'clock in the evening in their two white Yukons.

Drake drove the first Yukon with Liz riding shotgun beside him. Casey sat behind Drake with Nazir next to him, restrained and surprisingly looking dejected but also relieved.

"They were going to kill me when I did what they wanted me to," Nazir said. "Thank you for rescuing me. Jail is preferable to a bullet in my head, but where are you taking me?"

"What makes you think we're taking you to jail?" Drake asked. "You're a terrorist, Nazir. There's a special place in hell waiting for you."

"Then where are you taking me?"

"Somewhere we can have a talk without being interrupted," Drake told him.

"If I'm being arrested, I have the right to talk with an attorney. I don't have to talk to you."

"Suit yourself," Drake said. "Mike, do you have any duct tape left? Nazir doesn't want to talk to us and I don't want to listen to him. Make sure we both get what we want."

"My pleasure," Casey said and took a strip of duct tape from the roll in his pocket and slapped it across Nazir's mouth.

When they reached Steamboat Springs, the second Yukon stopped at the Rabbit Ears Motel. Morales checked them out and he and McRoberts got the luggage and loaded it in their Yukon. Norris stayed in the SUV with a pistol trained on a restrained and subdued Carl Landers. When Morales and McRoberts returned, they followed the first Yukon and drove to the airport where the PSS Gulfstream G-650 was waiting for them.

"When do we head back to Seattle?" Morales asked as he drove them out of the parking lot.

"They need us to babysit Nazir and this guy until they can be questioned separately on the plane. Kevin will have time to have another shot at Nazir's laptop on the way. If we're not needed after we get to D.C., we'll fly back to Seattle with Casey."

Landers was sitting between Norris and McRoberts in the second row of seats in the Yukon.

"Why are you taking me to D.C.?" Landers asked.

"Not our decision," Norris said. "There are some people there who want to know what you were doing on Danforth's ranch."

"Who's Danforth? I was told the FBI used the place as a safe house?"

"Who told you that, Oliver?"

"Are you saying Oliver's not FBI?"

"You're smarter than you look."

"If he's not FBI, who is he?"

"Are you saying you thought you were working for the FBI?"

"I think I need a lawyer before I say another word."

"As you wish," Norris said and slapped a strip of duct tape across Lander's mouth.

Morales turned on the radio and they listened to country music the rest of the twenty-five miles to the airport in Hayden, Colorado.

The PSS Gulfstream G-650 was parked outside the Atlantic Aviation FBO with the first Yukon next to it when they arrived. Morales pulled alongside and jumped out to see if Drake wanted

Landers brought inside. Special Agent Perkins was standing at the top of the stairs in the open door behind the cockpit.

"Go ahead and bring him in," she said, waving.

Morales gave her a quick salute and turned to open the door for Norris. "Let's bring him in; then I'll take the SUVs around front for Hertz to come and pick them up."

Norris got out and pulled Landers across the seat to stand beside him. "Time for you to meet the real FBI."

Norris and Morales each took an arm and walked Landers to the plane. Norris shoved him up the stairs ahead of him.

"Hi Kate, thanks for coming."

She stepped aside to let them pass and said, "Nazir's in the back with Drake. We'll keep him here in the main cabin until it's his turn."

Norris kept a hand on Lander's shoulder and walked him back to a forward-facing seat in the middle of the cabin and sat across from him in a rear-facing seat.

"As soon as we're in the air, I'll take the duct tape off. Until then, relax and get ready to politely answer some questions. Special Agent Perkins is a friend of mine. I'll take it personally if you're not polite and a gentleman. I can assure you that you do not want to behave that way."

Landers saw Special Agent Perkins coming down the aisle and looked her up and down.

Norris stood up and leaned his head down. "I told you to be a gentleman and perhaps you didn't understand me," he said and grabbed Lander's left arm with his right hand, pushing his right thumb into the pressure point in the forearm crevice at the elbow and wrapping his fingers around the back of the elbow squeezing hard.

Landers jumped at the sharp pain and nodded rapidly.

"Don't make me want to do that again," Norris said. "We both know you have many more pressure points than that."

Norris straightened up and turned to face Kate Perkins. "He's ready whenever you are."

"Let me see if Drake has learned anything from Nazir first."

Chapter Fifty-Eight

SPECIAL AGENT PERKINS continued down the aisle to the divided aft cabin with a pocket door.

Drake sat on a couch on one side of the aisle facing Nazir across the aisle on the other couch.

"He says when they landed in Montana, two FBI agents brought him directly to the ranch where he was kept in a storeroom in the basement until Oliver arrived," Drake told her. "That's all he'll tell me."

Perkins sat down beside Drake and studied Nazir for a moment. "Are you an American citizen, Mr. Nazir?"

"Yes, I am. When do I get to talk with an attorney?"

"That's what I'm trying to decide."

"I don't have to tell you anything unless my attorney tells me to."

"That's true; you don't if I'm trying to build a criminal case against you. If you're a terrorist, there are other ways for Mr. Drake to get you to talk."

"I have my rights; you can't waterboard an American citizen."

"I don't think you understand your situation, Mr. Nazir. Mr. Drake is not in the FBI or any other law enforcement agency. He's not CIA. He's a citizen like you and he thinks you had a friend of his killed in Portland, Oregon.

"He says you're a terrorist who tried to kill innocent Catholic parishioners while they worshipped in church and that he's sorry he didn't get to kill you then. He also says you betrayed your country when you agreed to work with Mikhail Volkov to start a civil war in America. He says he's sorry he didn't kill you when he found you in Volkov's villa in Hawaii.

"So, he has a lot of reasons to want to kill you. I won't let him if you cooperate with me and tell me everything I want to know. If you don't, then I'm afraid I was never here, and he'll get to do whatever he wants with you."

"She forgot a couple of things, didn't she?" Drake asked. "You tried to blow up my office in Portland. Fortunately for you, I wasn't there, and neither were my secretary and her husband. When you didn't succeed, you sent your Iranian commando friend to blow up my house while I was sleeping. I want very badly to put a bullet between your eyes, Nazir. Special Agent Perkins made me promise that I wouldn't do that if you cooperated with her. That's your situation, just so we're clear."

Nazir tried to look unconcerned with the veiled threats, but the way his Adam's apple bounced up and down several times when he repeatedly swallowed gave him away.

"Let's start with this," Perkins said. "Why were you being held at the ranch?"

"If I cooperate with you, what's in it for me?"

Perkins turned to Drake and smiled. "I thought you understood. Mr. Drake keeps his promise to me and you get to live."

"I don't believe you will let him kill me."

Special Agent Perkins stood up and said to Drake, "I'll go tell our pilot to land in Denver and I'll fly back to D.C. by myself. Leave him alone until I'm off the plane."

Before she had the pocket door all the way open, Nazir said, "Oliver wanted me to launch a cyberattack on the banks."

Perkins stood still with her back to Nazir and asked, "How were you going to do that?"

"He gave me the malware to launch an ATM 'cash-out' strike."

Perkins turned around and sat beside Drake. "I understand what an ATM 'cash-out' strike is. Do you expect me to believe Oliver wanted you to do this all by yourself?"

Nazir nodded his head up and down as if to say, "Yes," but his pursed lips told them he was withholding the truth.

"Cooperating means telling me the truth. If you want me to stay on this plane, you need to stop lying to me," Perkins warned.

Nazir looked down at his feet and shook his head from side to side. "I can't. How do I know you won't kill them like Oliver's friend said they would if I didn't do what they wanted?"

Perkins leaned forward with her forearms resting on her knees. "Look at me, Nazir. Who is Oliver's friend? Who was he threatening to kill?"

Nazir took a deep breath, sighed and said, "He said he'd gone to a lot of trouble to retrieve my laptop and bring it to me. He knew all about me and the things I'd done for Volkov and Bradley, but he never said his name."

"I think we may know who he is. Now tell me the rest; who did he threaten to kill?"

"My friends, the members of my council."

"Tell me about your council."

"They're hackers like me."

"Does your council have a name?"

Nazir straightened up and said proudly, "The Islamic Revolutionary Council of America."

"Let me guess," Drake injected, "you're cyber jihadists. That's why Oliver knew you and the members of your council that, working together, you could handle the ATM strike."

"How far along are you in what Oliver wanted you to do?" Perkins asked.

"We were waiting for Oliver to tell us when to launch the strike."

"You mean the other hackers in your council have the malware and are waiting for you to tell them to initiate the strike?"

"Yes."

Drake slapped his knee. "That's why your laptop has been so important. They needed it in your hands to get the malware to your council and tell them to launch the strike."

"Oliver's friend may have wanted it for another reason," Nazir offered. "The file that was sent to the FBI Tipline was my diary had everything I did with Volkov and Bradley. Oliver's friend said he wanted to have my laptop 'examined'. I thought that was probably what he was interested in examining."

Perkins stood and said to Drake, "That's enough for now. Have someone come back and keep an eye on him."

Perkins waited at the open door of the aft cabin until Morales came back to take her place before following Drake to Casey sitting in the main cabin at a conference table.

"It looks like you just saved the country from a catastrophic financial meltdown," she said. "An ATM 'cash-out' strike involves waves of synchronized fraudulent withdrawals to drain bank accounts and shut down financial systems.

"A group believed to have been a front for the government of Iran tried a similar cyberattack in 2012 on five large banks. With the malware Oliver supplied Nazir and the hackers he's in contact with, they could have caused one of the worst terrorist attacks on the country since 9/11."

"You said this 2012 cyberattack was thought to have been orchestrated by Iran," Drake said. "The guy Nazir sent to kill me was an Iranian commando. Could this be another attempt by Iran to hit us?"

"If Oliver and Danforth are involved, then we're dealing with two very high-level traitors," Casey said.

"If they are, it would explain the murders I'm investigating," Perkins said. "They'd be willing to do whatever was necessary to keep from being exposed."

"Do you have enough to arrest Oliver and Danforth when we get to D.C.?" Casey asked.

"If Nazir is telling us the truth, I have enough to bring them in for questioning about a cyberattack on our banks. I don't have any solid evidence to link then to the murders."

"You have the laptop that's been in the hands of everyone that's been murdered," Drake pointed out.

"There could have been someone else after the laptop," Perkins said. "Danforth doesn't seem to be the kind of guy who would get his hands dirty by killing someone."

Casey pointed his thumb at Landers sitting up the aisle across from Norris. "Maybe, but he could hire someone like him."

"Are you ready to talk with him?" Drake asked Perkins.

"I am. While we're doing that, let's have your young hacker see if there's anything on Nazir's laptop that proves he's telling us the truth."

"I'll get him started on it," Casey said and headed up the aisle toward McRoberts.

"How do you want to handle this?" Drake asked.

"The only connection we know about is him being at the ranch guarding Nazir for Oliver," Perkins said. "Let's see what he can tell us about Oliver and Danforth and if Danforth was the one who brought the laptop to the ranch. Let him think they're the ones were interested in, not him."

Drake drummed his fingers on the conference table before saying, "I haven't mentioned this before, but he may have been working for Oliver on something else. When we flew Nazir here from Hawaii, we had arranged for investigators from DHS to take him into custody in Montana.

"When Casey landed with him, two FBI agents were there instead to take custody of him. The FBI has denied that Nazir was in its custody and we now know he was on the ranch in Colorado.

"Senator Hazelton tried to find the two FBI agents and the two DHS investigators. He learned they'd all died under suspicious circumstances. Colorado is close to Montana. What if he's the one Oliver or Danforth hired to kill the four agents?"

"If he is, then I'm investigating seven murders, not three."

Drake smiled. "Aren't you glad you agreed to work with us? I'm thinking there might be an accommodation in your future, if you solve seven murders."

"Until they find out I agreed to work with you without getting permission to do so. I might wind up losing my job instead."

"That won't happen, Kate."

"You don't know the bureaucrats in the FBI like I do. Before we talk to Landers, I want to make a call and see what I can learn about his background. If Oliver trusted him to watch Nazir and kill four federal agents, he would have a resume that qualified him for the job. I want to know what it is."

Chapter Fifty-Nine

SPECIAL AGENT PERKINS used the G-650's Iridium satellite communication system to call her assistant in D.C. and asked her to dig into the background of Carl Landers. She quickly learned that he was a former Army Ranger and had worked for the CIA before becoming a freelance security consultant.

She shared the information with Drake and Casey and asked them to bring Landers back to the conference table.

Casey had Landers sit closest to the window and scooted in beside him. Perkins and Drake sat across the table from them.

"How long have you worked as a security consultant?" Perkins began.

"Ten or eleven years," Landers said. "Why is that important?"

"Is that how long you've worked with James Oliver or did you work with him in the CIA?"

"Who says I ever worked for James Oliver?"

"But you do know him."

"I know a lot of people."

"May I call you Carl?" Perkins asked.

"You can call me whatever you want."

"Carl, you would be wise to answer my questions truthfully and completely. Let me introduce myself. I'm FBI Special Agent Perkins. I'm trying to decide if I should arrest you for just kidnapping or for conspiracy to commit a terrorist act and murder as well."

Landers visibly paled. "I'm not a terrorist."

"But you are a kidnapper and a murderer, aren't you?"

"What is it you want?"

"Were you the one who brought Nazir to the ranch?"

"Yes, I brought him to the ranch."

"From Montana?"

"Yes."

"Did you kill the FBI agents who turned him over to you?"

"Wait a minute. The two FBI agents were alive when I left them at the airport."

"Was that the airport in Bozeman, Montana?" Casey asked.

"Yes, that's where I was told to pick him up."

"Who told you to pick up Nazir in Bozeman?" Perkins resumed the questioning. "Was it Oliver?"

"It was."

"What did he tell you to do when you took custody of Nazir?"

"I was told to bring him to the ranch and keep him safe until they got ahold of his laptop and brought it to the ranch."

"Did Oliver tell you what he wanted Nazir to do with his laptop?"

"He didn't say."

"Did he tell you that you were working as a security contractor for the CIA?"

"Oliver never tells me specifically who I'm working for, but I believe it's probably the CIA."

"Does Oliver pay you himself or does the CIA pay your fee?"

"It's usually the CIA, but this time Oliver paid the first installment himself."

"What was Oliver paying you to do?"

"He hired me to provide security at the ranch and keep Nazir safe until he got there."

"Nazir says he thinks you were going to kill him when he

finished doing what Oliver wanted him to do. Is he right to think that?"

"Oliver told me that Nazir was never going to leave the ranch and that he would pay me to make sure he never did. I never said that I would."

"But he wanted you to kill Nazir, is that correct?"

"Yes."

"Do you know Thomas R. Danforth, III?"

"I've met him, but I don't know much about him."

"Where did you meet him?"

"He came to the ranch with Nazir's laptop."

"Is that the only time you met him?"

"Yes, it is."

"Did he tell you he was CIA like Oliver?"

"He didn't say. I assumed he was."

"Did Oliver tell you why the CIA was operating in the U.S. when it doesn't have jurisdiction to do so?"

Landers chuckled. "Do you really believe the CIA only operates overseas? Most of the stuff I do for them is here at home."

"When you do stuff for Oliver, is it always here at home?"

"For Oliver, yes."

"And that's so the CIA can plausibly deny your actions, correct?"

"I believe that's why they use freelance contractors most of the time."

"One last question, Landers," Drake said. "What were you going to do with my friends that you tried to kidnap?"

"Oliver wanted to know why they were snooping around the main gate at the ranch."

"What did he tell you to do once you got them to the ranch and found out?"

"Oliver told me they wouldn't be leaving once they were there."

Drake leaned across the conference table and poked Landers hard in the chest. "Then you're a lucky man you weren't able to find them."

Landers was taken back to his seat in the main cabin for Norris to keep an eye on him while Perkins decided what to do with him.

"If he's telling the truth about the FBI and DHS agents," Perkins said, "kidnapping Morales is all I can arrest him for. If he really didn't know what Oliver and Danforth were doing, conspiracy to commit an act of terrorism would be a long shot."

"Oliver and Danforth won't know that," Drake said. "As soon as Danforth knows Nazir and the men on his ranch are in FBI custody and that we have Nazir's laptop, they'll assume the worst."

"How will you prove that Danforth and Oliver were acting together in all of this?" Casey asked. "What if they each had their own agenda?"

"What do you mean?" Perkins asked.

"We know Danforth's been after the laptop for some reason. We don't know if he's involved in a cyberattack on the banks. That sounds like something the CIA would be involved in," Casey explained.

"We also don't know why the CIA would want to mount a cyberwar attack on U.S. banks," Drake added.

"I agree we're not done with this yet, but we'd better figure out what we're going to do with what we know before we land," Perkins said. "All hell's going to break loose when we do."

Chapter Sixty

THE PSS G-650 touched down at Ronald Reagan Washington National Airport thirty minutes past noon on October 24th, one week before Halloween. A cab was waiting at Signature Flight Support DCA to take FBI Special Agent Perkins to the Washington Field Office of the FBI (WFO) alone.

She had decided that she wouldn't have to immediately explain why she had allowed Nazir and Landers to be flown by PSS to Washington, DC, instead of having them arrested in Colorado, if she was waiting to arrest them herself at the WFO when they were driven there from the airport.

By having Nazir and Landers held at the WFO for questioning, instead of the FBI headquarters, she hoped it would delay Danforth and Oliver finding out what exactly had happened to them. When Landers didn't report in, as she had learned he was required to do twice a day, Danforth and Oliver would surely know something was wrong.

Before the two could react, however, she was confident Drake and the men from PSS could keep them under surveillance until the FBI's surveillance could take over until they were arrested.

Before they landed, Kevin McRoberts had examined Nazir's laptop and confirmed there was cyberattack malware on it that had been forwarded to nineteen members of the Islamic Revolutionary Council of America. She had the IP addresses of the nineteen from Kevin but needed some time to organize for their simultaneous arrests around the country.

Explaining how her investigation of three murders in the district had uncovered a terrorist plot for a devastating cyberattack on the nation's biggest banks had taken two grueling hours with the special agent in charge of the WFO and another hour with the assistant director in charge.

They had listened carefully while she detailed her investigation and seemed to accept her reason for not keeping them informed. They both struggled, however, with the idea of authorizing the arrest of Thomas R. Danforth, III.

The FBI had become so politicized they all realized that such an arrest without an air-tight slam-dunk indisputably strong case would get them all fired.

The compromise Perkins' superiors agreed on was for her to interrogate Nazir and Landers more completely in the WFO. She was then to prepare a detailed report about the murders and the cyberattack plot for review by the Department of Justice before any action would be taken against Thomas Danforth or James Oliver.

It was five o'clock in the afternoon when she closed the door of her office and called Drake.

"I just walked into a bureaucratic brick wall," she said. "The assistant director in charge and the SAC want me to more completely interrogate Nazir and Landers here at the WFO and write a detailed report that has to be reviewed by the Department of Justice before any action will be taken against Danforth or Oliver."

"Does that include surveillance?" Drake asked.

"It does. There's no way they won't hear about Nazir and Landers being in FBI custody and make a run for it."

"Oliver might make a run for it, but Danforth's the kind of guy who will try to talk his way out of this."

"Any ideas?"

"As soon as we bring Nazir and Landers to you, we can split up and watch Oliver and Danforth until you get the green light."

"That could be a while."

"I know. We'll figure something out. Can you get the home addresses for Danforth and Oliver for me? We won't be able to watch them when they're at work, but we can sit on them when they're coming to and from."

"That won't be a problem," Perkins said. "Sorry about the delay. I thought I'd get them to move faster to deal with a couple of traitors, but all they can think about are their careers."

"Not your fault. You did the best you could. I'll send Nazir and Oliver your way and then we'll find a way to help the government do the job we're paying them to do."

———

DRAKE PUT his iPhone in his pocket and stood with his hands on his hips in the galley aisle. It wasn't the first time the government had been slow to act, if it acted at all, when he'd been involved. He should have expected it with someone like Thomas R. Danforth, III.

Liz walked up behind him. "Is Kate okay?"

"Kate's fine. Her superiors are slow-walking her request for action on Danforth and Oliver. They won't even put surveillance on either of them until the DOJ reviews her report."

"I was afraid of that. What does she want us to do?"

"She wants us to take Nazir and Landers to the Washington field office. I said we'd find a way to keep an eye on Danforth and Oliver until they give her the green light to bring them in."

"How are we going to do that? We don't have the personnel for two surveillance teams and none of us have slept much in two days."

"I know, Liz. Maybe we skip surveillance and go on offense."

"What does that mean?"

"The FBI wants to proceed carefully so that no one jeopardizes their career, if this all goes sideways. That's not a concern we have."

"What about jeopardizing our futures, as in jail time? Whatever you're thinking could be construed as interfering in a federal criminal investigation."

"Then we'll have to find a way to do what I'm thinking of doing without it being construed as interfering."

Chapter Sixty-One

AFTER NORRIS and Morales called taxi cabs and escorted Nazir and Landers separately to the Washington field office and were back at the Kimpton Glover Park Hotel taking naps, Drake invited Casey and Liz to the hotel's bar for a drink before dinner.

Liz had chosen a massage in the hotel's spa over a nap and Casey had gone for a run. Drake was left alone in his room to think of a way to convince Danforth or Oliver to turn themselves in before they were arrested for treason, conspiracy and murder.

He didn't know enough about the relationship between the two men, but he did know that survival was a powerful instinct. He'd observed it firsthand as a prosecutor in Oregon watching criminals scurry to be the first in line to confess when a plea deal was offered.

Danforth and Oliver weren't simple criminals facing drug or robbery charges and the charges against them would be far worse than years in jail. They were terrorists participating in a plan to wage cyberwarfare against American banks and co-conspirators in the murder of seven people.

Getting them to turn on each other without them knowing he was involved was one key. The only way he could think to do that was by sending them a message that couldn't be traced back to him.

He knew there was a way to do that because that was the bread and butter of hackers and he knew one of the best hackers in the world.

The other key was coming up with a message that would force one of them to betray the other, in hopes of saving himself. It was the message that he was having trouble with.

Liz and Casey were sitting in the bar waiting for him when he got there.

"You two look refreshed," he said to greet them.

"You look like trouble to me," Casey said. "Liz told me you want to go on offence."

"Liz is concerned that it means interfering in a criminal investigation. That's not what I'm thinking about. The FBI will be investigating this plot to strike at the banks and the murders. I agree that getting involved in that would be interfering in what Kate's doing.

"I want to find the person or persons in the government who tipped off Volkov. That's why we brought Nazir back and why we kept his laptop.

"We still have his laptop and I think there's something on it that Danforth and Oliver didn't want us to see. What else would explain the efforts they made to get it back? Once they had Nazir, they didn't need his laptop for a cyberattack on the banks. Oliver was the one who provided the malware to Nazir for that. Nazir could have used any laptop to launch the attack."

"Okay, I follow you so far," Casey said. "But how do we use the laptop to prove Danforth and Oliver are traitors?"

"We offer to sell it to them for an exorbitant price."

"There's evidence on the laptop that Kate will need. Putting the laptop at risk in any way would certainly be interfering," Liz said.

"That's why we won't offer them Nazir's laptop. We'll offer them one that's exactly like his."

"How do we get them interested?" Casey asked.

"Kevin told me the file Nazir sent to the FBI Tipline is on the laptop. Danforth has, no doubt, seen the Tipline file, maybe Oliver has too. Kevin says there are other files that diary what Nazir was doing for Bradley and Volkov that Danforth will not have seen. We send them bits and pieces from the other files. They won't be able to resist getting their hands on the rest of Nazir's files."

"They've killed a lot of people to get the laptop," Liz pointed out. "How do we get them to admit their involvement with Volkov before they try to kill us first and save their money?"

"We do it like we handled the exchange for the laptop the first time. We bug the laptop case and listen to them when they think they're safe and celebrating. What do you think?"

"If you can find a way to do this safely from a distance, I'm in. I don't want any of us exposed to the contract killers the CIA is fond of using, the kind of men Oliver knows. The safer alternative is to let Kate prosecute them her way."

"What do you think, Mike?"

"I agree with Liz that the safer alternative would be to let Kate handle this. I also know that you're not going to rest until you identify the ones in the government who aided Volkov last summer. If you can come up with a way to satisfy the concerns Liz has and promise me that we do this together, I'm in."

Drake waved for the waitress to come over to take an order for a round of drinks to seal the deal. When they each had what they had ordered, Drake proposed a toast.

"Here's to making sure that justice is not delayed or denied."

Chapter Sixty-Two

DRAKE'S ATTEMPT TO get some sleep that night was a bust. He ran a hundred scenarios through his mind that might work and rejected them all. When he finally fell asleep, two hours before the sun came up the next morning, he'd given up on the idea of getting Danforth and Oliver to convict themselves.

At seven thirty, he heard Liz taking a shower in their suite and sat up, rubbing his sleepy eyes that felt like they'd been polished with sandpaper.

Liz peeked around the corner from the bathroom and watched him trying to wake up. "You look terrible. Maybe a cold shower will jump-start your morning."

"That's the worst suggestion I've ever heard. You're just trying to make sure I don't come over there and rip that towel off your naked body."

"Would that help you wake up?" she said batting her eyes and smiling.

At eight o'clock, half an hour later, he was fully awake and hadn't taken the cold one Liz had suggested. Sitting at the small table near the window, enjoying a cup of coffee Liz had ordered for them from room service, he told her about the idea that came to him in the hot shower he had taken.

"I gave up on the idea of using Nazir's laptop to get Danforth and Oliver to implicate themselves and force the FBI to go from slow-walking its investigation to perp-walking them both from their offices this afternoon.

"I'm convinced Danforth is the man I need to take down," Drake continued. "I think he's the one who tipped off Volkov. I just don't know how to prove it.

"I also believe Danforth is behind the MS-13 gang from Chicago who tried to kill us at the restaurant. There's a way to prove that. I remember reading in Danforth's file that Senator Hazelton put together for us that Danforth put away the MS-13 leader in Chicago. That gang leader is in a federal prison in Colorado. Danforth was in Colorado when he brought the laptop to the ranch.

"If I can prove that Danforth visited the federal prison in Florence, Colorado, I think there's a way to prove he tried to have us killed."

"I'm afraid to ask how you plan on doing that," Liz said.

"The MS-13 gang in Chicago lost men and have three men in jail here. Why not have them shake down Danforth to pay for their troubles?"

"How do you get them to do that?"

"We don't have to. We just have to make Danforth think it's the Chicago gang that's demanding the money."

"Then what?"

"When he shows up with the money, we give him a choice; confess to attempted murder or admit you were the one who tipped off Volkov."

"What if he refuses?"

"He won't. I can be very persuasive."

"I don't like it. You're putting yourself in harm's way. I said I can't go along with something like that."

"We've both done that before, Liz. Dropping in on Volkov's villa in Hawaii wasn't the safest thing I've done recently, and you went with me."

"There has to be another way."

"The only dangerous part is when I confront Danforth. We'll have the upper hand and we'll make sure I'm well protected."

"I still don't like it," she said, looking out the window and shaking her head. "Mike was right, you're not going to let go of this, are you? I'll go along with this on two conditions. You prove Danforth visited the MS-13 gang leader and you let me accompany you when you confront Danforth."

"I wouldn't have it any other way," Drake said and kissed her on the cheek as he got up to leave and run his plan by Casey.

Casey and the rest of the PSS crew were in the restaurant for breakfast when he found them.

"Where's Liz?" Casey asked.

"Putting on her makeup, she'll be down in a minute. I think there's a way we can take down Danforth and not interfere with the FBI investigation."

"If I say I want to hear it, will it ruin my breakfast?" Casey asked as he stopped a piece of bacon on the way to his mouth.

"Listen and find out."

Drake outlined his plan for Casey. When he finished, Casey called Kevin McRoberts over to their table.

"Kevin, I know you're careful when you visit a government site, but do you know if there are any additional risks for a visit to a federal prison?"

"What would I be looking for if I visited such a site?"

"Probably the visitor logs," Drake said. "I want to know if Thomas Danforth visited the federal prison in Florence, Colorado recently. If he did, I'd also like to know who he visited, if you can find out."

"I think I can do that. How soon do you need the information?"

"As soon as you're finished eating breakfast will be soon enough. Thanks, Kevin," Casey said and turned to Drake. "Is Liz on board with this?"

Drake looked around to see if she was in the restaurant yet.

"Mike, you know I love her, and I value her opinion. How did I get myself in a place when I need her consent for everything I want to do?"

Casey laughed. "You mean you haven't figured that out yet?"

"How do you handle it? Do you get Megan to agree with everything you want to do?"

"Depends on what it is. If it's something to do with her or the family, you bet I do. If it involves PSS, I may or may not. The problem you have is you're both involved in what we do at PSS. If she's your partner in both areas of your life, you get her to go along with whatever you're planning or risk sleeping on the couch when you disagree."

"There wasn't anything Kay and I disagreed on in the three short years we were married. This is new to me."

"You weren't doing anything more dangerous than putting criminals behind bars back then either. If you had been, I'm sure Kay would have been every bit as protective as Liz is being."

"You're right," Drake said. "I guess I should be happy that she cares."

"Happy that who cares?" Liz asked as she walked up behind Drake.

"Happy that my pistol-packing lady is going to have my back when we take down Danforth," Drake said as he stood and pulled out her chair.

"Right answer, cowboy. Good morning, Mike," Liz said as she sat down with a satisfied smile on her face.

Chapter Sixty-Three

KEVIN MCROBERTS CAME BACK to the restaurant with his laptop under his arm before Drake and Liz finished eating their breakfast and pulled out a chair to join them.

"Thomas Danforth did indeed visit the federal prison in Colorado last week," he reported. "The visitor's log does not indicate who he was there to see, but I was able to follow him on the prison's CCTV system to a meeting he had with this man."

They all leaned forward together to get a closer look at the tattooed man sitting across a table from Danforth. There was no one else in the room with the two men.

"That's Angel Torres Garcia, the leader of the Chicago branch of MS-13. I was able to identify him from coverage of his trial that's still available online," McRoberts said proudly.

"I'm having a hard time believing Danforth would use someone like Garcia, but there it is," Liz said. "How in the world did he think he would get away with it?"

"If those gang bangers had been successful, who would have thought to connect Danforth to what would have looked like random gang shooting in D.C.?" Casey asked. "We wouldn't have any of the evidence we brought back from his ranch and Nazir and

Landers wouldn't be in the custody of the FBI. He came close to covering up his involvement in all of this."

"Is there anything more I can help with?" McRoberts asked.

"No, this is great," Drake said. "Thanks, Kevin."

"What now?" Casey asked.

"I think Danforth should get a message from MS-13 that Angel says hello and he needs compensation for the loss of four men and money for lawyers for his men who are in jail," Drake said and flashed the MS-13 Devil's Horn hand sign.

"He'll mess his pants when he gets that," Casey chuckled.

"How are you going to get the message to him?" Liz asked.

"How would MS-13 deliver it?" Drake asked.

"In a way that says they mean business, maybe a severed horse's head in his bed," Casey said and chuckled again.

"That's a little much, but I like the idea. Why not something like a crime scene photo of some MS-13 atrocity we find online with directions and time for a meeting?" Drake asked. "He'll understand that."

"But will he come?" Liz asked.

"He'll come, probably not alone even if he's told to. We'll need a place where we can control the area. You know your way around here, Liz. Can you think of a place MS-13 might want to meet Danforth?"

"It would need to be somewhere MS-13 is feared, somewhere with a lot of immigrants. Ward 4 has a large Latino immigrant population. Fort Slocum Park would work. It's an old Civil War fort with a lot of green space and an urban forest."

"Mike, why don't you take Morales and check it out? When I meet Danforth, I'd like to have a sniper covering me," Drake said.

"Covering us, you mean," Liz said. "I'm going with you."

"Why? All we need is for him to show up."

"You said yourself he probably won't come alone. Besides, he'll expect more than one gang member to be there."

"If he doesn't come alone, he'll have people spread around to cover him. I need your eyes in position to look for them," Drake said firmly.

"This isn't a request, Adam," Liz said sharply. "I have to see his face when he realizes it's over. I was proud to be an FBI agent. This dirt bag gives anyone who's ever worked for the FBI a bad name."

Casey signaled the end of the round by asking how they were going to deliver the MS-13 demand to Danforth. "If you want to meet with Danforth before he's in FBI custody and has a lawyer, we need to contact him as soon as possible. How do you suggest we do that?"

Drake looked away from Liz and turned to his friend. "What are you thinking?"

"He has to receive the message directly, without anyone else having a chance to see it or inspect it," Casey suggested. "Having it delivered to FBI Headquarters won't work. I'm sure Kevin can find his private email address. He could make sure it's untraceable."

"Will Danforth believe MS-13 has the expertise to send him an untraceable email?" Liz asked.

Drake nodded his head. "Liz has a point. There can't be any doubt that it's coming from MS-13."

The three sat silently considering the problem until Casey's face broke into a broad grin.

"What if the email came from the federal prison in Colorado? If Kevin can hack the prison's system to see the visitor log, why not have him send the message from there?" Casey asked.

"Beautiful!" Drake slapped Casey's shoulder then said to Liz, "You want to see his face when he knows it's over; I want to see his face when he gets an email from Angel Garcia!"

Liz stood up and said, "I'll go find Kevin and get him started on the email. You two find a way to make sure this works the way we want it to."

They watched her leave the restaurant before Casey admitted the obvious. "There's no way to make sure this works the way we want it to. There are too many variables, especially if you want to make sure Liz isn't at risk."

"I don't see how we're going to avoid it, if she insists on being there to confront Danforth."

"She might be a rusty former FBI agent, but she did all right when you two walked into Volkov's villa in Hawaii."

"She was great, wasn't she, wearing that halter top and short shorts to distract those Spetsnaz goons?"

"She was indeed. You trusted her then, you'll have to trust her again. Besides, your old sniper buddy isn't going to let anything happen to either one of you. Even if it means I have to take out the assistant director of the FBI and anyone he brings with him to do it."

Chapter Sixty-Four

JAMES OLIVER KNEW something was wrong. He hadn't been able to reach Carl Landers at Danforth's ranch for twenty-four hours. It was time to implement Plan B and make sure no one ever found out what he had been trying to do at the ranch.

That meant making sure Thomas R. Danforth, III wasn't around to tell anyone.

It also meant making sure Danforth didn't know that something had gone wrong and decide to hang him out to dry to hide his own involvement.

Shortly after Danforth had identified him from FBI surveillance film buying drugs from a MS-13 dealer, Oliver had made it his business to know everything possible about the man who held his drug use over his head for what Danforth called "an occasional favor".

As the head of the FBI's Counterintelligence Division, Danforth thought he knew more about what was going on in the country than anyone else. That made him a sucker for information he could use to make everyone convinced that he was the sage he claimed to be.

With the intelligence Oliver collected as the CIA's associate deputy director of the Directorate of Digital Innovation (DDI), both abroad and at home, he always had classified intelligence that Danforth couldn't resist meeting him to hear about.

This was why Danforth would come to J. Gilbert's Wood-fired Steak and Seafood Restaurant tonight, as invited, to collect the latest tidbit of intelligence he was offering. Oliver thought it was only fitting that his relationship with Thomas R. Danforth, III would end where it had begun, in the parking lot of the CIA's favorite watering hole just two miles south of the George Bush Center for Intelligence in Langley, Virginia. It was where he'd been filmed by an FBI surveillance team buying cocaine.

Danforth's routine never varied, which was foolish for a man in his position. After he left FBI Headquarters from the underground parking garage in his Mercedes, he drove the same route to his home in McLean, Virginia, unless he was meeting someone for dinner or staying in the capital at the Four Seasons where an escort would be waiting in his room.

When he left work today, Oliver would be watching to make sure no one was following him. If his ranch had been under surveillance, which it must have been, Danforth would be under surveillance now. How closely he was being watched would determine whether a silenced Ruger SR22 was used to kill him up close or an M4A1 and the new Sig Sauer upper receiver and integral suppressor from a distance.

Either way, Danforth had to be killed, if there was any chance of getting out of the country and reaching Europe where he could disappear. The evidence he'd left at Danforth's ranch would convince everyone that Danforth had been responsible for snatching Nazir from the FBI and killing the FBI agents and the DHS investigators.

That and the USB flash drive with the recordings from Danforth's encrypted iPhone he'd bugged containing his calls to Mikhail Volkov. Danforth would be remembered as a traitor to his country as well as a corrupt murdering bureaucrat.

———

THOMAS R. Danforth checked for new emails on his iPhone that was synced with his laptop at home, as he always did before leaving work, and fell back into his chair in shock.

> **Meet my men at Fort Slocum Park tonight, 7:00 p.m. at covered seating area. Bring money for men I lost and lawyers for men in jail. $250,000 for now. Angel.**

His heart raced in anger at the audacity of the man, reaching out from prison to shake him down! He'd given him information that would keep his sister out of prison. Angel didn't care about his men! He'd killed some of them himself for failing him.

And he damned sure didn't need the money. MS-13 were drug dealers who used their brutal ways to intimidate other drug dealers they competed with and they were very profitable in their line of work.

His secretary opened the door of his office and saw his red face. "Are you all right, sir?"

Danforth waved her away.

It was 4:30 p.m. How did Angel expect him to come up with a quarter of a million dollars by 7:00 p.m.? Drug dealers might have that kind of money lying around, but he certainly didn't.

He wasn't even sure this was about money. Maybe something kept Angel from helping his sister with the information about the informant's drug history or the location of the safe house. If that was the case, he could still help Angel keep his sister out of jail.

But he wasn't going to give Angel's gang members a promise that he would and have even more men with something to blackmail him with.

They would just have to take a message back to Angel; "You're messing with the wrong guy," delivered in a way Angel would understand. He wouldn't use a machete; he would use something far more powerful. His favorite new toy that he'd gotten his hands on was a Heckler & Koch MP7A2. The submachine gun's 4.6m x 30 cartridge could penetrate Kevlar/titanium body armor from 200 meters.

Danforth expected to be much closer than that when he emptied a forty-round magazine on the gang bangers.

Chapter Sixty-Five

FORT SLOCUM PARK IN WASHINGTON, DC was one of seven forts built by the Union Army to protect the city during the Civil War. Its open fields and urban forested land were largely neglected by the National Park Service and now overgrown with weeds. There were dog trails, picnic tables and covered seating areas scattered around and at night, it was a perfect place for a gang like MS-13 to arrange a clandestine meeting.

At least that was the report that Mike Casey made when he returned to the hotel with Marco Morales to brief Drake and Liz in their room.

"The covered seating area we found online is surrounded with large trees and up a slope. Behind it is a dense thicket of trees. There are plenty of positions for us to cover you from and you'll be able to see anyone approaching your position."

"Where will you be?" Drake asked.

"I'll be in the thicket of trees with a one-hundred-eighty-degree field of fire. Norris and Morales will be in flanking positions to the left and right of the covered seating area. We'll be in position an hour before Danforth's supposed to show up. You and Liz should be at the covered seating facility before he gets there, say fifteen or twenty minutes ahead of him."

"Do we need to worry about someone calling the police when they see you entering the park with weapons?" Liz asked.

"I have folding stocks for our M4s. It's not hard to keep them out of sight, but it is a possibility. I don't expect anyone to be in the park after dark. We'll be careful," Casey assured her.

"Should we let Kate Perkins know what we're doing?" Liz asked.

Drake shook his head. "I don't think we should. Kate's got her hands full with Nazir and Landers in custody and trying to keep Danforth from finding out that she has them. Danforth's going to find out sooner or later. Our only chance to find out if he was the one feeding Volkov information is get to him before he's arrested. He'd have an attorney and make a run for it and we'd lose him."

"What if he already knows and figures out he's being set up?" Casey asked. "We could have Norris call her and find out how she's doing with the interrogations?"

"Why have Norris call her?" Drake asked. "Liz could call her."

"Liz doesn't have a reason to call her, Norris does," Casey said with a smile. "I'll go and give Norris his assignment."

After the door closed behind Casey, Drake checked his watch, an Omega Seamaster Liz had given him. "We have some time to kill before we leave for the park. Anything you'd like to do?"

"As I remember, you like crab cakes. Why don't we stop at Clyde's of Georgetown for our lunch? Then I'll need to buy a hoodie somewhere for tonight."

"You think a hoodie will make you look like a gangbanger?"

"Do you have a better idea?"

"Ok, let's get you a hoodie."

Drake left to get keys for one of the Yukons and saw Casey coming out of Dan Norris's room.

"Has Dan called Kate Perkins?" Drake asked.

"He called her this morning to see if she wanted to have lunch with him, but she said she's too busy. He said she's angry that we still have Nazir's laptop."

"I was afraid of that. I wanted Kevin to have a little more time to search for any evidence on the laptop. He hasn't found anything. Does she know about the malware Nazir was going to have his hackers use against the banks? Without his computer, Nazir doesn't have a way to launch the attack."

"I'm not sure that's going to justify keeping Nazir's laptop from her," Casey said.

"Are you willing to trust the FBI to look that hard for evidence to prove that one of their own might be a traitor? It isn't pertinent to the murders she's investigating. It's not even pertinent to whatever Danforth and Oliver are up to, as far as we know."

"I understand, but we have to consider the blowback if Kate Perkins decides we've gone too far."

"I'm willing to take sole responsibility for this, Mike, if it comes to that. She doesn't know that Danforth sent the MS-13 shooters after us and that we found out about it by hacking the federal prison in Colorado. The only way we can prove that Danforth ordered a hit on us is if he shows up tonight. Danforth is going to pay for that. If we give her the laptop, as well as the evidence to put Danforth away for attempted murder and treason, she'll understand."

"She'd better or you're going to be in a lot of trouble."

Chapter Sixty-Six

AN HOUR before Danforth was expected to arrive at Fort Slocum Park, Casey, Norris and Morales entered the park separately from the north and west and south. They all wore black jeans, black windbreakers that hid their M4s with folding stock attachments and black baseball hats.

When they found positions that offered concealment and a clear line of sight to the covered seating area and the open area around it, they confirmed their locations to each other using the same Motorola combat radios and tactical headsets they'd used on Danforth's ranch in Colorado.

"Settle in, gentlemen, and keep eyes and ears open," Casey said. "From the looks of the stuff I stumbled across on my way in, this place gets all sorts of visitor. The weeds were up to my knees in places and the trees more like thick brush. Someone could crawl up to you and you wouldn't see them until they jumped up to cut your throat."

Morales pushed his PTT button. "From the trash I saw, they've had homeless living here at times."

"Were you the guy who picked this place?" Norris asked Casey.

"No, Liz did. She used to run one of the trails that crosses through the park."

"That must have been a while ago, as overgrown as this place is now," Norris said.

Morales trained his night vision monocular on two visitors coming across the open field south of his position. "A man and a woman walking a Jack Russell. It's not our guy and a date."

The dog walkers were the only people who entered the park until Drake and Liz entered the park at twenty minutes to seven.

Norris pushed his PTT button to report two more visitors. "I have two people wearing hoodies who just came into view east of me. Looks like a man and woman."

"Good call, Dan," Liz said into her lapel microphone.

"You guys having any fun yet?" Drake asked.

"Only seen two people walking a dog so far," Casey reported. "You see anything on the way in?"

"No one paid any attention to us when we walked here from two streets over where we parked the Yukon," Drake said.

"Go get comfortable," Casey said. "We'll let you know if he shows up."

"Copy that," Drake said. "I'll be greatly disappointed if he doesn't."

Drake and Liz walked on to the covered seating area on the knoll. When they got there, they sat on the top of one of the picnic tables there, facing the open field to the west and south of them.

At five minutes after seven o'clock, a solitary figure marched across the open field to the south.

"It's Danforth," Casey reported.

From his position to the east, Morales had a clear view of Danforth's right side. "He's got an HK MP7 hanging from his right shoulder."

Drake kept his eyes on Danforth as he approached them, leaning forward with his forearms resting on his knees. "Let him keep coming until I stop him. If he brings the HK up, let him see a green dot on his chest, Mike."

"Copy that."

Drake waited until Danforth was twenty-five yards away before greeting him. "That's far enough, Danforth. Lower the HK to the ground and approach."

At the sound of Drake's voice, Danforth started moving his hand back to the grip of the short-barreled submachine hanging from his shoulder.

"Don't do it, Danforth. Look at the green dot on your chest. I won't tell you again to drop the HK to the ground."

Danforth looked down at his chest and froze. "Who are you?"

Drake pulled the hoodie back off his head with his left hand and stepped down from the picnic table. "I thought you'd recognize my voice."

"Drake!"

"I told you I'd find out what you were up to, but I didn't think it would be you colluding with MS-13 to kill us."

"You'll never prove that."

Liz jumped down and stood beside Drake. "We already have. How did you get Angel to send his guys here from Chicago?"

"Who's Angel?"

"That's good," Liz said. "Angel is the guy you visited in the federal prison in Colorado. What I don't understand is why. Getting in bed with Angel just upped the possible penalty for the people you've had killed here in Washington."

"You've got it wrong, Strobel. I haven't had anyone killed."

"Yes, you have," Drake said, "starting with the people who died this summer because you helped Mikhail Volkov get his hands on a shipment of AK-47s. How did you find out about the shipment?"

"I don't know what you're talking about."

"I think you do. Was it your friend in the CIA, James Oliver, who told you the AK-47s were about to be intercepted in Seattle?"

"Why do you think that little queer is a friend of mine?"

Drake started to slowly nod his head up and down as the pieces of the puzzle fell into place. "That's it, isn't it? You and Oliver were in it together and there's something on Nazir's laptop that will prove it. You're trying to keep us from proving that you aided and abetted a Russian meddling in the domestic affairs of your country. Why, Danforth?"

Danforth glared at Drake for a long moment and started laughing. "You'll never know how really screwed up this country is. If you did—"

Danforth went down like an unprotected quarterback hit from behind by a charging defensive end and didn't move.

Drake and Liz ran around behind the picnic table and turned it over for cover.

"I didn't hear the shot, but I caught movement at nine o'clock from my position just after Danforth went down," Norris reported.

"You see anything, Marco?" Drake asked.

"Yes, in pursuit," Morales said, breathing heavily. "He's running west across the park along the tree line toward 3rd Street and the row houses."

Chapter Sixty-Seven

DRAKE CHECKED DANFORTH FOR A PULSE. "He's alive. Call 911, Liz, and get him to a hospital. Better let Agent Perkins know he's been shot."

"What should I tell her?"

"That he's been shot. We'll fill her in later," Drake said and took off running toward 3rd Street and the row houses.

He hit his PTT button and told Casey and Norris that Liz was staying with Danforth and he was on his way to help Morales.

Drake couldn't see them, but he knew Casey and Norris were ahead of him and were also chasing after Morales. As he got closer to the west side of the park, he could just make out their dark forms converging ahead of him behind Morales.

"He's crossed 3rd Street and is running into that open space south of Madison Street NW," Morales radioed. "I've lost sight of him."

"He's got a car nearby. Get a license plate if you can't catch up to him," Drake directed.

Casey and Norris ran across 3rd Street ahead of him. He saw them split up to search what looked to be a small park with large trees whose leaves were changing into fall colors.

"I'm on the sidewalk over on 3rd Place NW," Morales reported. "The brake lights of a Mercedes sedan just went on. It's pulling out and driving south. It's got to be the shooter."

"Did you get the license?" Drake asked.

"Too far away for me to make out, but I used my cell phone. We'll see."

Morales was looking at his phone's screen and trying to expand the image on it when Casey and Norris and then Drake ran up and gathered around him.

"It's not real clear," Morales said. "Three numbers, an image of what looks like the dome of the Capitol and three more numbers."

"That's a bicentennial license plate for Washington, DC." Norris said. "I had one on my car when I lived here. Hold the screen up for me and let me get a shot of the license. I have a Samsung Galaxy K zoom smartphone for my outdoor photographer hobby."

Norris took three quick pictures of the screen Morales was holding up and zoomed in on the license plate of the Mercedes. "561…959," he called out. "Do you want me to call Kate and see if she'll run it?"

Drake hesitated before saying, "Go ahead and get the address of the registered owner as well. I think I know who the owner is, but we need to be sure before we go see if he's home. Let's get back and see how Danforth is doing."

Norris stayed behind to call Kate Perkins while Drake and the others jogged back to Fort Slocum Park. Flashing overhead lights from three patrol cars surrounded an ambulance parked in front of the covered seating area on the other side of the park.

"How are we going to explain our presence here?" Casey asked as Drake stopped and looked back to see how far behind them Norris was.

"I'll join Liz and you three head back to the hotel," Drake said. "Danforth isn't going to say anything about why he's here in the park. I'll find out what Liz has said and follow her lead. We have permits for our guns, but we'll have a hard time explaining the M4s you three have. Find out who the Mercedes is registered to and wait for us at the hotel."

Casey and Morales waited for Norris to catch up while Drake entered the park and jogged across the open field to the growing number of DC Metro patrol cars.

He was stopped at the perimeter being set up around the crime scene and told to leave the park. When he explained he'd been with the woman being questioned next to the ambulance, he was escorted to a lieutenant listening to what Liz was saying to his captain.

"I used to come here when I was the executive assistant to the Secretary of DHS. I wanted to show it to my friend, and we stopped to read the historical marker. He's a history buff. We saw this man on the ground and a man running away. I called 911 and my friend chased after the other man. He might know more, he's right here with your lieutenant."

The captain turned to see Drake standing with the lieutenant and noticed a woman behind him, wearing a blue windbreaker and holding her credential up for an officer to examine.

"FBI," he said softly to the lieutenant. "Keep them separated while I see why she's here."

Liz stayed where she was, and an officer was summoned to walk Drake over to the covered seating area.

Drake watched Special Agent Perkins assert her authority. The two talked for a minute and he was surprised to see the captain step back and motion for the officer to bring him over.

"Special Agent Perkins tells me you've helped her with a murder investigation. She's also telling me that I can rely on whatever you and your lady friend are telling me happened here. Since you haven't told me anything and she says Ms. Strobel is former FBI, I'm willing to trust her with that. She'd like a word with both of you."

The captain waved Liz over to join Drake and walked away.

Special Agent Perkins stood silently, looking down at her shoes, until Liz got there. "Which one of you is going to tell me what really happened here? Dan called me to run a license plate for him, which

I'm sure you asked him to, and told me that Thomas Danforth had been shot here in the park. I assume the two are connected."

"Danforth was behind the MS-13 gangbangers who tried to kill us," Drake said. "He went to Colorado and met with the leader of the Chicago branch of MS-13 in the federal prison, one day before we were attacked at our hotel. We sent him an email that said it was from that leader and to bring money to this park to make up for the men he lost and for the attorneys for his men in jail. If he came, it would prove he'd commissioned MS-13 to kill us. Someone didn't want him talking to us. The license plate probably belongs to the man who shot him. That's what really happened here, Kate."

Chapter Sixty-Eight

SPECIAL AGENT PERKINS' penetrating stare searched for any sign of deception coming from Drake and then did the same with Liz.

Turning back to Drake, she said, "I told you not to interfere in my investigation."

"This is a separate matter. I wasn't willing to wait for you or your bosses to investigate Danforth and MS-13. We gave you Nazir and Landers. What are they saying about the murders you're investigating?"

"Landers doesn't know anything about the three murders here in DC. He says he was hired by James Oliver for security on the ranch to keep Nazir safe but says he doesn't know anything about what Oliver and Nazir were up to."

"What's Nazir saying?"

"He's not talking. He said he tried to warn us before about someone trying to start a civil war and we didn't do anything, why should he tell us anything now? Do you know what he's talking about?" Perkins asked.

Drake and Liz exchanged looks and then Liz stepped in between Drake and Perkins.

"Kate, there's a lot to this whole thing we haven't told you, but here and now is not the time," she said. "Take us somewhere we can talk privately, and we'll tell you everything."

"What do you suggest I tell the captain?"

"Tell him the truth, just not all the truth," Drake said. "We're still assisting you with your murder investigation and you need to find out if Danforth being shot is in any way connected. Danforth's FBI, you have jurisdiction, don't you?"

"Probably, but I don't want to be tied up with this shooting just yet. Stay put, I'm going to tell the captain I'm taking you two in for questioning and find out where they're taking Danforth."

Liz turned around to face Drake. "This is getting complicated. What do you want to do?"

"Find out who shot Danforth. I think it was Oliver and we need to find him. Kate can help us if she'll agree to join forces."

"How do we get her to do that?"

"We help her tie this all up with a nice red bow; what Danforth and Oliver were plotting, the murders and Danforth working with Volkov this summer. She'll be a hero."

"The FBI won't let that happen. It only allows a special agent to take the spotlight when the FBI gets all the credit. When Danforth is arrested, the FBI will have to take responsibility for harboring a traitor and admit that you were the one who brought him to justice."

"We'll make sure that doesn't happen."

"How?"

Drake saw Perkins returning and put his arm around Liz and pulled her close. "We have friends in high places," he whispered in her ear.

"The captain has agreed to let me take you in for questioning. He'll handle Danforth's shooting for now," she said. "Let's go."

"Where to?" Drake asked.

"Some place where I don't have to explain why I didn't bring you in for being involved in the attempted murder of a senior FBI assistant director."

"The restaurant and bar at our hotel?" Drake asked.

"Fine," Perkins said. "My car's over here."

Drake opened the door for Liz when they reached the black Ford Explorer Perkins was driving, seating her up front to keep the FBI agent engaged in conversation while he sat in the back and sent a text to Casey.

Agent Perkins is bringing us to our hotel to hear what we know about everything that's going on. We didn't tell her you three were at the park. See if Dan can find the owner of the Mercedes so she doesn't have to. I think it's James Oliver. If it is, keep an eye on him until we finish with Kate and we'll pay him a visit. I don't want him slipping away.

Casey's response was immediate.

Roger that.

While sharing a quattro formaggi pizza and two rounds of wine in the Casolare Ristorante and Bar at their hotel, Drake and Liz told Kate Perkins about everything they'd been involved in since the terrorist attacks on Catholic churches in Portland.

Nazir was the cyber jihadist who had supplied and assisted the wannabe women jihadist college students who tried to slaughter parishioners while they attended mass. Drake had prevented the attack with help from PSS and an FBI agent who'd been killed in the effort.

Nazir was also the cyber jihadist who helped a Russian oligarch, Mikhail Volkov, and a radical professor from Berkeley try to start a civil war in America the previous summer. Nazir was behind the social media fake news campaign that was designed to inflame passions with his jihadist hackers he called the Islamic Revolutionary Council of America.

Drake and Liz and the PSS team had raided the Russian's villa in Hawaii, found the radical professor dead after being tortured by Russian Spetsnaz and Nazir being held there. They'd returned Nazir to the mainland with his laptop to be questioned by investigators from DHS, only to have him intercepted by two FBI agents and taken to Danforth's ranch in Colorado. The two FBI agents and the two DHS agents involved in the transfer of Nazir had all died in suspicious circumstances. Danforth was believed to have aided and abetted Mikhail Volkov at some point in the plot.

Now Nazir had been found on Danforth's ranch working on James Oliver's plot to use Nazir and his council to launch a cyber-warfare attack on America's largest banks. Drake and Liz and the PSS team had found Nazir there and turned him over to Perkins in Colorado.

She knew the rest, Drake told her and that he believed the murders she was investigating had occurred while Danforth was trying to recover Nazir's laptop they'd brought back from Hawaii.

"You have Nazir and now Danforth," Drake told Perkins. "If I'm right, James Oliver is the man who shot him and the owner of the Mercedes we saw running from the park. We need to find Oliver before he disappears, Kate. Will you allow us to help you do that before it's too late?"

Chapter Sixty-Nine

SPECIAL AGENT KATE PERKINS presented her FBI credentials to the front desk attendant at the Watergate West and asked to be shown to the tenth-floor condominium apartment belonging to James Oliver. She was accompanied by three of her associates; Drake, Liz and Casey.

While they waited for a security guard to take them to Oliver's condo, Perkins also asked for the parking space number where Mr. Oliver kept his Mercedes. Norris and Morales were to be stationed there in case Oliver made it past them and tried to leave from the parking garage.

Perkins looked like an FBI agent, wearing a black wool and cashmere peacoat and tan khaki pants. Her three associates were still wearing the jeans and black windbreakers they'd worn at the park as they followed Perkins and the security guard to the elevators.

No one said anything in the elevator on the way to the eighth floor. When they stepped out of the elevator, Perkins asked the guard for Oliver's apartment number and told him he wasn't needed to escort them any further. They would take it from there.

Perkins led the way down the hall to the carved mahogany door of number 851 and pressed the Venetian bronze ring video doorbell in front of her. Casey stood to the left of the door and Drake and Liz stood to the right.

"Mr. Oliver, this is FBI Special Agent Perkins," she announced. "I need to speak with you."

Ten seconds later, a male voice said, "You are speaking with me, Agent Perkins. How can I help you?"

"I'm investigating the death of Tony Yamada. His bank records show that he worked for you in the past. I was hoping you could tell me about the kind of work he did for you so that I have some idea who might have wanted him dead."

Another ten seconds passed. "This isn't a good time for me to talk with you about Tony, Agent Perkins. Could we do this tomorrow?"

"This will only take a few minutes, Mr. Oliver. I really would like to speak with you tonight."

"May I see your credentials? Just hold them up to the video camera."

Perkins took out her FBI badge and held it up to the camera.

"Please come in," Oliver said and opened the door.

Perkins stepped forward and before Oliver could begin to close the door, Drake blocked the door from closing with his foot and entered behind her.

"What is this?" Oliver demanded.

"We didn't get a chance to talk with you at Danforth's ranch," Drake said and shoved Oliver away from the door.

Liz and Casey came in behind Drake and Casey closed the door.

Oliver stood his ground, surrounded by his four visitors in the foyer of his condo.

He reminded Drake of an aging Ben Affleck, with dark hair, a Van Dyke beard and wearing oval wire-rimmed glasses.

"Why do you think I was at Danforth's ranch?" he asked.

"I have Carl Landers in custody. He says you were," Perkins said. "Are you saying that you weren't?"

"I'm not saying anything. Are you arresting me, Agent Perkins?"

"That's why I'm here, Mr. Oliver."

"For what?"

"For a number of things but most recently for shooting Thomas Danforth tonight."

"And you think that was me?" Oliver said with a grin. "Good luck proving that. Let me put some shoes on and we'll go get this over with. I'm looking forward to turning my attorney loose on the FBI for barging in here tonight."

Oliver turned around and started across an open area with a galley kitchen on the right, lined with stainless steel appliances, and an entertainment area on the left.

"Don't try anything, Oliver," Drake said, "I'm right behind you."

Oliver raised his hand above his shoulder walking forward to acknowledge Drake and turned right toward a door. When he lowered his hand, he clapped twice, and the lights went out in the apartment.

Drake sprang forward, but Oliver was already through the door, locking it behind him.

Casey clapped twice, and the lights came back on. "Have this at home," he said as he ran to Drake's side.

"You're not getting past us, Oliver," Drake shouted. "You may as well come out."

When there was no response, Liz ran across the entertainment area to the gray solar shades along one wall. She tried to pull the shades back, but they were on an automated overhead tract that didn't require cords or chains to open.

Then she saw a HunterDouglas controller on the end table next to the black leather sofa and picked it up.

"I think there's a sliding door behind the shades," she said and pushed the single button on the controller. The shades separated in the middle and pulled back. The condo had a large balcony patio with potted plants and a gurgling waterfall beyond the sliding glass door.

Perkins ran over with her Glock service pistol drawn. "He may be armed and out there."

Drake shouted, "Oliver, last chance, we're coming in."

Casey got the nod from Drake and kicked in the door. They rushed in, with Casey sweeping the room to the left with his Glock and Drake doing the same on the right with his Kimber.

Oliver's master bedroom, decorated like the rest of the apartment with stark white walls and a king-size bed on a pedestal with a white satin bedspread, was empty.

A frosted glass door with an eagle etching was open onto the balcony.

"Tell Liz and Kate to wait and we'll all go out on your signal," Drake said to Casey. "He has to be out there, we're on the eighth floor."

Casey left the master bedroom and joined Liz and Perkins at the sliding glass door.

"Three, two, one," he called out loudly.

Drake opened the frosted glass door and slipped out, hugging the wall to the left.

There were three large maroon ceramic pots with plants in them on the patio, head high and tall enough to hide behind.

Drake slid along the wall until he could see around the two pots on his end of the balcony patio. "Clear on this end."

"Clear on this end," Perkins called out.

They met at the waterfall at the center. "He's gone," Drake said. "Liz, call down to Norris and Morales and let them know he might be headed their way. If he doesn't make a run for it, he could be anywhere in one of these other apartments. Let's find out how he got off this patio."

It didn't take long to find out. A fire escape ladder just outside the frosted glass door from Oliver's bedroom was hanging over the patio wall. Below it was the patio of the apartment below on the seventh floor.

Moving back inside, Perkins, "We don't have a search warrant, but since he invited us in, anything in plain view is fair game."

They fanned out to look for something that might tell them where Oliver was headed.

Drake and Liz went to Oliver's study while Casey and Perkins walked through the rest of the apartment.

The only things they found on Oliver's glass-topped desk were a closed silver MacBook Pro and a brochure for an AmaWaterways river tour of Europe.

"That would be one way to disappear in Europe. Travel under an assumed name and get off the boat anywhere you wanted without ever passing through an airport," Drake said.

"Maybe he just has good taste and is planning a nice—" Liz's phone chirped.

"Oliver's in the parking garage walking to his car. What do you want us to do?" Norris asked.

"Oliver's in the parking garage," Liz told Drake. "What do you want them to do?"

"Tell them not to let him leave. We'll be right down."

Chapter Seventy

NORRIS AND MORALES watched Oliver open the stairwell door and walk toward his Mercedes parked in the middle of the row closest to the wall. The gray moccasin slippers Oliver had on kept his footfall from making any sound.

Morales was standing behind a cement pillar at the far end of the row and Norris was standing beside a black Cadillac Escalade a row over closest to the exit ramp.

Norris motioned for Morales to move in from his position behind Oliver. When Oliver was one car away from his Mercedes, Norris stepped away from the Escalade and moved forward.

"James Oliver?" Norris asked.

Hearing his name, Oliver ducked into the space between his Mercedes and the car next to it and crouched down.

"Who's asking?"

"I'm here to assist FBI Special Agent Perkins," Norris said. "She asked me to make sure you didn't leave."

Oliver saw where Norris was standing and pulled a baby Glock out from the pocket of his khaki pants.

"Can't let that happen, friend," Oliver said, aiming the gun at Norris.

"I think you can," Morales said, stepping out from behind the pillar at the other end of the row of cars. His pistol was pointed at Oliver.

Oliver swung his gun away from Norris's position and took aim at Morales; he turned his head back to make sure Norris hadn't moved and saw that he had a gun aimed at him as well.

The stairwell door slowly opened and Special Agent Perkins stepped out. Seeing Norris with his gun out, she moved to her right and got behind the nearest car. Drake and Casey followed her out and ran forward to the second row of parked cars, moving down the row closer to Norris. Liz stayed behind the half-opened stairwell door.

"James Oliver, you're under arrest for the attempted murder of Thomas Danforth," Perkins shouted.

"Attempted murder." Oliver laughed. "You mean that SOB is still alive?"

"Alive and singing like a canary," Perkins bluffed. "Is that why you tried to kill him, to keep him from telling us about the cyberattack on the banks?"

"I tried to kill the commie bastard because he deserved to die," Oliver shouted.

"Were you the one who tipped off Mikhail Volkov that the shipment of AK-47s was going to be intercepted?" Drake asked as he moved behind two cars to get closer.

"That was Danforth. He wanted Volkov to succeed, to shake things up in this country."

"What did you want? You were working with him, weren't you?" Drake continued.

"The country needed to change course. I didn't care how it happened, so yeah, I helped him."

"Oliver, put your gun down and walk out," Perkins called out. "Tell us what you know about Danforth and the Russian. We can work something out if you cooperate."

"Not a chance. I'm CIA. I know I would end up in some dark site somewhere being tortured. This way is better," he said and walked out shooting toward the sound of Perkins' voice.

A shot rang out and Oliver's head jerked back. He dropped to the cold cement floor as a cacophony of car alarms began echoing off the walls in the parking garage.

Perkins stood like a statue, frozen in a two-handed Weaver stance with her Glock still pointed at the spot where Oliver had been standing.

Norris was the closest to her and ran to her side.

"Kate, it's okay," he told her as he put his left hand on top of her pistol and gently lowered it.

When she released her grip, he took the weapon from her, leaned in close and said, "He resisted arrest and you defended yourself. Remember that. People are going to come to turn off their car alarms and we need to preserve the scene. Stay here with Liz while we do that."

Norris ran to Drake who was standing over Oliver. "I'll go up the ramp and wait for the police. It might be someone I know. This is going to get crazy, with these car alarms, but we'll have to keep people from going to their cars to shut them off. You guys will have to keep them out of here."

"How's Kate?" Drake asked.

"I think this is her first. She's tough, she'll be okay."

Norris jogged toward the exit ramp and Drake waved Casey and Morales over.

"I'll keep anyone from entering the garage from the stairwell," Drake said. "Why don't you guys go help Norris and keep anyone from coming down the ramp until the police get here?"

"You got it," Casey said, and he and Morales jogged off to help Norris.

When he jogged by Perkins on his way to the stairwell door, he saw that she had her phone to her ear and was talking with someone. He assumed she was calling the FBI field office for assistance.

Ten noisy minutes later, he learned that he had assumed correctly when the special agent in charge and eight other FBI agents showed up.

By the time the FBI field Evidence Response Team finished their work and Oliver's body had been removed, it was midnight. During that time, statements had been taken from Special Agent Perkins and each of her civilian assistants that included a separate walk-through of Oliver's apartment with an assigned FBI special agent taking notes.

With all the new information the FBI field office was hearing about, Special Agent Perkins' "friends" were told to remain in DC for the foreseeable future.

Chapter Seventy-One

WITH HIS STAY in the capital extended, Drake had time to think about what he was going to do when he returned to the Northwest. The two parts of his life that he needed to reconcile were his personal life and his professional life.

The aspect of his personal life that required a decision centered on Liz and where he wanted to live. As much as he loved Oregon and his farm, it was becoming easier to be away from it for longer periods of time. The vineyard had been replanted and he'd already talked with his neighbor and vineyard manager about a joint venture to take care of it.

Lancer, his German Shepherd and running buddy, had been raised on the farm and he couldn't see either of them living in the city. But he knew there were plenty of places in and around Seattle where they would enjoy living. He'd taken a ferry ride once when he was in Seattle and always considered living on one of the islands in Puget Sound.

He didn't know if Liz would consider living on one of the islands, but that was something they could talk about later.

What was more immediate was what he wanted to do with his law practice in Portland. With each new responsibility he'd taken on for PSS, he felt more and more distanced from his traditional law practice. Serving as special counsel for PSS and the special projects that kept coming their way made him feel alive again, like he'd felt when he and Casey had served together in Delta Force, and he knew he didn't want to give that up.

The idea that kept surfacing in his mind was to keep the office and the condo above it and let Paul Benning use it for his burgeoning private investigations business. He would miss working with Margo certainly, but she seemed to enjoy working with Paul in the office where she could an eye on him.

He'd also thought about talking with Casey about adding an expanded investigation capability to PSS and Paul Benning would be a perfect fit. It was possible that he could even work out of the office in Portland. PSS had offices around the Pacific Rim, why not in Portland, Oregon as well?

Drake slowed his pace on the treadmill for a five-minute cool down in the hotel's fitness center when he saw Liz walk in.

"Kate's here," she said. "She wants to talk with us."

"Do I have time for a shower?"

"Towel off, you're fine. She's buying Bloody Marys for all of us in the bar."

"She must have good news. Go ahead; I'll be there as soon as I cool down."

Kate Perkins was sitting next to Dan Norris and laughing at something he'd said when Drake joined the others in the hotel's restaurant and bar. Six loaded Bloody Mary drinks were sitting in the middle of the table.

Drake sat down and admired the creativity of their bartender. His Bloody Mary had the obligatory celery stalk and skewer of olives and pickled peppers, accompanied by two strips of crisp bacon, two pickled green beans and a pink shrimp and lemon slice hanging from the rim of the glass.

Kate picked up her glass and raised it to each of them in turn. "You guys deserve a medal for what you've done. My murder investigations won't take long to wrap up and you've exposed two men who betrayed the country."

"It wouldn't have happened without you, Kate," Drake said. "You trusted us when we weren't sure who we could trust."

"How's Danforth?" Liz asked.

Kate shook her head. "He's unconscious in intensive care with a collapsed right lung and massive internal damage. Oliver missed his heart by an inch. They're not sure he's going to make it."

"We'll never know, will we, what Danforth was up to?" Liz asked.

"Actually, that's why I'm here buying a round of Bloody Marys for you guys," Kate said. "We went back and searched every inch of Danforth's ranch and found a hidden flash drive that recorded calls he made to the two FBI agents that snatched Nazir and brought him to the ranch. There's a call Danforth made to Carl Landers, telling him to kill the two FBI agents as well as the two DHS agents. And there are recorded calls he made to Mikhail Volkov."

"Why would Danforth record calls he was making?" Norris asked. "He's too smart to do something like that."

"We don't think he did," Kate said. "We think Oliver did. The phone Danforth had with him when he was shot was bugged."

"Oliver needed something to make sure Danforth didn't turn on him," Casey said. "Bugging his phone and recording incriminating conversations would guarantee that. So, it was Oliver's flash drive you found."

"What a couple of snakes!" Morales exclaimed.

"The calls Danforth made to Volkov, is there enough on them to go after Volkov?" Drake asked. "He had a role in all of this."

"We're working on that," Kate said with a smile. "He has dual citizenship. I've been given a green light to investigate him for treason."

"You're having quite the year, FBI Special Agent Perkins. If you ever decide to make a change, come see us. There will always be room for a famous FBI agent at PSS," Casey promised.

"Thanks, I appreciate the offer. When are you heading back to Seattle?"

"As soon as you tell us we're free to leave DC," Casey said.

"I'll make a call, but I think you're free to leave now, if you want."

"Then I guess this little vacation is about over. Megan wants me home to get ready for all the little ghosts and goblins that will come trick or treating next week," Casey said.

Drake had to laugh. "MS-13 gangbangers this week, little monsters wearing masks next week. You sure live an exciting life, my friend."

"Thanks to you," Casey said, "it's more exciting than it needs to be."

"I've been wanting to talk to you about that. I have some ideas I'd like to discuss."

Chapter Seventy-Two

ONE WEEK after the mid-term elections in the United States, the *New York Times* reported in its lead story that billionaire philanthropist Mikhail Volkov had been arrested.

Philanthropist Mikhail Volkov Has Been Accused of Treason

Monday morning, at seven thirty, Mikhail Volkov, the billionaire

Russian oligarch whose generous donations to thousands of

progressive non-profit organizations around the world, was seen

being perp-walked through the lobby of building One57 in midtown

Manhattan by FBI agents.

Trusted sources in the FBI are reporting that Volkov is accused

of treason for inciting civil unrest as an agent of Russia to start

a civil war in America this summer. Volkov's attorney

denies that his client is a Russian agent and says the arrest is

an attempt by the president to silence his most-prominent critic.

Later that day, the *New York Times* reported to its digital subscribers that the United States Senate Select Committee on Intelligence would hold hearings to investigate recent activities by members of the FBI and the CIA.

United States Senator Hazelton, the Chairman of the Senate

Select Committee on Intelligence, Announces Hearings To

Investigate Foreign Meddling in America's Civil Affairs

The chairman of the U.S. Senate's Select Committee on

Intelligence announced this afternoon that hearings would be

conducted to investigate reports that two senior officers

in the FBI and the CIA had aided and abetted an alleged agent

of Russia, billionaire Mikhail Volkov, by providing him

intelligence that assisted his efforts to start a civil war in America.

The directors of the FBI and CIA have pledged to cooperate

but say that senate hearings are unnecessary due to their own

independent and unbiased investigations that are already under way.

THE END

Next in the Adam Drake series

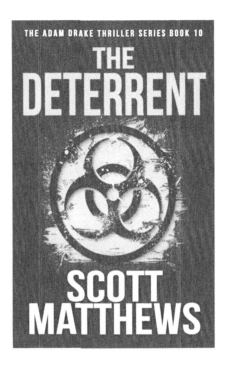

A live sample of the deadly H7N9 flu virus is the ransom terrorists are demanding from a research biologist if he wants his daughter back.

Adam Drake, lawyer and former Special Forces Tier 1 operator, has agreed to help a private investigator find the kidnapped victim and get her back. It's not clear who the kidnappers are, but Drake knows whoever they are, the ransomed virus can't be allowed to wind up in the hands of the wrong people.

The FBI's top priority will be to recover the virus before it disappears into the hands of terrorists or on the black market. If Drake decides not to get the FBI involved, he might improve his chances to get the biologist's daughter back alive but risk not recovering the sample of the virus.

Drake's decision will put lives as risk either way.

Printed in Great Britain
by Amazon

49534884R00158